MUSE

REBECCA LIM

HarperCollins *Children's Books*

First published in hardback in Australia by
HarperCollins*Publishers* Australia in 2011

First published in paperback in Great Britain by
HarperCollins *Children's Books* in 2011

HarperCollins *Children's Books* is a division of
HarperCollins*Publishers* Ltd,
77–85 Fulham Palace Road,
Hammersmith, London, W6 8JB.

The HarperCollins website address is: www.harpercollins.co.uk

1

Text copyright © Rebecca Lim 2011

ISBN 978-0-00-743607-1

Rebecca Lim asserts the moral right to be identified as the author of the work.

Printed and bound in Italy

To Barry and Judy Liu,
with thanks.

When the stars threw down their spears
And water'd heaven with their tears:
Did he smile his work to see?
Did he who made the Lamb make thee?

— WILLIAM BLAKE (1794)

CHAPTER 1

'Mercy,' I hear in the darkness behind my eyelids. 'Where are you?'

It's a young man's voice, achingly familiar.

My eyes flash open, and I raise my left hand to the base of my throat. The fingers of that hand seem to burn with a customary fire, a faint tracery of pain that dissipates almost immediately. The palest, pearlescent glow comes off the surface of my skin.

It's pitch dark in here, and I remember that I do that — glow — when there are no external sources of light around.

I take a long, trembling breath, expecting to feel a gunshot wound beneath my fingers, its edges ragged, bloody, fatal. But there's no wound, and no blood.

I lie here whole, and unmarked, breathing easily. Not dying on the floor of a dingy café, blood filling my lungs, crowding my airways, cradled in the arms of a man called … Sulaiman?

I feel my brow furrow. Everything's out of order; I can't make things line up. Because when I remember Sulaiman's stern face bent over mine, I see someone else there, inside him, inhabiting his body, lurking beneath his mortal skin. A shimmering being; one of the *elohim*: Gabriel.

And I am Lela Neill again, for one kaleidoscopic instant in which I feel the death rattle, the harsh susurration of her breathing. Feel myself mired in her body, which is cold and growing colder. Cold, too, the cracked linoleum upon which I lie.

Every sense is fading, the world turning to sepia before my eyes. Until there is a sensation, a sharp tug, as if some kind of cord has snapped, the bonds between myself and Lela's body beginning to loosen. I feel myself become something like mist, like fog.

But it is illusory, this confused jumble of imagery and sensation, already memory. That jump-cut moment in which I seem to be two people at once, in two places at once. Because I'm not really there.

I can't be. I know for a certainty, with a clarity that defies logic, that Lela is already dead.

And I give a single, piercing wail, my fingers flying up to my face in horror, the sound escaping before I can stop it. Its sonic aftershock seems to hover in this high-ceilinged room for an eternity. An elegy to the fallen girl.

I'm suddenly flooded with grief, with white heat, with a sensation like panic, and I fight my way out of the featherdown bedding I am inexplicably wrapped in, like a corpse in a winding sheet.

And though the blackness of the room should be impenetrable to my eyes, I see every chair, every ottoman, every vase, tasselled reading lamp, gilt-edged painting, porcelain ornament, every useless, luxurious appointment in this spacious chamber as if it is bright day and not night. Because I can see in the dark, like a cat.

No, I correct myself automatically, *better than a cat*. No creature under heaven can see better in the dark than I can.

The air in here is cold, the kind of sharp cold that presages snowfall. There's a window open somewhere.

I slide off the bed and make my way unerringly towards a set of deep curtain-covered windows, touch the plush, heavily embroidered fabric with my fingertips. Shove the whole mass aside until I encounter the icy glass in a partially raised sash window. I study the view over the rooftops of the moonlit city below and see that it is no longer truly night, but the early, velvet morning. Every star in the sky seems etched upon the inky blackness.

There is a catch in my breathing as I study the floodlit church that dominates the view from my bedchamber. I feel the pupils of my eyes contract in shock.

I know this place.

Like a crazy confection, a riot of arches, pinnacles, fretted spires, flying buttresses, statuary and stained glass; like a waking dream, a conundrum, the church is both steadfast and airy, hundreds of feet deep, wide, tall. Monumental. It is the Duomo, one of the greatest cathedrals in the world.

And the realisation hits me a second later that I am in Milan, in Northern Italy.

Milan.

A city of infinite treasures. A city I once loved and wandered at will. Though when, and as whom, I do not know. Again, I feel a brief jolt of dislocation, as if I am caught between past and present, fully inhabiting neither.

Then the sensation leaves me, and I realise that it is two hours before matins, before dawn.

In front of the Duomo, dwarfed by it, is a gleaming Christmas tree at least one hundred feet tall.

Glorious Milan. In December.

Before I can process anything more, there's a series of sharp taps upon the door.

I do not turn away from the window. Instead, I shake my long, unbound hair over my face, dig the toes of my narrow feet into the soft, plush pile of the carpet and pull the cuffs of my long sleeves over my hands. So that no part of my skin is visible from behind. It's become almost a reflex these days. Hiding this little light of mine.

The door opens behind me, before I can find my voice.

'Irina?' someone says blearily into the darkness. 'I heard you cry out — you scared me to death! Are you all right?'

Through the curtain of my long hair, I quickly scan the figure silhouetted in the doorway before returning my gaze to the city framed in the window.

A short, slender young woman — in her late twenties? — with jaw-length straight hair cut in a sleek bob stands there. The light behind her casts her face into shadow. I have no idea who she is. But she has a cut-glass accent, of a kind I've heard before. *English*, supplies my inner voice dryly. *She's English.*

How do I even ... *know* that?

'What's the matter with you?' the girl mutters. 'Cat got your tongue? Hard to believe.'

She snaps on a lamp by the door. The sudden flare of light makes the pupils of my borrowed eyes contract into pinpoints, but I adjust to the change in illumination instantaneously, without flinching.

The light of the lamp has extinguished the strange glow of my skin. I turn to face the stranger warily, uncurling my fingers from inside my sleeves, senses on high alert.

Who is she? What does she want from me?

The day can't come soon enough when I'll never again have to grope forward through the fog of a stranger's life, trying desperately not to give myself away.

The girl shakes her head in exasperation and tightens the belt of her patterned, blush-coloured kimono before heading purposefully across the room towards me. She stops a short distance away, looking me up and down critically.

'You don't need a PA, Irina, you need a nanny!

You've got *eight* hours of fittings ahead of you today, and that's just for starters. Hours of keeping perfectly still and taking direction, and we know those aren't your best skills. Now let's get you back to bed, okay? It's called "beauty sleep" for good reason, and even people like *you* need it.'

The girl has unusual eyes, one brown, one blue, and a cute pixie face, strong dark brows, a precision-cut slanting fringe — sleek silent-movie-star hair. But she's not, strictly speaking, beautiful. Not like ... 'me'.

I'm arrested by the reflection of the long, lean, exotic creature I see in the oval, gilt-framed mirror across the room. Touch the fingers of one hand to my face just to be certain that the young woman I'm looking at is me. Irina. *Us.*

Irina's unusually tall — a fraction over six foot, without shoes — with pale, clear, downy skin, large, wide-set, dark, feline eyes and fine features, almost elfin ears. A wide, mobile mouth, a small, heart-shaped face and thick, poker-straight hair the colour of burnt caramel that falls almost to the waist, worn with a blunt-cut fringe that slices straight across her forehead above wickedly arched brows.

Irina's clad in a fine, ivory-coloured cashmere sweater and bespoke matching trousers, very narrow, like cigarette pants, edged in pale blue ribbon. The most elegant sleepwear I've ever seen. Her build is lean and sinuous, narrow through the hips and shoulders, a swan's neck, collarbones very prominent above the V-neck of the sweater. In the mirror, Irina's knees appear wider than the midpoint of each thigh, and it's no trick of the light.

I'm inhabiting a beautiful stick insect. A freak of nature.

Irina's young. Younger than the stranger with the critical eyes.

But what's more startling than all this is the reflection *within* the reflection. There's another person framed in the mirror, even more preternaturally tall than the first. A ghost girl outlined in stardust, in moonlight. Who looks maybe sixteen on the outside, but seldom ever feels that way. With brown eyes, alabaster skin, a long, straight nose in an oval face framed by shoulder-length brown hair, each strand straight, even and perfectly the same. No will-o'-the-wisp like the other one, but broad-limbed, strong-looking. Stern-faced.

The second self, my true self.

The stranger laughs without amusement. 'Admiring yourself again?'

It's clear from her tone that she doesn't see *me* — just the human shell I'm inhabiting today. The girl I've soul-jacked.

'I suppose you can't help it,' she mutters, 'with a face and body like yours.'

I think Irina looks like a doll-faced alien with spidery limbs, but there's a sullen envy in the other girl's words. She should sooner envy Frankenstein's monster. For, despite her surface gloss, that's what Irina is today — a composite being, cobbled together from remnants.

The girl standing there giving me the evil eye isn't to know that the cycle that blights my existence has begun again: I've woken inside a new 'host' and am expected to rely on my wits, to hit the ground running, even though my entire world, my entire frame of reference, has shifted overnight. Though I call myself Mercy, I still don't know what my real name is. And I'm invisible to the world entire. Undetectable to any, save my own kind.

My own kind.

I feel Irina's brow furrow as I recall Gabriel disguised within the mortal, Sulaiman. The way I'm disguised now.

Eight of my own kind did this to me.

Unexpectedly, I'm assailed by monstrous images —

— of a steep, distant mountainside, a deadly crater upon one lonely slope, the soil scorched for leagues around, every tree, plant, animal and rock in the vicinity reduced to ashes, utterly destroyed.

— of a series of chambers, deep beneath the streets of an old city, piled high with the bones of the human dead. In the midst of this hellish domain — eight men. Each one unnaturally tall, preternaturally beautiful, youthful, ageless. Each one a being of pure fire, casting no shadow. They are gathered around a marble dais upon which something lies — blackened, twisted, burnt beyond recognition, barely alive.

What my inner eye sees there, upon that lonely tomb, brings another ringing scream to my lips.

The English girl covers her ears in pain, shrinking from me as if my cry has sharp edges to it, as if it's a noise loud enough to wake an entire sleeping city.

'Christ, Irina,' she gasps when the sound finally dies away. 'No need to scream the walls down! Everyone knows you can't pass a mirror without looking at yourself. It was meant to be a joke, okay?'

My left hand is flaring in agony, and I jam it beneath my elbow, against my right side, so the girl will not see it glow with a pale, white fire.

That burnt and blasted thing I saw? It was *me*.

I'd gone to that place of nightmare to die. Years ago. Centuries. I'd woken, instead, to find my fate in the hands of that righteous cabal: the Eight.

And I've been under their absolute dominion ever since.

Let me name them for you, for their identities are no longer a mystery to me. I saw them in my mind's eye, as Lela lay dying in Gabriel's arms.

Picture them, standing there, judgment in their eyes, every one. Each as beautiful as the next, but all so different. In form, in temperament, in abilities.

Gabriel, the herald of mysteries. Flame-haired, emerald-eyed. The self-same Gabriel who disguised himself, centuries later, as the mortal, Sulaiman, in order to watch over me.

Uriel: in face, in form, identical to me — the real me — save that he was created male. Which is a mystery in itself, one I have no answer for.

Fearsome Michael, the leader of them all, his flashing eyes as dark as his curling, black hair.

Selaphiel, sandy-haired and serious, absent, courteous, gentle, his quiet blue eyes fixed on things unseen.

Jegudiel with the waving, golden hair and dark, steely gaze, whose weapon of choice is a triple-thonged whip.

Silver-eyed, auburn-haired Jeremiel, who possesses a voice like exaltation.

Dark-eyed, dark-haired Barachiel, whose province is lightning, and whose emblem is a white rose.

And to close the circle of all those who passed sentence on me?

Raphael, the healer. Sable-eyed, dark-haired and olive-skinned. Whose mouth was made for laughter and compassion. The 'architect', so Gabriel had said, of my misery. The one whose plan it was, all those years ago, to hide me inside an unbroken succession of human lives. We'd been friends once. We might have been more, given time.

But Luc had changed all that.

I back towards an elegant armchair and perch unsteadily upon one arm as the memory of him takes me over.

Luc. My golden beloved. *My day star*, I called him, because he outshone all the stars, even the sun.

Luc — the one I have longed for. Whom I can never have, whom I can never find, because the Eight have pursued a policy, over these interminable centuries, of keeping us apart. I don't pretend to understand their reasons, because my memory has fault lines to it that have never healed, and may never heal.

Luc *loved* me, more than life itself. This much I know.

And, despite what I have become, he loves me still. He tells me so in my sleep, in my dreams — the only way we can ever be together these days. And Luc warns me, again and again, that the Eight wish me harm, that they cannot be trusted, that I must run from them. Keep running, and never stop.

But the Eight insist upon keeping me from Luc for my own good, the good of all things.

And the way this has been achieved?

I stare at Irina's remarkable face in the mirror. Touch her long-fingered hands to her extraordinary cheekbones.

There are two sides to every story.

But whose version of the truth should I believe?

Luc's?

Or Gabriel's?

Who lies to me? Who lies?

The English girl moves into the space reflected in the mirror, bringing my unwilling focus back. I get to my feet, uncomfortable that there's no longer any distance between us. She takes hold of Irina's sleeves impatiently, tugging her hands down, away from her face. Now I see three people reflected in the looking glass, although there are only two people physically present in the room. And even though I should be used to it by now, I feel a chill fall over me.

In the mirror, Irina's eyes are so dark, they seem almost black. They spark a fresh memory in me, a recent one.

Of a young man, with eyes so dark they had seemed almost black. He'd flown for hours to reach me, he'd been a whole day in the air. His face had been so pale with weariness, but he'd smiled the instant he saw me. That familiar fringe of dark hair had fallen into his eyes, and I'd reached out and brushed it back, as if my touch could banish his weariness. He'd embraced me and swung me about lightly in his arms, as if we were dancing. And I knew that he loved me, too, would have done anything for me. And in that moment, I'd felt an answering emotion.

Luc himself had pointed it out to me once, in a dream: that this mortal boy had somehow, beyond all understanding, fallen under my power, fallen for *me*, even though he has never seen me. When we first met, I had soul-jacked the body of a girl called Carmen

Zappacosta. And when the Eight had so cruelly shifted me out of her life and into Lela Neill's, that boy had come to me again as if nothing and no one on earth could keep us apart.

But then he'd watched me die, murdered in cold blood right before his eyes.

Or so it must have seemed to him, because I can still hear his screams.

I see him again, staring at me from behind police lines, through the front windows of a coffee shop. Me on the inside, staring back at him, all the longing in my gaze. And I relive the moment when a single bullet from a semi-automatic pistol entered Lela's body. The memory, the ghostly impact, is so vivid that I stagger backwards where I stand. I imagine I feel Justine Hennessy's hand in mine once again, hear myself whispering, through blood, through the great, pulsing wound in my chest, 'Tell him ... that Mercy shall come again ...'

In the mirror, I see Irina's expression of shock reflect my own. I watch all the colour leach out of her angular, unforgettable face as I suddenly remember his name. Catch hold of it, say it silently to myself, with reverence — *Ryan Daley* — as if the two words are a prayer.

And something seems to give way inside me, as if buried memories are struggling to the surface. The ground is shifting beneath my feet; time feels as if it is reeling away from me in all directions, and I must sift through the jumbled memories of five past lives to piece together what I want, what I need.

I *remember* Ryan. I remember everything about him. The way he looks when he's feeling impatient, the way I feel when he holds me close: messed-up, buzzy, wired. Like he's the greatest drug in the universe.

I need him for selfish reasons I can barely articulate. When I'm with him, I feel less like a freak. He makes me laugh. He makes me angry. He makes me feel alive, in the way I once was. But most of all, he *gets* me. And he makes me feel safe. He's the only person who doesn't treat me like a broken toy that must be fixed. And they're pretty potent things after centuries spent wandering the wilderness that is this earth: alone, deranged, damaged.

Did Ryan get my message? Or does he truly believe me … dead?

Is he grieving? My God, did I cause him grief? Did I *hurt* him?

I love Luc. That's a constant. He's always been

there, always. A face in my dreams, a voice in my head. We were meant to be together. We were *made* to be together. We have a connection that not even time, distance or remorseless exile can sunder. Some day, some day soon, we'll be together again. I know it. It's what's sustained me all along: the thought that one day this might all be over and I might be allowed to go home, to find Luc waiting for me. That hope kept me together, gave me something to steer by, even before I could begin to grasp again who he was, and what he'd once meant to me.

But right here, right now? There's Ryan. And I'm too afraid to name what I feel for him, because in no universe would someone like him and someone like me *ever* work out. What Ryan makes me feel is all an illusion, because feelings are for humans, and I'm not human. I know that much. My thing with Ryan can go exactly nowhere. But there's no crime against wishing, no crime against dreaming, is there? So when I'm with him — when circumstances don't transpire to tear us apart — I cheat and tell myself to take it one day at a time, to live in the moment.

But I also need Ryan to help Luc find me, if that makes any kind of sense. Because if Ryan and I are together, Luc will finally have some clue as to where upon the surface of this floating, teeming world I am. He had said so himself in my dream. *Find the mortal boy, return with him to Paradise and then we'll be together again.*

But I can't ever tell Ryan any of this. Because maybe then he wouldn't want to help me any more, and I can't risk it. If Ryan loves me, really loves *me* — and not just because I once helped save his twin sister's life — then I don't know what that would do to him, telling him he's got competition from a guy who was created to be peerless and immortal. Who needs to hear that?

He's been hurt enough for one lifetime.

I need to find him quickly. To apologise. To explain. To confess.

That he just may be my skeleton key, my wild card, my circuit breaker. My way out of this hot, damn mess.

CHAPTER 2

The girl with the two-coloured eyes crosses her arms, trying to catch and hold my gaze in the looking glass. 'You bloody well didn't, did you?' she snarls suddenly. '*Did you?*'

My eyes fly to hers in the mirror and I wonder why she's so angry.

'You've held it together for six months and now you go and start *using* again?' she yells. 'I'm not interested in all the stupid excuses you always have ready — *it just happened to be there; and how could I say no?*

'I warned you! You're not going to talk me out of it this time, because I can't do this any more! All the sneaking around for you, all the lying, when it's obvious to everyone what's wrong with you. You're even more out of it than usual. I quit. Hear me? I'm quitting.'

She turns and paces towards the rumpled bed, while I try to work out what I'm supposed to have done.

'Look at you!' She turns on me accusingly. 'You say you're "clean" but I've never seen you so spaced out and paranoid. I don't know how you got your hands on some, but after today — after those tedious, bloody fittings — we're done, we're through. You're a *junkie*, Irina. You need to get proper help, before you lose your mind. Or your life. I didn't sign up for this. I'm not prepared to walk in one day to find you dead on the floor.

'Are you getting any of this?' she says, sitting down on the edge of the bed, sounding defeated. 'And don't pretend your grasp of English has failed again, because I know you understand me perfectly.'

'You … can't … quit,' I reply with difficulty, the first words I've said since 'waking' here. Even to me, Irina's heavily accented voice sounds awkward, almost rusty, although the accent itself seems familiar.

'Because I'm …' I struggle to remember the word the English girl had thrown at me, '*clean.*'

I frown, still trying to make sense of the word's meaning in the context of her accusations. What is it exactly that I'm supposed to have … used?

Her answering laugh is shaky. 'Good try, but I've seen it all before, remember? The zombie eyes, the inability to conduct a logical conversation, the paranoid belief that something's trying to eat its way out through your skin. You probably woke everyone on this floor with your screaming. You must be coming down like a lead balloon. I still don't know how you managed it — I never let you out of my sight yesterday.'

Russian, my inner voice pipes up suddenly. *Irina's accent is Russian.*

'*Hello?*' she snaps. 'You're doing it again — spacing out!' She waves one hand in front of my face. 'You don't even remember me, do you?' she says softly. 'Gia? Gia Basso? Hired to make you look good? Hired because I speak enough Italian and French to give you an edge over all the other girls who'd plunge a dagger into your back and step into your shoes in a heartbeat given half the chance.'

'I am *not* spacing out,' I reply, a touch of anger creeping into Irina's husky voice. 'I'm thinking. There's a difference.'

Gia snorts. 'Where there's smoke there's always fire. I can't believe you'd jeopardise your comeback like this! We've only been working towards this day for *months*. Honestly, you *are* your own worst enemy.'

I feel a surge of irrational fury that makes the fingers of my left hand involuntarily curl into talons. I have to stop myself lifting the judgmental little twerp off the ground by the lapels of her cherry-blossom-patterned kimono and giving her a hard shake. She doesn't understand how far I've come just to get here; how I've started to do something that I've never been able to do before.

I'm beginning to *learn*. I'm beginning to accumulate knowledge; to make connections again, however random they may seem to you. Like how I seem to have an immediate geographical fix on where I am right now. And how I'm able to recognise Gia's accent, even Irina's. And how I'm walking and talking without feeling an ounce of physical distress. I could have been born in this body. It could *be* my body. From distal phalanges to metatarsals, from calcaneus to crown, it might almost have been mine, *ab initio*, from the very beginning. That gap that's always been present, between thought and deed? It's dissolving.

But most important of all is the fact that I can remember every second I spent as Lela Neill. She may be alive no longer, save in my memory, but I recall everything that happened when I *was* her. It's proof that I'm growing stronger, that I've started to circumvent the strange blockages in my mind, those obstacles that the Eight have somehow placed there. In some unholy way, I've begun to regenerate. Or mutate. Or evolve. And the process is getting ... faster.

I think that, like a machine, I used to be set to *delete*. That's why I've never been able to remember anything more than impressions really, sixteen, thirty-two, even forty-eight lives out of context. But something's changed. Some things are beginning to stick.

Or maybe, like acid, like flame, some kind of dangerous contaminant, *I'm* beginning to burn back through. And what's more, no one has any idea of the extent to which I'm back. Only me.

No matter how high the Eight might try to build up that wall of thorns around me, from now on, Sleeping Beauty is awake. And she's angry.

There's no reason I can't keep to the plan that I started when I was Lela Neill. The face, the body, even the specifics, may have changed, but there's nothing to stop me just picking up where I left off. Around me, time always gets misplaced, you know? It runs too fast, runs too slow. I've always had a problem with chronology, with the order of things. But starting today, I'm taking control before the sucker gets away from me. I ran out of time when I was Lela, and it's not going to happen again. As soon as I can get my bearings, figure out what Irina's story is, work out where the exits are, I'm going to reconnect with Ryan Daley and bust my way out of here.

Gia looks startled when I growl in Irina's heavy Russian accent, 'You want to quit? Go ahead. I'm not going to stop you.'

I stalk past her, calling her bluff, and fling open the first door I see. It leads into a spacious walk-in wardrobe containing an ironing board, half a dozen heavy white terry towelling robes, blankets, towels, slippers and umbrellas, all embossed with a fancy, crested hotel logo. You could comfortably house a small African village inside the space, but there's not a single scrap of clothing I could actually wear. I shut the door disgustedly.

'What are you, uh, doing?' Gia says uncertainly, as I try another door to the left of the first one. Again, I don't bother with the light switch. I don't need to.

I find myself staring into a luxury all-marble bathroom with its own flat screen TV and built-in sound system. It's covered in enough personal effects to bury a person alive, but there's nothing in here remotely resembling anything to wear, and even I draw the line at walking the streets in my pyjamas. Only crazies do that.

I might hear voices in my head, but that doesn't make me crazy.

I slam shut the bathroom door and turn to face the girl on the bed. 'Where are my clothes?' I demand.

Gia starts to laugh so wildly, she sounds like she's crying.

'Where are my clothes?' I say again, fiercely. 'I need to go out. There are things I have to do.'

Top of the list? Locate one of those all-night internet joints I used to frequent when I was Lela. I need to use that seething, wholly man-made 'web' I still can't get my old-school head around to draw Ryan to me, the way I did before. Across oceans, across time zones.

In all this time, I've never been able to find Luc and he's never been able to find me. But Ryan, at least, has a physical location on this earth. He comes from a small town called Paradise that's as far from it as it's possible to get. But it's a real place, perched on an ugly stretch of beach in a country I don't even have a name for yet. I'd been forced to leave Lela's body before I'd managed to find that out.

Even if Ryan hasn't reached home yet, he's going to be checking his emails. I can get a lock on him again, I know it.

Gia's still laughing. 'Where are my clothes!' she whoops. 'Listen to yourself! You sure you're "clean"?'

I frown, still unable to see the joke.

Gia leads me out of my bedroom and into a massive sitting room that's decorated in more of the same riotous rococo excess. There are too many occasional tables, mirrors, knick-knacks, table lamps, armchairs, divans, vases of scented, white blooms, hand-knotted silk rugs and footstools for one lone skinny female like me to use.

We pass a coffee table surrounded by deep, winged armchairs, and an elegant dining table with eight chairs around it that's been placed beneath a set of windows facing out onto the street to catch the light and the incredible view. I'm in part of an old Milanese palazzo, I realise, looking around. The proportions of the rooms are baronial. Beneath all the unrelenting froufrou, the place has old bones.

'Is all this all ... mine?' I murmur.

'We're sharing it,' Gia says over her shoulder, 'like we always do. Although you always make sure you give me the smallest room in the suite.'

We come to a stop outside two doors on the other side of the vast sitting area that are painted a discreet olive-grey colour, with inset door panels outlined in gold leaf. Both doors are closed.

Gia points at the one on the right. 'That one's mine and it's off-limits,' she says matter-of-factly. 'The last time you asked to borrow one of my vintage Jean Desses cocktail dresses, I found myself at Paris Fashion Week staring at a photo of it on the back of one of your supermodel "friends" at a hotel nightclub opening in Miami. You know, the one who always forgets to put on her underwear before she goes out. You swore you had no idea how it got there and when I finally got it back after threatening legal action, the dress had part of its skirt missing.'

I look at her blankly. She'd lost me at the word *vintage* and she knows it.

Gia sighs, opening the door on the left and flicking on the light. 'Does this answer your earlier question?' she says with heavy sarcasm.

I can see why she's incredulous. The vast room has had all of its furniture removed and is filled with matching bespoke luggage in an expensive-looking black, tan and white chevron pattern. There would have to be sixteen pieces of the stuff at least, and the initials *I.D.Z.* are emblazoned across the front of each one in large, bright green script, with a matching navy blue and green racing stripe running down the centre of each piece.

'Flashy,' I drawl in Irina's husky voice.

Gia gives me an odd look. 'These are just your "essentials",' she replies. 'We had a screaming match over the six other suitcases I forced you to leave at home because we're only supposed to be here for, like, five days.'

Spilling out of every open case is a wealth of coats, dresses, jackets, tops, skirts, trousers, shorts, sweaters, wraps, jeans, leggings, boots and shoes in every colour and texture imaginable, along with handfuls of filmy lingerie. It's a sea of leather, denim, fur, feathers, couture, vintage and velvet. Irina is clearly not averse to a sequin. The room is like an Aladdin's cave of high-end apparel. There's enough clothing here to dress an army of women for a week without anyone having to lift a finger to do laundry.

When I think about Carmen Zappacosta's one dingy sports bag, her little boy's clothes and her much-loved flat, grey toy bunny with its fur all worn-down in places, its reattached glass eyes, I feel almost misty. Ditto Lela Neill's haphazardly stored collection of threadbare second-hand clothing, most of it past its use-by date the first time around and dyed an unbecoming black, green or purple.

How could one person have so many … things?

'Are these all mine, too?' I say idiotically, knowing the question is basically rhetorical and that I fully deserve the look Gia is giving me now. The crazy-long inseams on the crystal-studded, low-rider jeans draped across the nearest case are a dead giveaway. Plus, Irina has long, bony, ballet-dancer's feet that match the pair of towering snakeskin stilettos slung carelessly near the door. Gia's feet are like something from the days of Imperial China: doll-sized.

'You know I'm not even going to dignify that with an answer,' Gia replies as she ushers me out of the room and back into the warmly-lit sitting room.

She paces across to an antique secretaire against one wall and retrieves a pile of glossy magazines from it, thrusting them in my direction.

'You're *Irina Zhivanevskaya*, remember? Super-model, tabloid darling. One of the most recognised faces on the planet? Women all over the world copy the way you dress, the way you wear your hair, the places you hang out. They follow your every move, every disastrous hook-up, with morbid interest.'

I quickly scan the covers in my hands and Irina's mesmerising face is on every one.

Gia gives a small laugh. 'You're one of the "one name" girls — like Gisele or Daria, Elle, Lara or Iman. You can't just "go out",' she says. 'You haven't been able to just "go out" for several years. It takes full hair and make-up and a decoy car or two for you to just get up and leave any place. Let alone here. And especially now.'

She takes back one of the magazines in my hands and flicks through it until she finds the cover story and hands it back to me. I frown as I read about Irina's latest battle with a very public addiction to drugs that's left her *dangerously erratic.* I look up to see Gia's cool eyes on me.

'It's mostly just old gossip hurriedly cobbled together because no one's quite sure how bad it really is, not even me, because you lie and lie. I've quit on you three times already and you've somehow always managed to lure me back. You always know which buttons of mine to push. And I'm no fame whore, but I still kind of like the crazy shit that happens around you. Nobody else on earth gets a chance to see what you see, be where you are …

'I expect you'll sack me now,' Gia says, looking down at the floor, 'for talking out of turn like this …'

I shake my head. 'On the contrary,' I reply in Irina's distinctive smoke-and-whiskey voice. 'I value your honesty.'

I didn't used to. When I'd first begun to realise there was something really wrong with me — that the face and body I happened to be inhabiting never seemed to bear any correlation to the person I was inside — I was so wound up and brittle, so wary, that I'd truly believed that honesty was for simpletons. But that was then, and this is now, and I could use more of it. The Eight? Luc, even? They're all keeping something from me, something bad. I can feel it in my bones.

I rifle quickly through the other magazine articles about Irina and it's clear that she may be famous, beautiful and rich beyond reason, but she's a monster. Irina's been pulled off an aeroplane for slapping a flight attendant who asked her to get off her mobile, she's thrown champagne and punches at a love rival in a Berlin nightclub, had nude photos uploaded onto the net by a vindictive ex-boyfriend, been filmed scoring, mainlining and passing out, and already labelled a *has-been* at the ripe old age of nineteen. She's a bitch-slapping, hair-pulling, tantrum-throwing piece of work.

As I hand the magazines back to Gia in amazement, she says, 'The fact you've had to give yourself a refresher course and don't appear to remember the highlights from your own life speaks volumes ...'

I'm silent for a long while. There's no getting around it. Irina must be some kind of highly-strung, celebrity clotheshorse. With a self-destructive streak a mile wide. I'm beginning to see the extent of my problem. Somehow, I need to locate Ryan again, vanish Irina right out of her very public life, and give the Eight the slip so that I can rendezvous with Luc back in Ryan's hometown of Paradise. Have I covered everything?

I curse the Eight under my breath for their eternal interference, the tests within tests they seem determined always to set me.

'You know this city better than I do,' I say cajolingly. 'I have to go out, I have to find someone. Couldn't we just go — you and me? Walk out of here right now?'

Gia meets my eyes in astonishment. 'You'd be screwed,' she replies. 'Even though the paparazzi are camped outside your usual hotel, as soon as you set foot outside here, a crowd of ordinary Italians with phone cams will be in your face broadcasting your whereabouts to the entire world. Everyone knows who you are and why you're in Milan. And they're all waiting for you to fall flat on your face.'

'I really am "clean",' I say simply. 'And I really do need your help. Because it's important I find this guy — you don't know how much.'

Gia rolls her eyes. 'They're always "important" until you leave them begging and broken and move on to your next victim. No way,' she says firmly. 'I'm under strict orders from management not to let you out on the street during the hours of darkness. You're too much of an insurance risk these days. It's not worth my hide to try and smuggle you out.' Her eyes soften a little as she stares into my mutinous face. 'I know it's seemed like a prison sentence lately, but the arrangements are in place for your own good. You know that, don't you?'

I feel a surge of anger at her words that makes the fingers of my left hand ache. Why does everyone think they know better than me?

Gia jerks a thumb at the bed. 'Ask me again in daylight, okay? It can at least wait until after sunrise.

Now get some rest. Final fittings begin in about three hours and they'll be brutal. Giovanni's already warned me that he won't stand any more tardiness or attitude from you or you'll lose the global print advertising contract, as well as the catwalk gig. Remember, you've only got this because your management called in all their favours. Somehow, the great Giovanni Re still has a soft spot for you even though you've always been a complete bitch to him. No one else is prepared to touch you right now, so don't stuff this up. Sleep. Now. *Capiche?*'

I climb into bed reluctantly and she stares down into my face. 'Let's just start over, okay? Let's just get through today as if none of this …' she gestures in the air between us, 'ever happened. I still might quit, you know. If I don't kill you first.'

Gia walks over to the windows and draws the curtains shut again before heading back towards the door. She snaps off the light and closes the door firmly behind her.

I pull the plump, feather-light bedclothes right up under my chin and lie there in the dark, looking up at the ceiling.

It's covered in an original Renaissance fresco, with lots of fine brushwork in gold and blue and blush pink. Maybe Tiepolo? Definitely in the style of Tiepolo, with all those luminous clouds and long-limbed, vigorous people. Who seem, like so much else, achingly familiar, but so very far beyond my reach.

CHAPTER 3

I'm unable to sleep, even though I want to so badly. In all these years, sleep has been my only source of solace. In dreams, I feel most like myself, capable of anything, not limited by the human face and form I happen to be wearing.

And in dreams, I have access to that most longed-for of things — time with Luc. Though even *that*, the Eight would deny us, if They could.

When Luc first picked me out of that throng of *elohim* — each more beautiful than the last — to be his love, he said, to be his queen, some small part of me had refused to believe that it would last. Because when I looked at him, and then looked at me, I couldn't understand what he saw in me, what set me apart from all the rest. But in a funny kind of way, we *have* lasted. Though it's been years since we last touched, or even met face to face.

Gabriel told me himself that while I sleep — when the linkages between soul and body are at their weakest — Luc somehow still has access to my thoughts, access to *me*. It's a connection that has persisted despite everything the Eight have done to keep us apart.

And though in my dreams, Luc sometimes seems more angry, more goading, more desperate, cruel and spiteful than I have ever remembered him to be, just the sight of him — golden-skinned, golden-haired, broad-shouldered, snake-hipped, long and lean, with eyes as pale as living ice, like broken water — is like a shot of pure adrenaline to the heart. He's the most beautiful thing in creation, more beautiful than the sun. Call me shallow — and I'm sure plenty have; it's just a feeling I get — I've always loved beautiful things.

I could use Luc's devious counsel now. There was no one better at getting what he wanted. No one. But for the past few hours, I've lain here, tossing and turning, unable to reach out to him, unable to conjure up the necessary pre-conditions for him to reach out to me. I've just been stuck in a kind of waking trance, replaying Lela's last moments — our last moments together — over and over. Feeling that fatal gunshot, wondering if there was anything I could've done differently.

There's a sudden, sharp rap on the door and Gia Basso enters the room again, dressed in street clothes this time. She marches across to the curtains and yanks them open with a skittering sound. It's still dark outside but lightening just a little, at the horizon. My internal clock says it's still very early: six; maybe six fifteen, at most.

Gia's wearing a tough-looking, black leather jacket with rows of brass studs on the lapels over a bunch of layered, artfully ripped tee-shirts and tank tops and a vintage-looking, beat-up waistcoat; skin-tight jeans and towering black leather ankle boots criss-crossed by a welter of leather straps. There's jangling silver jewellery at her ears and on her wrists, a couple of long and floaty patterned scarves slung around her neck, and she's wearing a striking dark purple lipstick and strong, smoky eye make-up combination that somehow work together, even though they shouldn't. With her glossy, China-girl hair, she's the most stylish creature I've ever beheld, and I say so, admiringly.

She frowns, giving me a sharp look as if she thinks

that I'm — what's that phrase I puzzled over so much when I was Lela? Ah, yes, *taking the piss*. Making fun of her. I'm not, but she ignores my comment and barks, 'As soon as people get a lock on your location, a huge contingent will materialise out of nowhere. It'll be like a flash mob, I guarantee it. You're "so hot right now" and not for the right reasons. Get ready to run the gauntlet. Breakfast is on its way up. We can plan our route with Felipe while you eat.'

She ruthlessly hauls the coverlet off my body, her eyebrows flying up in surprise when I rise immediately and head into the OTT marble ensuite to splash water onto Irina's perfectly symmetrical, heart-shaped little face, jumpy with nerves at the thought that Operation Get Me Outta Here is about to find itself back on track.

Gia watches me narrowly, exclaiming in a passable Russian accent, 'You're not going to call me a *heartless beeetch* today?'

I shake my head and look around. Scattered across the enormous stone vanity unit are at least a dozen hairbrushes in as many styles: barrel-shaped, paddle-shaped, oval, square, mini-sized, maxi-sized, natural or synthetic. I can't move without tripping over a plush white bath towel on the floor, and I pick up each one I come across, folding it quickly and neatly into a precise square, until there is a stack of them on top of the gilded footstool near the basins. Gia folds her arms and leans in the doorway. I feel her eyes follow me around the room.

Next, I pick out a large, flat brush that looks like an instrument of torture and yank it through Irina's long, caramel-coloured mane, her hair crackling beneath my brushstrokes.

The room is filled with towering floral arrangements, all in white; groupings of half-burnt scented candles with base notes of cinnamon, myrrh and orange blossom; and the heavy artillery of glamour — hair straighteners, large and small, curling tongs, hot curlers, eyelash shapers, hair dryers, tweezers, combs, hairpins, hair spray, lacquer, fudge, gel, mousse, styling wax, treatments for dry hair, damaged hair and coloured hair, bottles of perfume of every size and description, enough make-up to fill a store, not to mention all the gear required to take it off again. Clearly, it takes a lot to be Irina Zhivanevskaya. I frown. She looks okay to me the way she is. How much of this stuff am I expected to use? And how do I use most of it?

As I hesitate, I see that Gia wants to say something, then literally has to bite her tongue to stop herself.

I look back towards the massive stone vanity above which our three faces — mine, Irina's, Gia's — are reflected. I meet Gia's eyes in the mirror. 'I don't know what to do.'

Gia's eyebrows disappear into her slanting, razor-cut fringe. 'What do you mean you don't know what to do?' she exclaims. 'Do what you usually do. Do you know how *insane* you sound?'

She's right. Even a junkie supermodel is going to remember how to get herself dolled up for work. It's clear that I'm going to have to recycle the cover story I'd used when I was Lela. The last thing I need right now is for Irina to be sent back to rehab because she's making no sense.

'I'm clean, Gia, I promise you,' I say. 'It's just that I've never told anyone this before ...' I lower my voice so that she has to lean forward to hear '... but I can't ... remember things. It's a disease, you know? It's been happening for a while now, and lately it's been getting worse. But I'm too scared to have it properly checked out ...'

I'm no actress, but I make Irina's expression as scared and as mournful as I can. Gia looks genuinely shocked and I can tell she believes me.

'You mean all those times I thought you were strung out, you might actually have been ...'

I nod quickly. 'I haven't been very good at hiding my ... affliction. I have mood swings, you know? I find myself doing things I know I'll regret later. I'm so afraid I'm going to die that I deliberately do things I know might kill me anyway ...'

I have to bite back laughter. Once I get going, I'm pretty unstoppable. Luc used to say that I was almost as good as he was at making things up, that I was a natural. I frown at the sudden recollection.

Gia takes me by the sleeve, bringing my attention back. 'Why didn't you tell me sooner?' she says softly. 'You let me believe all those awful things about you. If the press knew about this ... brain thing of yours, then maybe they wouldn't make up so much shit about you all the time. You should let me feed the story to a couple of the more sympathetic editors. Make sure it gets around ...'

I shrug and look sadly at the floor. But the lie's worked. A little of Gia's ingrained wariness around me, her brooding irritation, seems to have dissipated.

'Come on,' Gia sighs, leading me back through the palatial sitting area into the room littered with luggage and clothing.

'Now, you've got just over half an hour to pull a look together,' she says crisply. 'Clothes first, war paint after. We *cannot* be late. It's Giovanni's fiftieth anniversary in the biz and he's rumoured to be retiring after the runway show is over, and announcing the new designer who's taking over from him. Which, if true, is *huge* news. And he's picked just *you* — not the usual battalion of hollow-cheeked fembots — to open and close. So act appropriately. No falling off the catwalk; no lewd or criminal behaviour at the afterparty — not unless you never want to work again.' She's already backing towards the door as she adds, 'And the faster we leave, the more chance we have of avoiding the press.'

She's on the verge of shutting the door when I call out, 'Wait!'

Gia gives me a wary look through the gap. 'What? What now?'

I scan this stranger's sea of belongings ruefully. 'Why don't you ... *help* me?' I say.

Gia goes incredibly still. '*Help you?*' she says finally, wrinkling her nose and stepping slowly back through the door. 'Like, what, physically dress you? I'm not supposed to touch "the presence", remember? And the last time I suggested you weren't rocking the outfit you had on, you threw a McQueen armadillo at me.'

I shake my head, bewildered by almost every word that's just emerged from her mouth, doubly bewildered by the sheer volume of clothing in the room. Working out whether I'm 'rocking' my outfit has always been the least of my troubles when I wake up in someone else's body with no memory of how I got there.

I look around the room, with literally no idea where to start. Most days, I have enough difficulty trying to blend into my immediate surroundings convincingly, without adding ambush photography to the mix.

'I'm not having a good day,' I plead, tapping the side of my head. 'Help me to look —'

'What?' Gia shoots back, hands on hips. 'Like a cashed-up, colour-blind rock chick meets vintage-boho, Euro-princess *slut*?'

'Say that again?' I'm taken aback at the venom in her words.

She shrugs. 'Well, you asked. And it makes a change from having my opinion completely ignored. The way you dress may have made you famous, but it's a little too schizophrenic and *look-at-me* for my tastes. You may have the "best body in the business" to go along with that "face of the century" of yours, but you kind of put too much information out there, if you know what I'm saying.' Gia's expression is a weird mix of envious and dubious.

She sighs. 'You're right though — you actually *do* need help. You've started appearing at the top of "What's Not Hot" lists in fashion magazines lately. People are saying you've lost your fashion mojo. Bad news in your line of work, *darling*.'

She moves through the sea of cases and bags with a critical eye and picks out a narrow pair of soft, leather trousers, low-rise, long and lean, in a warm chocolate colour. Then she rifles through some kind of jumbo-sized duffle bag on wheels and pulls out a crew-neck, long-sleeved, body-skimming, dusky-olive cashmere tunic that falls to mid hip. 'These will have to do.'

She comes to a standstill and scans the room for several minutes until she finds what she wants — a hard travelling case that comes up to just above her waist, filled to the brim with shoes stored in neat pairs. 'Just what I was looking for,' she says as she draws out a gleaming pair of black patent heels — so shiny, I can see my face in them — with criminally high heels, six inches at least, and bright red soles.

'I can't move in those,' I protest. They look like the claws of some alien creature.

'You'll have to,' Gia replies, distractedly. 'You know as well as I do that flat shoes won't lift the ensemble the way these will. Plus, you're *Irina*, and *Irina* never wears flats. Wedges maybe, clogs at a stretch.' Gia wrinkles her nose at the idea.

'Always something with a heel,' she insists, 'to make you seem even less like the rest of us mere mortals when you stalk by with your head in the clouds.'

'Where is it?' Gia mutters, as she grabs a matched set of silky, floral-print lingerie and throws it at me, too. 'Did we pack them in the medium trolley case? Or cram them all in the hatbox?' She laughs triumphantly as she unclasps the fastening on a hatbox as big as a bass drum and draws out a midnight-black felt cloche hat with intricate pleating extending over one ear so the leading edge extends upwards slightly, like a bird's wing.

'Perfect. It'll look fantastic against the warm, neutral tones and all that long hair of yours. And let's finish it off with that long, black, military-style shearling overcoat Andreas sent you from his studio in Madrid last winter. It's the only one he ever made in that particular design. You've never worn it and I know that hurt his feelings enormously. When I ran into him backstage at the London shows this year, his lips were practically trembling as he asked after you.'

Gia locates the overcoat in a huge case that opens outwards like a mini wardrobe complete with hangers. She drapes it over her arm with the other pieces she's selected for me, the little hat perched over one small fist. 'Hop to it,' she says, wending her way back through the cases and holding her selections out to me.

'What?' I say, startled. 'Right now? Here?'

It's Gia's turn to look shocked. 'You're, like, a model?' she exclaims mockingly. 'You stand around in your underwear all day — if you're lucky — while fifteen people work on your hair and make-up and shove fabulously expensive clothes over your head. I'm the one who's always telling you to put some goddamn clothes on, remember? So, needless to say, I've seen it all before. But I'll look away from "the presence",' she snorts loudly, 'if that'll help.'

I have no choice but to scramble out of the cashmere sleep suit I'm wearing and into the things Gia's chosen for me, in record time. She looks at me clinically when I'm done, turning me in the direction of a full-length mirror set up in the corner of the room. The colours she's selected highlight Irina's cream and roses complexion, her toffee-coloured hair and huge, wide-set, dark eyes fringed by extravagant dark lashes.

Gia tugs the black cloche hat onto my head, twisting and pulling at it until she's satisfied with the angle of the delicate bird wing arcing above one brow. She pulls a set of bobby pins from a large, monogrammed vanity case and secures the hat firmly.

'Fabulous,' she murmurs as she jams the last pin in place. 'And put these on when we get outside or you'll be sorry.' She hands me a soft, sleek pair of short, hand-stitched, shearling-lined, black leather gloves.

I shove them into a pocket of my ankle-length coat and climb reluctantly into the shoes, feeling as if I'm going to tip forward onto my face at any moment.

'I can't do this!' I exclaim, screwing up Irina's small and exquisite nose.

Gia frowns as she takes in my awkward, slump-shouldered, turtle-necked posture. 'What you mean is, you can't do this *unmedicated*. Well, tough, because it's not my job to facilitate your self-harming tendencies. Stand up straighter, and it won't seem like you're falling downhill. You need to redistribute your weight. I can't believe I'm telling *you* this — your memory really must be shot to hell.'

I make subtle adjustments to Irina's posture until Gia stops frowning.

'That's better,' she says. 'It's perfect. A little bit rock and roll, a little bit minimalist-with-an-edge, and the hat is just quirky enough to signal that you're a fashion insider, you speak the language. You couldn't take a bad photo in that outfit. From any angle.'

'It feels like torture,' I respond dryly, feeling my feet going numb.

Gia laughs. 'Beauty hurts.'

She's about to say something else when a doorbell peals so loudly, I almost jump. I'm reminded of the small matter of locating Ryan Daley, which completely slipped my mind during the insane amount of time it took us to find me something to wear. Irina's heart gives a sudden lurch.

'You promised you'd help me find him, find Ryan,' I remind Gia.

She shakes her head warningly, already heading towards the door. 'Not now,' she says over her shoulder. 'That will be Felipe, and Felipe is not accustomed to being ignored.' Her tone is derisive.

I trail awkwardly after her in the crippling, shiny heels she picked out for me to wear. When she flings open the door to my suite, I see a handsome, sun-bronzed, strong-featured young man standing there. Mid to late twenties, with black, slicked-back hair. He's shorter than I am in my absurd footwear, and broad-shouldered, muscular, powerful-looking. He's wearing a single-breasted charcoal grey suit over a black turtleneck, a camel-coloured overcoat and expensive-looking, spit-and-polish black lace-up brogues. He's carrying a pair of cream and tan, perforated leather driving gloves in one hand. As he follows Gia into the stately sitting room of the suite, I see open admiration in his dark eyes. For *me*.

Even though I consider myself impervious to all forms of flattery, I find myself blushing suddenly under his appreciative and unblinking scrutiny. Even Ryan never looked at me the way this guy's doing now. Like I'm good enough to ... devour. I don't know whether to feel pleased, or revolted.

'*¡Querida!*' the young man murmurs in a low, musical voice like an auditory caress. '*Cómo ardo al pensar en su belleza, a pesar de su maldad infernal.*'

Gia shoots Felipe a scandalised look.

I feel Irina's face suddenly flush with a strange, hectic blood, her heartbeat kick into higher gear. It's *Spanish*. I actually recognise it.

But I don't recall any past facility with Spanish at all. So where is this coming from?

Literally, the guy had said —

Darling! How your beauty sets me on fire, despite your infernal evil.

I don't know how it's possible, but when I reach out for the words I need, the words I want to use, they're somehow there.

'*Qué simpatico … como siempre, querido Felipe*,' I reply tersely. 'But let's speak English, for Gia's sake, *¿le parece bien?*'

There are accents on all the wrong places, accents where there shouldn't be any, but from the looks on both their faces, I've just made perfect sense in a language I shouldn't even *know*.

'You're speaking English for *my* sake?' Gia says disbelievingly.

The confident smile on Felipe's handsome face falters for a moment, before it's smoothly re-established. 'Your Spanish, Senorita Zhivanevskaya,' he says, his perfect white teeth showing, 'he has improved very much.'

'Yes, "he" has,' Gia mutters. 'Out of sight. So tell me again, Irina, why you insisted on hiring that creepy translator for the Costa Rican swimsuit shoot last month?'

From the look on Gia's face, it's clear that the only languages Irina's supposed to have are Russian and bitchy conversational English.

'Sit,' I tell Felipe, still pretending I didn't hear Gia's question. I gesture at the two pairs of elegant winged armchairs facing each other either side of a monumental glass and steel coffee table bearing porcelain cups and saucers and a sleek, silver, lidded jug.

Gia and I take our places across from Felipe and, for a moment, I do not hear the icily correct small talk that the two of them are exchanging. Lela Neill hadn't spoken Spanish. Neither had Lucy, or Susannah. Or Ezra before them. But with a name like Zappacosta, I'm guessing that Carmen might be able to. *And now I can, too? Even though I passed through Carmen's body … two lives ago?* Or does this ability come from somewhere else, some *when* else? Some 'life' even further back than the time I was Carmen?

The cool-hued room seems to tilt. There's a sudden sensation that I'm freefalling, though my physical body sits here, unmoved. What's inside always so very different from what's outside.

As if from very far away, I hear Gia enquire frostily of our guest, 'Tea?', before picking up the silver thermos and pouring a shot of hot, dark amber liquid into one of the crested white teacups on the table before her. It's a trait so peculiar to the English, and as I direct my unfocused gaze at the steam coming off the surface of the drink, I can almost make out every particle rising.

Felipe shakes his head dismissively, unfolding a road map from a pocket of his overcoat. He spreads it out on the table between us with his tanned, long-fingered hands, before uncapping a gold and onyx fountain pen.

Something tugs away at my subconscious, begging to be made plain. That small voice inside me, that's always one step ahead of my waking self, murmurs: *Gabriel, Uriel, Michael, Jegudiel, Selaphiel, Jeremiel, Barachiel, Raphael.*

Eight names more familiar to me than my own. Eight names that could be a poem. Or … a prayer.

Inexplicably, that YouTube clip of Uriel walking on water, the one Ryan had told me to look at, replays itself in my head. He was gliding across the surface of an icy Scottish loch, searching for something or ... someone?

And on the heels of that thought — the recollection that when I touch someone — someone unguarded, someone human — their thoughts and emotions, even their memories, become like an open book to me.

How are these things even remotely connected to the fact that when I'm pushed to the brink I can hurt people with my bare hands?

Twice now, I've almost torn myself free of the body I've been placed in. It happened once when I was Carmen, when I was wild with fear and anger. It happened again when I was Lela. I'd placed a hand upon Lela's mother as she lay dying and had somehow seen *inside* her cancer-ridden body. I'd even tried to heal her from the inside out — before I'd been forced to return into Lela.

I hadn't been able to save Karen Neill, because Azraeil had already marked her for his own.

Azraeil. I frown.

Like the Eight, he's one of the *elohim*. But one thing sets him apart from the others. His touch can bring ... death. Or restore life in equal measure.

Traits. They're all traits, I realise suddenly. These things I can do that I can't explain. Even that strange ability Azraeil has, which no one else possesses — mastery over death itself. All these are traits. Peculiar to our kind. In us, when we were first ... created.

I squeeze my eyes shut, chasing down thoughts that refuse to come clear.

Gia turns to me and queries, 'Irina? What do you think of braving Via Broletto today? Too risky?'

I shake my head blindly, waving at her, at Felipe, to decide.

When I was Lela, I met a rogue *malakh* — a kind of supernatural messenger — who'd chosen exile on earth rather than fulfil the task for which it was created. Somehow it had glimpsed me inside Lela's skin; had claimed that it could detect the protective mark of the *elohim* upon me. It had begged me to intercede with the *elohim* on its behalf because it needed a human body in which to live out its days. For in turning away from its original purpose, it had doomed itself to an eternal and painful half-life as a wandering, formless spirit.

It had envied me — *me!* — and the fact that I was constantly being reborn in a succession of mortal bodies.

Elohim. When I was Lela, even probing the meaning of that word had caused me unimaginable pain.

But now, that small voice inside me, which is always, always, one beat ahead of my waking self, whispers: *Most holy, most high. Together with a thousand others that no mortal alive has ever seen, or could ever give name to. Whatever you may be now, however estranged you have become from each other, you were all once created ... equal.*

And to you all: the ability to speak in tongues, both new and ancient.

And to you all: the power to bend matter and spirit, the laws of nature, to your will; to suspend time, move matter, occupy objects both animate and inanimate; mimic both the living and the dead; transport yourselves from place to place in the space between two heartbeats.

The very embodiment of paradox.

My eyes fly wide as I finally *see* — what I should have seen all along.

Grief enfolds me suddenly in its wings, grasps my borrowed heart in its black talons. When I lost Luc, when I lost any notion of context, of history, of 'home' — that casual ability to bend the laws of nature to my will — I lost my way. In one moment, I lost everything.

All of us were created with extraordinary abilities

no human being could ever comprehend. And most extraordinary of all these? The ability to atomise and re-form at will. Like water, like an unstable element that can shift between phases, I should be able to change states in a heartbeat. To become permeating yet impermeable, boundless yet infinitesimal.

It's much, much more than just the ability to possess another living creature or to shape-shift. It's — how do I put it? — the ability to turn the burning matter of which I am made into a weapon, a living sword, pure and directed energy. Will it and it is done.

It's something unique to all of us. We who are unkillable and immortal, unless one of our own kind seeks to destroy us.

Ah, yes. The rules — and there *are* rules, one must know them in order to contravene them — come back to me, unexpectedly, from some long buried oubliette in my mind.

The Eight. Even Azraeil. What they are, I am. What they are, Luc is, too.

We *elohim*.

We High Ones.

We ... *archangeli*.

Archangels. It's the name for *what I am.*

At the realisation, I seem to catch fire within, and I wonder how it is that Gia and Felipe cannot see me burning.

What *happened* to me?

CHAPTER 4

Gia and Felipe continue to argue over potential routes and traffic conditions, road surfaces and the forecast for rain, while inside Irina's slight and mortal frame my spirit burns and burns.

How had I not seen this before?

How am I able to see it now?

When I was Lela, it was as if certain things had been placed off limits by the Eight, were deliberately ringed around, in my mind, by fire. Just probing the meaning of the word *elohim*, even the name *Carmen Zappacosta*, had caused an electrical storm in my head, raw and immediate pain.

But not ... today.

And soon, maybe, I'll again be able to control that strange process of atomisation that happened to me once when I was Carmen, and once when I was Lela. And when I'm able to do that? Nothing will ever stop me again.

I'll be free.

I'm suddenly gripped by a ferocious urgency. Luc thinks that I need negative emotions like rage or fear to trigger the process of atomisation, of unbecoming. But what I'm feeling now? Is a terrible sense of hope, of ... possibility. And maybe that's enough.

While Gia and Felipe continue to argue, I turn inward, seeking to separate the burning strands of myself from the mortal vessel I've been forced into. I follow them down.

Down.

I am as a dark maze, a tangle of roots. Disorder masking some kind of pattern, deliberately broken, deliberately ... twisted.

Behind Irina's eyes, within her rigid body, I'm shivering into a billion pieces as I reach out for that strange, dissociative state in which I seem capable of *anything*.

Felipe's and Gia's voices, the contours, textures and colours of the real world, begin to bleach out as I dissolve inwards, fade down, even though concrete reality is in evidence everywhere around me — in the seated figure to my right lifting the teacup to her purple-stained mouth, in the museum-quality furnishings, the lovely costly floral arrangements that already smell, to me, as if they are in a state of advanced decay. My perspective grows hazy and the room, the voices, seem to stretch and warp in different directions around me as if time, space, light, sound, all can yield, all can bend.

And I know that it's happening again, that I'm actually pulling it off, and it's no accident. I'm beginning to *atomise*. I'm following the linkages, the switchbacks, the false trails and complex whorls and spirals, the broken pattern that the Eight have somehow cast me into. As if I am a cave diver, a pearl fisher, seeking a source.

And I find it. All paths lead to a point that cannot be followed further, cannot be unravelled. Irina's body slumps against the seat back as I reach towards that anchor point and try to pull myself free.

But, though I'm like mercury now, like vapour, some part of me remains knotted tightly in place, tethered to Irina's body, by some diabolical means I cannot unravel. Though I gather myself over and over with increasing desperation, I cannot sunder the knot that keeps me chained to her. And I know that it is the vital part, the part that is keeping me earthbound.

A small choking sound escapes Irina's lips.

So small that Gia's cup pauses only momentarily on its way to her mouth, before she completes the action and leans forward to point at the map spread out before her.

As I rage through the nerve endings and sinews, the flesh, wet matter and bone that Irina is made of, seeking a way out, a flaw, a loophole, I feel Irina's soul in here, too. Locked away tightly, like a kernel, a hard knot, her soul twisted and turned in on itself, like a möbius strip. To keep it out of harm's way. To free up this vessel for my use.

And if I am released? I have to hope that her soul will be freed at the same instant. Or the body will die.

Abruptly, the weird sensation of unbecoming reverses, as if I am pulled back by a cord, by an elastic band, and I coalesce again inside Irina's skin, behind her eyes, as if I am her, and she is me, and there is no gap, none at all, between us.

How long have I been gone? A heartbeat, maybe. Surely nothing more. But I'm breathing heavily and my sudden anguish burns so fiercely and so bright that I must jam my aching left hand inside my coat so the others in this room will not see it glow with that telltale flame that is as corrosive as it is lovely.

But Gia sees that something is amiss — from Irina's posture? The muscles of her face? — because Gia has sharp eyes and is paid to see everything about her employer.

'You look so pale!' she exclaims. 'What's the matter, Irina? Are you unwell?'

Unwell?

I have to cover my mouth with my right hand so that the scream building inside me won't escape and destroy the physical world.

I want to tell them that I was never supposed to be here, that it's all some terrible mistake. That I'm still paying for something I did once, a long time ago, that I can't even remember.

And the ones who are making me pay are the eight most powerful beings in the universe, the highest among us all that were first created, the ones to whom all but Azraeil must bow down, because death bows to no one, death is a force unto itself. Only these eight archangels might guess at what is in the heart and mind of our absent creator, for They were formed to be His regents, His princes, and to call us all to order. It is They who have done this to me.

I hear Gabriel's voice again, as clearly as if he were here, now, in this room: *I would rather have been put to the sword myself than endure what you have.*

What crime? What crime did I commit to deserve this?

I want to tell Gia all of this, but there's no point, because she would never understand. Never believe how it could even be possible for a vessel as small, as narrow, as a human body to contain everything that I am, everything that I was before. I'm like a centaur, a gorgon, a harpy. Something ancient, mythical, made up. A cautionary tale, a fable. Unreal.

I'm bent over my burning left hand, struggling to contain the pain, and Gia reaches out to me, but I pull away sharply. When I'm feeling this way, I'm dangerous, and people invariably get hurt.

Once — two lifetimes ago — I made myself a promise that my time would soon come. That one day, not too far away, it would no longer be about just surfing the next wave, just holding on, just surviving; it would be about *me*. And that time is *now*. Because staying safe, doing nothing, keeping out of sight, has never been my way. I know it now for a truth. The Eight have forced me to be so many things that I'm not, for far too long.

'I can't do this any more,' I tell Gia and Felipe

fiercely through my pain. 'If I don't get out soon, I'm going to go mad. You both work for me, right? I hold the purse strings, I call the shots?'

Gia nods, frightened by something in Irina's expression. Felipe is very still, watching guardedly with his dark, arrogant eyes.

'So you're going to start doing things *my* way,' I rasp. 'I'm done with waiting. I don't care how you do it, or what it costs to make it happen, but I want you to find someone for me and bring him here. *Now*. His name is Ryan Daley.'

Gia's unusual eyes widen at the unexpected request, and her dark brows snap together as I rattle off Ryan's mobile number — committed to memory two lives ago — and the URL for the social networking site Lela Neill befriended him on.

'Bring him *here*? Now?' Gia mutters. 'With the schedule you have?' She pulls a slim, black device out of a pocket of her leather jacket and inputs all of the information I've thrown at her, jabbing furiously at the device's seamless face. 'What if he won't come?'

'Make him,' I snap. 'Tell him: *Mercy is alive and badly needs your help* — use those exact words and I guarantee you'll have his immediate and undivided attention. Book him on the next plane out of wherever he is. I mean it. The next plane. Got that?'

Gia stops tapping for a moment, her eyes mystified. 'He really is that "important" to you?' She makes talking marks in the air with her free hand. 'I didn't think you were serious. Everything's always a matter of life and death with you, even when it isn't. You go through guys like they're bottled water, like they're completely disposable. It honestly can't wait until after we leave Italy? It'd be a lot less complicated to set up.'

I shake my head. 'Find him for me. It's the most important thing I'm ever going to ask you to do. Ever. So don't mess it up.'

Gia's eyebrows shoot up. 'But we've got three more full days of commitments here in Milan. Final fittings; dress rehearsal; runway show; dinner and afterparty. Even if we get the guy here, like, *today*, you can't just walk away from this thing. You'll never work again. You know that, don't you?'

I give a short laugh, half-way between amusement and despair. 'Just get him here, and Irina Zhivanevskaya shall meet her commitments.'

Gia gives me an odd look before nodding and jamming the hand-held device back into her jacket pocket. She turns to Felipe.

'Irina's right,' she says briskly. 'We need to *move*. I can go looking for this Ryan guy as soon as we're on the road. The sooner we leave, the better. We'll take the route I marked out originally, no arguments. You weren't Irina's driver the last time we were here. I know what I'm talking about, so you may as well put the map away.'

Felipe's eyes clash with Gia's as he angrily gathers up the road map and shoves it back inside his overcoat along with the status pen. He rises to his feet with barely concealed irritation.

Gia turns to me and says reassuringly, 'Okay, the deal is: we get through today, then the next day, and one more day after that, and then we'll go home. It's nothing, right? We'll pare back your schedule after this job, I promise. I'll talk to your management — they'll have to listen if they know what's good for them. No sense killing the golden goose, right? And if they don't? We'll find someone else who will. You're *Irina*. Everyone wants you, everyone loves you. This feeling you're having … it will pass.'

She's only being kind, but I can't stop myself from snarling, 'Do *your* job. Find him. What are you waiting for?'

'Straight onto it,' Gia says soothingly, 'I promise. As soon as we get to the cars.'

I don't need to touch her to know I've hurt her feelings, but I'm no good at modifying my behaviour when something I want is almost within reach.

'Felipe,' Gia snaps. 'Your car has to be waiting by the emergency exit. I need Irina to be inside and on the move before anyone gets a good look at her. Giovanni's security team can handle things from his end, but we can't be seen to be arriving a second late or she loses the booking. It's in the contract. Fast, fast, *fast* today. No dawdling, no unscheduled stops.'

'It is understood.' Felipe's tone is now openly hostile. His dark eyes flick to her face for a second before he resumes studying the gilded frescos on the ceiling, his mouth a sulky line.

Gia continues to badger him. 'And you've spoken to Bertrand? He's clear that Natasha's to leave Irina's usual hotel an hour after we leave here, wearing the wig and dark glasses? And he's to drive her all over Milan so she gets to Atelier Re well after we've gone inside?'

'*Sí,*' Felipe says, not bothering to hide his boredom. 'The decoy, she is ready. We have been through it many times. You must think us stupid, Senorita Basso.'

Gia doesn't bother to refute him. 'And Irina's security detail? Have you confirmed the personnel, the numbers?'

Felipe's reply is sullen. 'It, too, is in hand. Gianfranco recommends three cars today. One to go ahead, one to follow. You will travel in the last car, Senorita Basso, with Carlo and Jürgen. Myself and Senorita Zhivanevskaya in the second car, and Angelo and Vladimir in the first car. To give her enough time to get inside without unnecessary ... complication.'

Gia's expression is suddenly furious. '*Complication?* Is that what you think of me? And what? Separate us? Whose idea was that? Look at the condition she's in today — I can't leave her alone! Especially with the mob scene she'll have to endure outside Atelier Re. She's too fragile. We can't risk a relapse.'

Felipe shrugs, his expression unreadable. 'Do not ask me. It is Gianfranco's orders. I am just the driver. Ring him if you like.'

'Just the driver!' Gia expostulates. 'What are you plotting, Felipe?'

Felipe studies the fingernails of one tanned hand. 'If that is all, *Miss*?'

The doorbell peals again, and Gia looks up sharply. 'That'll be breakfast. Finally. When I call down, Felipe, have the engine idling. Hotel security has organised for us to exit through the basement levels. There's to be no waiting time. None at all.'

Felipe gives a mocking half-bow in Gia's direction. 'You worry too much, Senorita Basso,' he replies insolently. 'She is in good hands. The best, no?'

He gives me a lazy, lascivious wink and walks quickly to the door of the suite with long strides.

'You'll find Ryan?' I remind Gia again, feeling strangely uncertain. 'Bring him to me?'

She nods and I can feel my heart rate begin to slow, my breathing even out, my left hand stop aching. I flex my fingers gingerly and take my hand out of my pocket, sit straighter in my armchair.

At the door, Felipe lets in a dark-eyed young woman with dark, curly, chin-length hair wearing a crisp white shirt and sober, maroon skirt suit with the hotel crest picked out in gold thread on the jacket's front pocket. She's pushing a linen-covered trolley bearing a raft of breakfast things, including two dome-covered plates. She's so flustered at the sight of me that she runs over her own foot in her hurry to get the trolley to the graceful dining table near the street-facing windows of the sitting room.

The woman takes a pot off the trolley, lifting the

lid with unsteady hands to show us the hot coffee inside, before repeating the action with the second pot, containing boiled water. There's a small dish with slices of lemon arranged on it in a pretty pattern, and another with butter and two small pots of different varieties of jam. She places these on the table, darting quick, self-conscious glances in my direction.

She lifts the first silver dome, revealing a plate of mixed warm pastries and toasted bread. Under the second, there's a small white bowl with a couple of tablespoons of dry oatmeal in it, mixed in with a type of seed and dried berries I can't identify. She sets these down, blushing beneath my scrutiny, then unrolls two heavy, linen placemats and lines each one up with a dining chair.

Out of the warming area inside the trolley, she pulls a plate bearing a lavish, English-style breakfast — scrambled eggs, fried bacon, grilled sausages, tomatoes and mushrooms — and places it on one placemat. Then she pulls out another plate, which appears to hold a couple of tablespoons of scrambled egg-white and sets it on top of the other mat. Finally, she removes a small jug of hot milk.

The woman clumsily lays out two sets of silver cutlery, puts a folded cloth napkin beside each plate before practically bowing her way backwards out of the room. Her eyes are fixed on me so attentively as she lets herself out that she bounces off the doorframe and almost falls in a heap in the hallway outside. Blushing furiously, she staggers upright and shuts the door to the suite behind her with one last anguished look in my direction.

'What was *that* all about?' I say.

Gia follows the direction of my astonished gaze and shrugs. 'Just another case of insta-girl-crush. People are more accident-prone around you. Remember that reporter from the *Argus* who followed you around during the London shows three years back when you really began to take off? He wrote an article about it; said you were the human equivalent of walking under a ladder. Total bad news from start to finish. And I should know!' She gives a burst of genuine laughter before her expression grows wary again, as if she's said too much and can't understand how it keeps happening.

The smell of the food is strangely welcome. I don't often feel hungry, but today, for some reason, I'm ravenous.

'Let's eat,' I say, pulling out the dining chair in front of the loaded, cooked breakfast plate.

Gia clears her throat. 'Uh, that would be mine? You're the one with the agent who insists you limit your daily calorie intake to keep you "competitive". Your definition of breakfast is two tablespoons of raw oats, linseed and goji berry, slightly wetted with hot, soy milk, capped off with some cooked egg-white washed down with hot lemon water.' She pulls a face. 'Yummy.'

'I don't do starvation diets,' I exclaim. 'And the pastries?'

Gia's expression is half-sceptical, half-amused. 'Um, they'd be mine, too. But I'm happy to share.' She grins. 'If, for a change, you do as you're bloody well told.'

We split the pastries and hot breakfast down the middle, returning Irina's usual cheerless fare to the trolley. As we eat, I can feel Gia's eyes on me. But whenever I look up, she glances away.

'Coffee?' she asks, pouring herself a cup.

I wrinkle my nose and shake my head. 'Can't stand it.'

She stares at me for a second. 'That's not what you usually say.'

I shrug.

'You know,' she says finally, when we place our cutlery down, having eaten our way through everything worth eating, 'you seem so different today. I can't put my finger on it. But I like this version of you. Much as it pains me to say it, you seem more in touch with your ... humanity today. You seem more like the rest of us.'

I laugh, genuinely amused by her words.

She can't help giving me an answering grin. 'You look startled by the suggestion.'

'You have no idea how much!' I grin back.

Then Gia's smile dies, and she pushes her plate away firmly, as if she's about to walk into battle. 'You ready?'

I lift Irina's narrow shoulders again in a shrug, let them fall. How can one ever be ready to live another person's life? To go forth into another person's day?

Gia stalks over to the gilt-edged console table by the in-room surround-sound system, her silver jewellery jangling. She picks up the house phone, dials a number and says curtly into the receiver, 'We're coming down.'

After replacing the handset, she walks across to an elegant, button-back armchair near the door and picks up a huge, tan-coloured, crocodile-skin carryall, holding it out to me as she picks up her own shiny, black patent-leather tote off the floor. It's bristling with external pockets and silver buckles. 'Okay?' she says. 'I mean it, are you ready?'

I loop the handles of the holdall over one thin shoulder. 'As ready as I'll ever be, *darlink*,' I say in Irina's husky voice, as Gia holds the door open to let me through into the hotel corridor.

CHAPTER 5

As I teeter down the hallway after Gia, my eyes feel grainy and the ground seems wavy and distorted and way too far away.

I should have slept last night, but I couldn't. Sometimes I forget that the human body — as miraculous and complex as it is — is not a machine and cannot be dictated to. Not in the ways that really matter.

We stalk down miles of lush royal blue and gold patterned carpet, beneath enormous hand-blown Murano glass chandeliers of breathtaking beauty, past hundreds of thousands of dollars worth of original art, statuary and antique *demi-lune* tables with delicately carved clawed feet, like the feet of predatory animals. As we move closer to the lifts, I see a man holding a lift door open for us with a hand the size of a dinner plate. His eyes seem to linger just a fraction too long upon my face.

He's dressed like a suit, though he looks like a thug made good, with a heavy-set frame and a nose that's slightly left of centre. He's sporting a five-o'clock shadow that must be pretty much around-the-clock, has scarred facial skin and a serious case of perma-tan. His long, thick, unnaturally black hair is pulled tight into a low ponytail and he's wearing an earpiece. He's taller than average, and it's clear from a quick visual inspection that he enjoys a workout. Big head, big hands. Bull-necked. Neat, clipped nails. Expensive gold watch. Expensive shoes for someone in his line of work.

With a nod, the man indicates we should enter the lift. 'Irina,' he rasps, his Russian accent unmistakeable. '*Zdravstvujte.*'

Hello, he's saying, and I don't know how I know this, but it's the formal way. The way an employee, say, would address his employer, even though this guy has thirty years and about two hundred pounds on Irina, at least, and looks like a wise guy, a hit man.

'Vladimir,' I reply, thinking back quickly to the names that Gia and Felipe had bandied around. That was the only Russian name they'd mentioned.

I don't recall ever speaking a word of Russian, but it's Irina's first language and it seems to be making perfect sense to me so far. So to hell with it — what have I got to lose? It's like how Carmen could sing, and Lela was good with people; and when I was them, I could somehow do those things, too. Because some things the body just remembers.

A fine sweat breaks out on my forehead as I close my eyes and channel myself inwards, chasing the words I'm looking for down the unreliable pathways of Irina's brain. When I open my eyes again, it's like I've always known them.

'*Kak ... tvoyo zdorovie?*' I say — accents on all the wrong places, accents where there shouldn't be any — testing the unfamiliar weight and feel of the words on my tongue. I think I've just said: *How's your health?*

The man-mountain nods slowly, gratified that I seem to remember him. '*Neplokho,*' he says, shrugging. *Not bad.*

I feel a surge of elation, a chemical rush. Maybe I was wrong. Maybe the human body *is* a machine that may be harnessed, after all. If you just work out how.

Gia's eyes are on me again as we take our positions at the back of the high-shine mirrored lift. Perhaps Irina's voice sounded weird. Hell, maybe I forgot to conjugate a verb properly and Gia zeroed in on the error. But at least Vladimir understood what I was saying. I casually flip Irina's unbound caramel-coloured hair back over her narrow shoulders, hitch her handbag higher and pretend not to notice Gia staring. The lift doors slide shut and we begin our descent.

Vladimir addresses something small and round pinned to the lapel of his killer suit. 'I have them,' he says, tilting his head to one side as he listens to an answering voice in his almost-invisible earpiece. I watch his small, pale blue eyes watching the numbered wall panel light up in descending order.

We sink down past the ground floor without stopping and on past the basement into the lower basement. The lift doesn't even stop on the way; not a soul tries to get in. Clearly, being a world-class bitch can come in handy.

'Coming up through the laundry in five,' Vladimir mutters into his mic as the doors glide open.

Another of Irina's hired security goons is standing there — the man's colossal build, tiny earpiece and bespoke-tailored suit and expensive shoes are a dead giveaway, although I have no idea if it's Carlo, Jürgen, Angelo or even Gianfranco himself that I'm looking at. The guy's got a platinum-blond buzz cut and a face like hewn granite. When his cold, grey eyes meet mine, something seems to leap in them, even though the muscles of his face remain motionless.

Everyone wants you, everyone loves you, Gia said. And I see that it's true.

I study the large space before me with fascination. It's filled with steam, shouting and mechanical noises, the smell of soap powder mingled with disinfectant and wet wool. Everywhere I turn, there are laundry bags and open trolleys piled high with dirty linen or clean, folded linen. An automated drying and sorting system snakes its way around the perimeters of the cavernous room, and almost all the clips are filled. The space is packed with busy migrant workers in disposable headgear and identical hotel uniforms.

Vladimir leads the way through the vast, humming room at a brisk pace, the second guy falling in wordlessly behind Gia and me.

Much the same way the woman who served me breakfast did, every single person in the place turns to stare at me as if I've just descended from the sun on a golden chariot. *Dazzled.* That's the way I'd describe the universal reaction to Irina's presence; although they've all clearly been ordered not to approach or address her because when I try to meet anyone's eyes, they look away immediately.

Still, there's talk, talk, talk in at least a dozen different languages. And in every accent I hear the word *Irina* repeated and amplified until it seems to break in a wave against the heavy beams of the ceiling that separate this stifling underworld from the gracious apartments above.

One law for the lion and ox is oppression. The words come to me unexpectedly as I look around at all the busy worker bees in the room. It's so true. And such a sad truth. I mean, I should know; who better than I? But still it bothers me that we can't all be lions, or all be oxen; that equality was not one of the necessary pre-conditions of the closed system that we know as the universe. Because how is that fair? It's just asking for trouble from the get-go.

Our tight, mismatched little group has almost made it to the exit across the room when a starstruck middle-aged woman spills a huge bag of dirty laundry straight onto Vladimir's expensive shoes. We're forced to stop as she gets down on her hands and knees in front of us, desperately trying to stuff an avalanche of wet towels back into the bag.

'Jürgen!' Vladimir snaps and the platinum-blond giant immediately scans the room for threats.

'Didn't I tell you you were bad luck?' Gia murmurs out of the side of her mouth as Vladimir starts shouting at the woman in English to get out of our way.

'Vladimir, *dostatochno*,' I caution. Enough.

He glowers at me, growling into the mic on his lapel, 'There's a delay.' He kicks out at the soiled laundry nearest his feet as he listens to the reply.

I stamp my own feet in my towering, alien heels. It feels as if my legs are dying from the soles upwards.

Gia shoots me a warning look. 'Don't get involved!' she hisses.

Vladimir insists loudly, 'No, no, I'm handling it.'

What he *isn't* handling is the dirty laundry, and I can feel the worker's mounting distress. It hangs about her like a detectable odour, like a cloud, as she scrabbles desperately at our feet. I wonder how it is that people like Irina and Gia could become so divorced from ordinary life. I catch everyone by surprise when I dump Irina's oversized croc-skin holdall against Jürgen's knife-pleated trouser leg and crouch down, reaching for the nearest towel.

Jürgen kicks the handbag out of his way with unnecessary force and a gold-plated mobile phone falls out with a sharp clatter onto the ancient, stone-flagged floor.

'Irina, *nyet!*' Vladimir roars over my head.

The laundry worker lets out a wail and rips dirty towels out of my hands as fast as I can pick them up.

'That's a two hundred thousand dollar, one-of-a-kind bag,' Gia says to Jürgen mildly as she bends down and gathers up Irina's things. 'But of course you'd know that.'

Workers begin darting over from everywhere to help the woman and me repack the laundry bag. Though I pretend not to notice, I feel their hands brush mine deliberately, feel their eyes raking my face. *Everyone wants you, everyone loves you.* It's making me feel kind of queasy, all the attention.

Gia helps me to my feet and the people around me fall back reluctantly. 'Don't even get me started on your *But I must have eeet* little phone that you haven't even learnt how to use properly yet, which is now probably broken thanks to Tyrannodon here ...' She hooks Irina's bag back onto my shoulder, nodding at the crowd.

'You're attention-seeking again in some bizarre way I can't fathom,' she says. 'I've *never* seen you lift a finger to help anyone if there wasn't something in it for you. But now that you've picked up the germs of hundreds of past hotel guests, can we *go*?'

Vladimir claps his hands dismissively and the crowd scatters. He extends a spotless handkerchief in my direction and I wipe my hands with it. He takes it from me with his thumb and index finger and drops it disdainfully on the floor beside him. We continue through the room, to a doorway on the other side that leads to an internal staircase, away from that sea of expectant, devouring eyes. As we move up the stairwell, it's suddenly eerily quiet and our footsteps echo on the uneven stone stairs, worn down from centuries of use. We walk up in single file, past two landings, not a single, living soul around, until we reach a pair of heavy steel doors. Vladimir pushes down hard on the panic bar running along the inside of the door on the right, meeting with unexpected resistance. He turns and exchanges a look with Jürgen over our heads. Together, both men put their shoulders to the door and force it open, hissing with the effort.

We stagger out onto Via Victor Hugo, into the teeth of a building gale. Even as I watch, black clouds hurtle across the sky, covering the sun. A long shadow seems to blanket the wide thoroughfare we are standing on, sweeping down its face, across the exteriors of all the graceful buildings crowded on either side, like a river of darkness. In the distance, through the man-made stone canyon, I catch a glimpse of the Piazza del Duomo — the Duomo Square — the Christmas tree and the softly gleaming cathedral rising at its far end like a mirage.

We're quite some distance from the recessed circular drive of the hotel's official entrance. According to plan, there are three glossy black luxury sedans with dark tinted windows illegally parked against the kerb, engines idling, each sporting a silver hood ornament in the shape of a delicate winged lady in flight. The cars are longer and wider than normal, with two rear doors instead of one, and they seem to be riding a little low to the ground, as if they might be armoured.

I wonder again how one lone skinny female could merit all this protection, be the centre of so much attention. I don't know how Irina can stand living like this. It's beginning to give me the creeps, the way everyone stares and whispers and desires.

Standing beside the first car is a heavy-set older guy in a tailored navy overcoat, who can only be Angelo. A younger coat-wearing giant, with a head of short, tight dark curls, who must be Carlo, is holding open one of the back doors to the third car. The eyes of both men light up when they see me, but then they dart anxious looks at the leaden ominous sky.

'Is about time!' Angelo calls out, looking back at me longingly.

'*Subito!*' Carlo snaps, though he, too, cannot look away from me for long.

The fierce gusting wind tears at the ends of my hair so that it ripples out behind me like a bright banner. All the fancy awnings and shutters along the street snap and creak, as the wind buffets them. The sky is an unnatural colour — steel grey with a hint of yellow in it — and the arctic conditions are enough to stop Gia in her tracks so that I almost collide with her back. With an oath, she knots her fancy scarves tightly around the lower half of her face before zipping her leather jacket right up under her neck. Vladimir and Jürgen scowl as they hunch their heavy shoulders against the bitter conditions and pull on matching pairs of black leather gloves, scanning opposite ends of the street continuously.

Vladimir moves forward and opens the back passenger side door to the second car, gesturing urgently for me to get inside as the wind throws grit in all our faces and threatens to snatch the stylish cloche hat right off my head and over the rooftops. Still, I hesitate, unwilling to be dragged back inside, back into Irina's claustrophobic, over-protected, hothouse little life. I close my eyes and tilt my head back as if I could drink in the approaching tempest, transcend it.

'What are you doing? Get moving!' Gia yells through her veil of scarves as she stumbles in the direction of the third car. 'See you at Giovanni's. *Just be prepared.*'

'Wait!' I scream, raising my black-gloved hand in her direction.

Gia stops, looking back at me quizzically, and I shriek 'Ryan!' into the teeth of the wind. It's not a question.

Gia hesitates as Carlo plucks at her arm. She throws his hand off and pivots on one heel, back in my direction. Carlo snarls in guttural Italian, but remains where he is, watching me, because that's what he's supposed to do, and what he can't help doing.

Gia leans in towards me as I yell, 'Bring him to me. As soon as you can.'

In reply, she shouts: '*Mercy is alive and badly needs your help* — have I got it?'

I nod vigorously and she gives me a thumbs-up, then shoves me in the direction of the second limo before stumbling back towards the third car and climbing into the back seat. Jürgen gets in beside her and Carlo swings into the seat facing theirs. The two rear doors slam shut in unison and I can no longer see them all behind the car's blank, dark windows, though I can still feel their eyes on me.

Angelo's waiting impatiently for Vladimir to get into the first limo, but the older man continues to watch me narrowly. There's impatience in his voice when he suddenly bellows, '*Býstro*, Irina! *Býstro!*' *Hurry*, he's saying. *Hurry*. But there's still that reluctance in me to re-enter Irina's heavily regimented existence.

And something's telling me to look around. It's like an itch, like a small and nagging cut dragging at my attention. Something; but nothing I can really place.

The entire length of Via Victor Hugo is weirdly deserted. The old buildings lining both sides of the street have taken on a cold and sinister cast. They seem to loom inwards in the failing light, as if we have stepped into a painting by Dali, or Magritte.

I see that while I was talking to Gia, a cumulonimbus cloud of terrifying proportions has filled the sky immediately above us. Its ragged, billowing shape seems as wide as it is tall, and it's outlined in a strange and brilliant corona, as if it has swallowed the sun. There's distant lightning flickering at its heart that maybe only I can see. The strange mass seems to frame the graceful triangular Palladian roofline of the three-storey grey stone building across the road in a brilliant, numinous light. The extraordinary cloud formation is so beautiful that I can hardly look away. It seems almost familiar, like a portal to another world.

'Irina!' Vladimir shouts, but his voice seems remote and inconsequential, as if heard in a dream.

I can almost smell the approaching storm. There's heavy rain on the way, a massive front that will hit the old city like a bomb, and I know with certainty that it will last for hours and obscure everything in its path. That cloud, it's just the beginning of something terrible. A storm for the ages. They'll talk about it for years to come.

I rip my eyes away from the sky and take a small grudging step towards Vladimir. But then I see something. A gleaming blur moving in an illogical fashion. Like a mobile patch of sunlight. Light where there shouldn't be any light. I turn my head towards it, though when I try to follow it with my eyes, I don't see it any more. Perhaps the surface gleam of slickly shining paving stones, or the electric light spilling out of the interiors of cafés and storefronts, is playing tricks on my senses.

Or maybe, remarks my inner demon, *it does not wish to be seen. Not this time.*

I frown.

Appare! I think. *Show yourself.*

And that's when I feel it, faint but insistent. Like an energy at once hot and cold, hair-raising, like a hum, like vinegar in my bones. I know that feeling, have felt it before. Know its source. And it's coming closer.

I scan my surroundings intently, see nothing. Though I can still feel it, almost hear the grating *zing*, *zing* of its movements. It's far weaker, far fainter, than when I first encountered it on a city street in Australia a lifetime ago. It's the same entity, I'm sure of it. And the *malakh* is following me, for some reason only it knows.

Quid est nomen tuum? I think. *Tell me your name.*

'Irina!' Vladimir repeats. He steps forward and places one hand under my elbow, ushering me insistently towards the open car door so that I have no choice but to follow, though I continue searching the air, the sky, for that familiar, errant gleam.

Inside the car, Felipe's mouth is smiling as he beckons me forward, but his eyes are cold with annoyance. '*Senorita*,' he calls, leaning through the gap between the front seats with his smiling mouth and cold eyes. '*Por favor, Senorita.*'

The icy wind tears at my hair, at my clothes, as if insisting that I stay. And I *want* to stay outside on this steel-grey thoroughfare, under this steel-grey sky, with the temperature falling fast towards freezing. The cold has never bothered me. But I don't see how I can, because there's no freedom for Irina from these people who've been instructed never to let her out of their sight. I feel a stab of pity for her — even though she's a bitch-slapping mess-in-a-dress. What else can you expect if you cage a wild animal?

Vladimir applies subtle pressure to the bones and nerves of my elbow. I'm leaning forward, placing one foot on the running board of the limo when I catch a glimpse of something else. It's up on that roof across the way, the one outlined in glory. And though it feels as if Vladimir is crushing the bones of my arm to pieces, I dig in my impossible heels, and lift my head to look at it.

The moment I do, the faint, achy sensation — that hum I can feel way down in my bones — it all abruptly ceases. And time itself, the flesh-rending wind, the whole world around me — they all stand still. Because it's not a light I'm seeing, up on that roof. Not a transient gleam. It's a man's shape. Broad-shouldered, long-limbed, perfectly proportioned, like something out of a classical painting, a living statue. He's appeared so silently it's as if he stepped out of that radiant cloud. There's a corona all around him.

Even from where I'm standing, way down on the ground, I see that he has tawny, wide-set eyes — like the eyes of a young lion — and olive skin, long, dark gold hair. He's wearing ordinary-looking street clothes: a long-sleeved grey and white plaid shirt over a white tee-shirt and blue jeans; a pair of battered, dark red Converse on his feet. There's even a black satchel on his broad back, a beaten-up leather belt around his waist. But I know they're all fake. Just props. He may look like a pitch-perfect human being in his late teens or early twenties, but he's not human.

This guy in the ordinary clothes is standing on the stone pinnacle of a roof that's about sixty feet off the ground. And he's more beautiful than anything in creation has a right to be. He's bound by light.

It seems to come off his skin in shimmering waves of pure energy, as if he's made of it. The gathering darkness can't hide what he is.

He's an archangel.

CHAPTER 6

Te gnovi, I address the being upon the roof silently, as the *malakh* had once addressed me. *I know you.*

And I do. Forgotten all these years, but recalled in the beholding, as if scales have suddenly fallen from my eyes. He's one of the archangels who rally to Michael's bright presence. A lieutenant, if you like, loyal unto death. He'd stood with that shining multitude arrayed against me, against Luc, all those years ago, for reasons I can no longer remember, but want so badly to recall.

K'el. As I remember his name, something seems to ignite in me. The two worlds — one 'real' yet fallible, one unseen and infallible — converge once again in a single, watchful figure upon a distant roofline. Seeing him causes me an almost physical pain. I feel a wave of longing so intense that it's like a kind of sickness. For *home*.

Where the great universe wheels and turns, and turns about. Where planets, stars, suns, moons, the greater and lesser bodies, fly by; comets, black holes, supernovae, strange fissures in time and space, twist and curl overhead like a painted, yet living, ever-changing dome.

I should be wary, I should be angry. K'el is in some way implicated in this, my banishment. But there's something like giddiness, like glee, in my expression as I say his name again. I savour the sound, the feel and weight, of the word. It is an indictment of my peculiar ... condition that I could have forgotten someone I once knew so well.

But there's no answering joy in his face as he steps off the roof — sixty feet, at least, above the surface of the earth — and drifts weightlessly towards the ground, until he is standing across the street from me, disdain in his golden eyes.

You are betrayed, he says directly into my mind. And his voice is as chill and unwelcoming as the arctic wind that plagued Via Victor Hugo only moments ago. *He comes for you and you must cleave to us, cleave to the Eight, else evil be given free reign and the war begin in earnest.*

I step away from Irina's limousine, away from the frozen figures of Vladimir and Angelo poised on the street like life-sized, plastic action figures, away from Felipe's motionless form, still twisted towards me inside the vehicle, anger touching his aquiline features. Away, for a moment, from the trappings of Irina's cosseted life.

I cross the street towards K'el, arms outstretched, as if I, too, am floating. Or sleepwalking.

I wonder whether he will let me touch him. The need to place my hands upon one who is my kin, my brethren, one who knew me *as I was*, who recognises me inside this stranger's body, is so physical that I'm shaking with it.

I step up from the street's irregular surface onto the footpath and it's as if I hit an unseen wall of force. It's immovable. When I push forward, seeking to pierce that seamless web of energy that surrounds him, there's a crackle of intense blue-white light at the point where I make contact with his invisible armour, his deliberate shell. For an instant, there's the sensation that I'm touching eternity, absolute power. And I must step back, or else Irina's tender human skin will begin to *burn*.

I can go no further — he will let me get no closer — and the surge of disappointment I feel is like a spurt of acid in my heart.

We look upon each other, one foot of space all that separates us. It may as well be the width of a galaxy. He will not let me touch him, though his eyes seem strangely intent, almost hungry, as he looks upon my face.

'No time for sentimentality, *Mercy*.' His voice is acid, belying the luminosity of his gaze. 'The universe no longer revolves around your wants or desires. Luc will soon be here. Despite all our best-laid plans — plans involving more time and more of us than a single being should ever warrant — he's found you. Or one of his spies has. And now he hastens here to claim you. But we will not let it happen.'

Luc knows where I am? He's coming *here*?

I stumble, almost fall, at the implication.

Immediately, the force-field that K'el has placed between us vanishes and he grips my wrist with his cool, steadying fingers. The gesture is telling: in some way, he must still remember me the way I was, he must still care.

I look down at his glowing hand upon Irina's skin. And it's like marble or alabaster, without flaw, smooth as fired glass or porcelain. Unlined on any surface. Uncorrupted and incorruptible. Though he's touching me, I get no sense of what's in his mind because his guard is up. He does not wish me to know.

As tall as Irina is, K'el is taller, constructed like a figure out of myth, looming over me, almost blocking out what remains of the weird half-light. I feel dwarfed and strangely frail in his glowing presence where once we were … equals.

And I cry, 'Not one of you — not Uriel, not Gabriel, not even Luc — has ever told me *why*. Why can't I be "claimed"? Why can't I go home, when it's what I want more than anything in this world? What has this elaborate plan — involving so much time, so many of "us" — all been for? *I don't understand*, K'el. I don't understand what came between us all to cause this rift. Weren't we *friends* once, you and I?'

K'el gazes at me with his liquid gold, burning eyes, and I see something at war within him. He *wants* to tell me; but something — some stricture, some pronouncement, some fatal consequence — prevents him. And he's struggling with it.

But my bewilderment, my absolute sorrow, is genuine, and his gaze softens, though his hand upon me remains like iron. 'Once friends, yes, though in time I almost came to … hate you and was glad when you … left us.'

I frown at his words, the things left unsaid in the pauses, and he adds softly, 'I see that you don't understand, don't even remember that day. Nothing's ever been the same, for any of us, since then, did you know that?' He leans forward and smooths a strand of long hair out of my eyes, so gently that I barely feel his touch. 'It's better this way. There's nothing in that memory for you but grief, and it's best if …'

His voice falters, and I see that he's trying to say the right thing, choose the right words, the less hurtful words.

'It's better this way,' he repeats more firmly, gripping my narrow shoulders. 'You don't want to remember what happened. It would only destroy you all over again.'

I find myself trembling, and K'el's fingers tighten on me as if he'd like to pull me close. 'Luc's no good for you, he's never been good enough,' he murmurs, looking down into my upturned face with his glorious eyes.

I close mine, thinking he will wrap his arms around me at last. But then he gives a small, hard laugh and lets go of me, almost pushing me away.

'And that's got to be the understatement of all time,' he snarls. 'But you've always had this ability to ... unsettle me and I see that you haven't lost that power. I came here to warn you. That's what I'm here for.' His tone is self-mocking.

Feeling strangely bereft, I wail, 'But I still don't understand what I did wrong! Why was I cast out?'

K'el's beautiful mouth twists a little and he paces away, as if standing too close to me might be dangerous. 'You did nothing but fall in love with the wrong one,' he says, suddenly refusing to meet my eyes. 'You picked Luc when you should have picked ... Raphael. Well, that's the accepted wisdom, anyway.' His voice is bitter.

I recoil at his words. 'That's it? For something so simple I was ... *banished?*'

He hesitates. I can see him struggling for the right words, the right way to frame an explanation I've waited aeons to hear.

'You were guilty of being young and overly ... malleable,' he says finally. 'You let passion be your guiding principle. You let Luc twist you, let him change your character from everything that was light — all the bright, good things that were in you from the moment you were first created — to a creature motivated by cruelty, perversity, vanity, the principles of pleasure without thought or care of repercussion. Together, you and Luc were a divisive force, and so destructive. More devastating even than life forms like these.' He gestures at my human face, my human shape, dismissively. 'Raphael would have been a more fitting companion for someone as high-spirited, as strong-willed, curious and questioning, as you were,' he says, his eyes never leaving mine for a moment. 'He would have strengthened you in beauty, in wisdom, in compassion, in every way that matters. Any one of us would have been a better match for you than Luc. Even me.' His mouth twists again.

I feel my face flush with angry blood. As if *alone* I was nothing. I was only something when I was someone's companion, someone's consort.

'The heart will have only what it wants,' I spit. 'And so I was judged and cast out because I was young and foolish? Because I chose the *wrong one*?'

My voice flies up the scale, breaking on the words, and K'el's eyes darken with something like disgust.

'*Not for us*, that "lifelong partnership" that's said to unite mortal woman and mortal man in heart, in mind, in body. We are *elohim*, Mercy. We were created first among angels; first among all things that were created. Some of us were sworn to protect the holy throne; some to govern the order of the universe and all life within its boundaries; some to bear witness, to keep history, to mark the passage of time; some to fill the skies with glory, to sing praise even when there seems little reason to do so. Everything in its place, or else it is chaos. It is our creed.'

For a single, disorientating moment I'm Lela Neill again, hearing Sulaiman/Gabriel telling me the same thing, and I feel the same fury. *Know your place.* What kind of stupid creed is that?

K'el's voice is low, almost menacing. 'We were created to maintain control, not surrender it. You were so far out of line that you threatened us all.'

'Ah yes, the "line",' I say bitterly, staring at my feet with strangely stinging eyes.

I'm feeling a strong sense of déjà vu, as if I've been admonished in just this way before. By K'el, by others.

'You're all the same,' I snap. 'And you wonder why I chose Luc over any of you?'

K'el moves closer almost reluctantly, tilting my chin up to draw my gaze back to him, his eyes curiously intent. 'We're not supposed to love just *one* other, to the exclusion of everything else — duty, fellowship, faith, principle. We *are* love — for each other, for all things. An impartial love, it's true; we can't hope to do anything more than maintain a rough equilibrium.' His eyes flash and there's something like loathing again in his expression.

'You changed everything,' he says accusingly. 'When you saw Luc for the first time, things were never the same again.'

'And yet everything changes, everything evolves,' I argue hopelessly. 'Why should *we* remain forever rigid and unchanging when even the universe itself does not? Nowhere is it written that it's a crime for one such as I was to fall in love!'

'Yet we were created to be eternal and perfect and changeless.' K'el's voice is bitter. 'You never would have looked at me, at any of us, the way you looked at *him*. You were *obsessed*. As he was with you.'

I close my eyes briefly, feeling Irina's face flame in memory of the way we were together, Luc and I. Like two suns colliding. Who wouldn't want a love like that? Who couldn't survive on the embers of such a love, for centuries, if one had to?

So they'd all thought Luc was wrong for me, that together we were a colossal, destructive mistake. And no one had ever told me. They'd just arranged for me to be summarily removed from everything I'd ever known, because I'd become inconvenient and embarrassing, not quite up to par.

'So I was exiled by committee, with no recourse to anyone? Given no avenue of appeal? I had no chance to defend myself before you cast me out!' I cry.

K'el's gaze is troubled as he replies slowly, 'That's not the way it happened; don't go putting words into my mouth. What's happened to you — the way we have been forced to keep you hidden — was born of necessity. It was the best we could do, given the circumstances — can't you understand that?' There's another odd pause. 'Luc knew of our disquiet. And he chose not to tell you. Instead, he isolated you, kept you away from us deliberately. What does that say about him?'

For a second, I'm pierced by a vision of Luc and me entwined in each other's arms within a living bower of flowers, the air heavy with the fragrance of a thousand different blooms that no human hand could possibly have put together. It was our place, our world, the hanging garden he created for me alone. Dust now, ashes.

'It wouldn't have changed anything,' I answer in grief, in defiance. 'I wouldn't have given up a second I spent by Luc's side. He's what's sustained me, all this time, in the wilderness that is this earth. My only true friend, my constant companion.'

K'el's lip curls as he crushes my upper arms so tightly in his hands that I gasp out loud.

'Then, foolish creature,' he roars, and his voice has a steely, ringing edge to it, 'you do not need an explanation for this eternity of drifting — in which you claim you've had *no* friends, *no* sustenance, no support of any kind. In making your choice, you damned yourself to countless lifetimes of human misery. Your fault, all of it. Free will — that thing you hold in such sacred regard — always comes at a price.'

He raises his right hand, glaring at me with his preternatural lion eyes, and I'm suddenly very afraid, remembering that our kind may only kill and be killed by each other.

As if he's reading my thoughts, K'el gives a bitter laugh and rakes his tawny hair with his gleaming upraised hand before letting it fall harmlessly to his side.

'Many times over the years I've wished you dead, if only to throw the burden of you off my back. You've been a millstone about the neck of many,

Mercy. I will not lie. For each life you "live", one of us must watch over you — as though we have nothing better to do than witness you blundering through the human world, stirring echoes enough for Luc to follow. I wanted to forget you, more than anything. But I haven't been permitted to do so.' He scowls. 'You were dangerous then, and you're even more dangerous now, only you don't know why. But I didn't come here today to destroy you.'

He looks away, then back at me. 'Michael's on his way, but he's been … delayed. He sent a messenger, one of the *malakhim* — though a *malakh* unlike any I've encountered before, one that was strangely weak and formless. I was asked to deliver Michael's message to you, in person. And that's never happened before, Mercy; do you appreciate the seriousness of the moment? Even while we stand here, idly conversing on this city street, the game plan is changing all around us. In life after life, the one whose task it is to watch over you has *never* been allowed to reveal themselves to you. But here we are, face-to-face, on Michael's orders. These are interesting times, are they not?'

I don't tell K'el that the rule has been broken before, and recently. By Uriel — who'd appeared to me when I was Carmen. By Gabriel — who'd appeared to me when I was Lela. *One law for the lion.* Though even amongst lions, it seems equality is in scarce supply.

'Interesting times indeed,' I reply more coolly than I'm feeling. 'And the message?' After all this time, Michael himself — the Viceroy of Heaven, the Commander of the Army of God — has a message … for me? There's a sudden tight feeling in my chest, a terrible anticipation.

K'el's face is grim. 'His message? Not all of the Eight will be gathered here before Luc arrives. But as many of us as are able will keep you from Luc, or die trying, and that *is* no lie. Whatever you do, do not touch Luc, do not go to him, do not go with him, or allow yourself to be taken by his forces. I cannot speak more plainly than that. Everything turns on it.'

'Or what? What happens?' I ask, still strangely breathless.

'Hell happens,' K'el says, so quietly that I think I must have misheard him, until he adds, 'Everywhere. Not just on earth. Everywhere.'

I frown, unable to process what I'm hearing. From what I'm able to recall, Hell is a place for unruly souls who don't pass Azraeil's test for admittance to the sweet hereafter. It's a way station for the imperfect, a holding pen for those without the right stuff.

'Who *cares* if Hell happens?' I say slowly. 'The ghosts of the mortal dead would hardly pose a threat to any of us. They're just light and shade, fragments of emotion and memory that have become stuck in an endless fugue and refuse to die.'

K'el is silent for a long time and though he's close enough to touch, he seems very far away. 'Things have changed a lot since you've been … gone,' he replies finally. 'These days, Hell is run by the Devil and his legion, the *daemonium*. At its core is his lethal personal guard of one hundred demons; every single one of them beautiful, evil and more powerful than you would believe possible. Our opposites, both in attitude and appetite. We maintain, they destroy. That's roughly how it works. The defining difference between us and them is that the Devil and his lieutenants permit themselves the act of … creation.'

My eyes widen at his words and K'el nods.

'Yes,' he says softly. 'The creation of new "life". Something we are forbidden to do; it is the right of only one, the maker of us all. Yet they,' K'el seems to shudder, 'create such monstrous parodies of life that we ...' His voice dies away. 'We *elohim* may outnumber the Devil and his strongest demons something like nine to one, but some days it feels as if the *daemonium* may yet overwhelm us all.'

I rack my brain for what little I know of Hell and the Devil.

'Do they really exist?' I challenge. 'To the living here on earth, Hell is more a figure of speech these days, a curse word: *Hell yes, Hell no.* And "the Devil"? Is he even real? When the universe was young, *we* were there, but no "Devil", no "demons".

'Isn't the Devil just a figure made up to frighten small children?' I say. 'Just a name, a concept, something folkloric, not real?'

K'el's reply is sharp and swift. 'The way most mortals think of us, you mean?'

'Isn't "the Devil" just a convenient name for the very darkest aspects of human nature?' I insist stubbornly. 'Something to pin the unimaginable upon?'

K'el sighs. 'If that's what you believe, then you've been too long on this earth — as the Devil himself has been. He was banished not long after you left us, and confined to this world as eternal punishment, together with one hundred of our number —'

'Those demons you spoke of,' I interrupt, comprehension dawning. 'The very strongest *daemonium*? They were once *elohim*? Archangels?'

K'el nods. 'The self-same hundred who chose loyalty to the Devil over a place in Heaven. Finding resistance on earth, but no resistance in Hell, the Devil set up his "kingdom" there with the help of his faithful. Together they built a legion of *daemonium* — not born of light, as we were, but of absolute evil. But the Devil longs for dominion over the world of the living, too, and you see the results of his dark longings in "the news", daily. For what use is an army without an empire? Moment by moment, his reach grows longer, his power greater. The underworld is no longer enough for the Devil; he must march on the overworld, *this* world, and at long last, make it his.'

K'el spreads his arms wide to indicate the bleak city street we are standing in, the frozen figures of the men behind us. For a split second, I recall that terrible dream in which I glimpsed a jumble of technicolour horrors — human wars without number, acts of genocidal madness, death on a scale so large that I gasp, 'Someone is actually *responsible* for those things?'

K'el's voice is sombre. 'The Devil both rules and emanates that which mortals call "Hell". You're right in saying that when we were made, there was no "Devil", no "demons". But neither were there unquiet spirits, fell creatures, monstrous things, events, catastrophes, *wars*. These came after us. Now there's more evil on this earth than there are *elohim* or *malakhim* to deal with it. Those tormented fragments of memory and emotion, light and shade you speak of? They may be manipulated and controlled, used to create an army both animate and foul. And I've seen it. It *exists*.'

I know Irina's eyes are suddenly huge in her pale face. 'But why?' I mutter. 'Why would such a thing even be … necessary?'

'Let's put it in human terms you'll understand,' K'el says impatiently. 'The Devil and his legion are bent on a "hostile takeover" not only of this realm, but of Heaven itself. Which, of course, has always been the goal.'

'But what does the Devil have to do with *me*?' I whisper, feeling strangely fearful.

K'el looks at me with great sadness in his eyes. 'I've told you all I know. It's up to you to put the rest together, if you dare. But be careful what you wish for. You don't want that missing puzzle piece. Take it from me.'

'Have you ever considered that this elaborate plan that Raphael came up with for me is just a form of revenge?' I say quietly. 'Just payback for me choosing Luc over him in the first place?'

K'el steps back from me in dismay. 'Over centuries, over *millennia*, it has taken all Eight — physically gathered together — to wrestle your rebellious energy into each and every one of the human vessels we have procured for you. And *every time* Raphael has argued that you have learnt your lesson, that there must be some other, kinder, gentler way to protect you from Luc that will not involve twisting you out of true. And now Raphael — who loved you best, who only wanted your happiness — is missing. Taken while on his way to meet the others, taken before he could help them place you inside the body of a young woman called Irina Zhivanevskaya ...'

I recoil in disbelief. 'But there are few as powerful as Raphael in all of creation. How could he be taken?'

'Believe it,' K'el retorts, eyes flashing. 'He was taken almost the instant Gabriel drew you forth from the dying body of Lela Neill and called the others here to Milan to meet with him. But Raphael never arrived, and the others could not wait; for when you aren't coiled like a sleeping serpent inside the body of a human host, your spirit is like a beacon: detectable to those who know how to look for it. And not only is Raphael missing, but Selaphiel, too — gentle Selaphiel, the most unworldly of us, concerned only with the mysteries of creation, the regulation of the stars, suns, moons, planets. He vanished almost a year ago — taken just before you were placed inside a mortal woman called Ezra. For countless years, it has taken the might and power of all eight to hide you, though it's only ever taken one to draw you out again. But now, now there are only six to do the work of eight ...'

Ezra. The girl who'd fled an abusive marriage and changed her name. The one who came before Susannah, Lucy, Carmen, Lela. I realise now that I must have begun to awaken when I was her, because memories suddenly return: of me throwing her things into a car and driving away in the dead of night, the mark of her husband's fists upon her face. I must have these memories of Ezra because there were just seven to place me into her life and her body, instead of eight. And now there are only six, and I suddenly find myself able to speak Spanish and Russian, when before I could recall speaking only English. And Latin — the language of empire builders, slave masters, ecclesiasts.

And Selaphiel taken also? I can't believe anyone could wish him ill.

'What happened, K'el?' I ask, shaken. 'What really happened that last day I stood among you all with Luc by my side?'

Again, I recall Luc and I at the epicentre of something vast, a conflagration waiting to happen, an ache in time, a breath suspended. The Eight arrayed against us, weapons of power raised, a shining multitude gathered behind them. Behind Luc and me, another shining multitude. Two halves of a people that had once been whole and united. I remember Luc's defiance, though not its rationale. He'd spoken of faith and goodwill, made an act of barter, or surrender. And in that instant, I'd felt a searing pain in my left hand, and the world had gone blank and white, and all my memories had shattered like glass.

I find myself absently flexing the fingers of my left hand, like a street fighter who has already thrown a punch and connected.

'Please,' I beseech K'el in a low voice. 'Tell me.'

K'el shakes his head as he looks down at my upturned face, lays the back of one hand briefly against my cheek. 'You don't remember because some part of you doesn't wish to remember. It's self preservation.

We were all there — all the *elohim*, the *malakhim*, the powers, dominions, *seraphim*, all of us. It's no secret what happened; there's no reason we would hide it from you. Everything you want to know is still there, inside you.'

Always the same answer.

Red rage flares in me and I pound K'el's broad chest with Irina's thin fists. 'Tell me!' I scream. 'Tell me!'

He stands there, unmoved, beneath the sharp rain of blows. 'Unlike you, unlike Luc,' he murmurs, 'I'm no liar. I have no talent for it. So I'm not going to tell you, because I would never sugar coat such a terrible truth. And it would hurt you to hear it again, maybe even unhinge you. Search within yourself for the knowledge, but beware of what you see there. It may be your undoing.'

He releases me then, cupping Irina's face — my face — in a gesture so tender it seems almost final. And I remember, with a sudden, shocking clarity, that K'el had truly loved me, perhaps as much as Raphael had done. How could I have forgotten it? He had hoped I would choose him for my own. And yet I'd taken delight in tormenting him with my preference for Luc.

'If I had to rank you at all,' I remember taunting K'el, 'you wouldn't even *place*.' And I'd laughed.

I close my eyes briefly in shame. I recall the way K'el had watched me. He'd been like a lost dog, always at my heels. Ever hopeful, hopeless. Something Luc had never been.

K'el gives me a crooked smile as he takes in my expression of remorse. 'In many ways, Irina Zhivanevskaya reminds me a lot of how you used to be. Wild, self-centred, spiteful. Beautiful beyond belief. Though you've somehow convinced Raphael, Gabriel, even Uriel, that you've changed for the better. Maybe even me.'

He lays a warning finger on my lips when he sees a new question forming there.

'After this life,' he says quietly, 'Nuriel will be your watcher and you'll no longer be my concern — at least until the next time Michael calls on me to take up the burden. And no doubt there *will* be a next time. I don't think he's ever going to let me forget you — call it *my* penance.'

He turns away, as if preparing to vanish back into whatever vortex he stepped out of. I'm so afraid he'll leave me that I say the first thing that comes into my head to make him stay.

'I don't even know my name,' I wail softly. 'You didn't even leave me that much.'

He turns back to face me, arrested by my question, and I catch a fleeting expression cross his face before his guard goes up again.

But that expression had been enough.

In poker you'd call it a *tell*, which is funny, because that's exactly what he'd been debating. *Tell her? Don't tell her?*

And I'm staggered that he'd even show weakness that way. How did I get so good at reading him, when I never was before?

'Oh, you have a name, *Mercy*,' he says ruefully. 'Like me, like the Eight, the name of God is woven into its very fabric. It's ...'

When he utters it, my real name, my mind fills with a sudden, terrible screeching, as if some unfathomable chasm housing the soul of every person damned since the time of the Fall itself has suddenly opened in my head; as if Hell itself has somehow become lodged in there.

I am the only still point in a spinning, screaming world.

I fall to my knees, sweating and shaking, as if my own name has become a weapon with the power to slay me. Then, just as suddenly, there's silence.

I can barely lift my head to focus on K'el's glorious countenance so far above mine. I'm sure he's seeing abject horror in my eyes.

'Raphael called it "the last defence",' K'el murmurs, extending a luminous hand to help me back onto my feet. 'He said that if all else failed and you fell into the hands of the *daemonium*, they'd be unable to find any trace of your true identity inside you. Your name's so well hidden that only Raphael himself has the power to restore it to you.'

He regards me with his dark gold eyes, as if he's memorising every line of my face, before releasing me. 'Remember, if you see Luc? Just walk away like I'm doing now, but don't look back. And don't try to leave Milan before the six get here, because I'll find you.'

Then he turns and moves swiftly away down the street, towards the distant outline of the Duomo, head down, his hands buried deep in the pockets of his worn-in blue jeans. And it may be a trick of the light, but as I watch, he seems to grow smaller, to somehow scale down to mortal size, so that from the back he might actually be what he appears to be — a pitch-perfect human boy in nondescript clothing.

Without warning, the giant storm front breaks.

And though I can see in the dark like a cat, can see for miles, through sunshine or moonlight, rain or fog, though I rake Via Victor Hugo with my desperate eyes, the one who watches over me is suddenly no longer there, vanished like smoke. And there's only the torrential, blinding rain.

CHAPTER 7

I scream into the icy, driving rain, rain like needles, like nails, 'K'el! K'el! I'm so sorry!'

Sorry that I didn't love you enough; could never love you the way you wanted me to love you.

But there's no answer; only thunder like rolling war drums in the sky. Rain fills my mouth, and, though I was not formed to cry tears, I can feel them, hot and stinging, as they run down Irina's cheeks. They mingle with the water streaming down her face.

Time has recommenced again and the whole world around me, and I am drenched through in seconds, barely able to lift my head or open my eyes against the fearsome onslaught of the unnatural, keening wind, the vicious rain. The thunder is so loud now, it sounds like cannon fire. Lightning suddenly splits the skyline, briefly illuminating the now empty rooftop on which K'el had first appeared.

Luc is coming. He's on his way, that small voice whispers inside me, my inner demon.

This is only the beginning.

I can almost feel Luc's anger in the air all around. And there's that sense — as there always was when Luc was near — of terrible anticipation, excitement, at what he might do. Luc, who never toed any line, who questioned every received wisdom and, for better or worse, taught me to be that way, too. Luc, who blazed brighter than any of us. Rules had neither impressed nor bound him. I'd loved that about him — that he was different; that he recognised no bounds; that he was a risk taker.

And though I love Luc as much as I love the idea of freedom, all I am feeling now is *fear*. I want to stay, but I want to run, too. Because those of the Eight that remain won't simply let Luc take me. Someone I know, someone I love, or might once have loved, is going to get hurt. It's a certainty.

From behind me, a man bawls, 'What are you *doing*?'

I turn with difficulty, so disorientated that I can barely remember who I'm supposed to be today, how I got out here in the rain.

'Irina!' the man roars again from the opposite side of the street, and runs at me, soaked and scowling. He grabs me by the arm, and in the time it takes for him to drag me across the road towards a gleaming black limo with one back door open, I remember that his name is Vladimir, he's part of my security detail, and today? I'm supposed to be one of the most beautiful and desirable women on the planet.

I'm still laughing hysterically as we reach the waiting car. Vladimir forces my head down and shoves me inside, nothing courteous or gentlemanly about him now. 'Drive!' he snarls into Felipe's astonished face, before slamming the door on us and ducking through the pelting rain towards his own limo.

Immediately, my laughter dies. And I don't feel cold, but I can't stop shaking. Felipe hands me a snowy-white hand towel across the front seats, then releases the handbrake and accelerates into the road.

The rain pounding down on the closed fibreglass sunroof of the car sounds like falling gravel. As I fumble out of the heavy wet overcoat and take off the cloche hat, rubbing at Irina's wet face and hair with the hopelessly inadequate towel, Felipe depresses a button on his dashboard. It engages a mechanical ceiling panel that slides shut soundlessly, hiding the sunroof from view. The noise lessens a little but it still sounds like the world is ending outside. We're forced to move slowly because visibility is down to a few feet in every direction.

It's dark as night as we make a bewildering number of turns down narrow one-way streets — high beams on. For a moment, I see the dim, hulking shape of the Duomo reappear in the rear window of the limo before we do a sharp left and the cathedral is lost to sight.

There are few cars on the road and no people. Milan could be a rain-slicked ghost town at the end of time. The rain surges beneath the wheels of the car as if we have become seaborne.

I see Felipe's eyes rest on me momentarily in the driver's mirror before they flick back to the road ahead. 'You look like the drowned cat,' he says, an edge to his voice. 'We are alone at last, *querida*. As we planned.'

Planned? Is Irina involved with him in some way?

I lean forward, flipping Irina's long, wet hair over my head, towelling it vigorously to forestall any immediate need for conversation. I pretend I don't notice Felipe's impatient exhalation, the gear change he executes with a little too much force. Through the damp and obscuring strands of Irina's hair I feverishly scan the interior of the car for clues that might assist with the conversation we are supposed to be having.

It's unlike any other car I've seen before. There are lights in shiny chrome fittings near each of the headrests, and a mini-bar built into one of the doors. Two bench seats face each other, upholstered in a full-grain tan leather and offering more leg room between them than most people would actually need. Each seat is bisected by a wide, space-age-looking armrest that extends down to the floor. The limo is filled with the heady smell of white flowers and there's gleaming chrome and wood inlay everywhere I look. There's also a small silver serving tray on the armrest opposite mine, and on it, a faceted crystal carafe that's three-quarters full. Beside it stands a tall, matching drinking glass filled to the brim with a colourless liquid. No ice. No condensation.

The whole thing is about a million miles away from Ryan Daley's four-wheel drive and its smells of diesel fuel and mud-encrusted guy stuff. I suddenly wish so badly I was there with him — eating candy bars all over the front passenger seat, our breath fogging up the windows — that I have to close my eyes and take a deep and shaky breath.

I sit up and tuck Irina's damp, unbound hair back behind her shoulders, place the wet towel on the seat beside mine. I lean forward and pick up the faceted crystal tumbler and study its contents, lift it to my nose. It looks like water, but it smells like some kind of spirit ... vodka maybe? That's all I'm getting.

I place the glass back on the tray. Only a teenage Russian supermodel would contemplate drinking vodka before 8 am during the worst storm of all time. And K'el thinks that we're alike? I must have been some kind of major *prima donna* back in the day.

Felipe catches my movements in the driver's mirror. 'For you,' he says. Any trace of the coldness I imagined in his eyes before has vanished. Now, he seems almost excited. 'It is exactly as we planned. *Drink*. It will ... relax you.'

I glance back at the tray. That's the plan? A clandestine tipple before the day begins? I hadn't known I was tense, but I feel the line of Irina's shoulders relax. Something as simple as one lousy drink, I can handle. When I was Carmen, I'd chugged eight bourbon and Cokes in one sitting and they'd done nothing to me, nothing. Oh, I'd *pretended* to be unconscious afterwards, but Ryan had known all along that it was an act. To me, alcohol is like accelerant poured on a bonfire: easily consumed, leaving no aftertaste, no ill effects. I could drink and drink and never fall down, never pass out. I know it with a certainty that defies logic. Beer, spirits, whatever — bring them on.

'*¡Bebe!*' Felipe says eagerly. *Drink.*

Gia hadn't mentioned Irina having any problem with alcohol. Drugs, men, decision-making, modesty, notoriety — yes. But not booze. So, what the hell?

I raise the glass high enough for Felipe to see in the driver's mirror. Then I place it to my lips and scull its contents in one smooth motion, without pausing for breath.

I sit back, and seem to see — from a long way away — the crystal glass fall from my suddenly nerveless fingers. Immediately, I know that I've made a bad mistake.

Felipe winks at me in the driver's mirror and I know that I'm missing something. There's some kind of coded meaning in all this that Irina would understand, but I'm having trouble interpreting. I'm suddenly having trouble breathing, too; I can't seem to get enough air into my lungs.

The realisation hits me — way, way too late — that it hadn't just been 100 proof rocket fuel in that glass. There'd been something else in it, something chemical, synthetic, a world away from wine, beer or vodka. A foreign substance I can't identify that's carving a coruscating path through Irina's bird-boned body like acid.

I imagine I can feel the stuff actually hitting Irina's bloodstream like a toxic bomb blast. Poison? Has he *poisoned* me?

'What — have — you — done — to — me?' I gag, clawing at my neck and chest.

I feel my pupils dilate, the blood vessels in my face and body explode with heat beneath my pale, fine skin. I'm sweating and shaking now, and a muscle above my right eye begins to twitch uncontrollably. It feels as if my heart is going to burst. That I'm literally speeding up, or burning up.

The car hits an unexpected pothole and water sprays up in front like a wave hitting a ship. Even after the car rights itself, I still imagine the world is falling away beneath me. Felipe switches the windscreen wipers to maximum and the harsh, rhythmic sound makes me cringe. He gives me a sharp glance in the mirror.

'You're not … pleased?' he says, dark brows furrowing. 'You don't like it? It's A-grade. *De la mejor calidad.* I had to put in more, because when you take it like this, the high it is not so high.'

There's a pain in the centre of my forehead now as if I've been hit with an axe. Even the limo's soft interior lights are searing my eyes. I can't seem to control my head, and fall back against the seat.

'Ge …' I gargle. 'He …'

What I'm trying to say is: *Get help*. But I can't get the words out; it's as if Irina's turning to stone. I'd felt a similar sensation of paralysis when I was Carmen in that hospital bed, flooded with sedatives, on the verge of leaving Ryan for the first time. That awful gulf between thought and action, mind and body, that I thought I'd never again experience — it's returned. When I try to raise one of Irina's hands, it's become something separate from her body. I can't lift it off my knees.

More than ever, I'm trapped in here. And I remember that terrible feeling as Lela lay dying — of being mired in her body, entombed alive, while one by one her five senses slowly faded to black.

And yet … everything seems curiously magnified — the sound of the rain, the terrible scraping noise the windscreen wipers are making, even the vibrations coming up from the uneven road through the limo's four tyres, the slight fishtailing of the back wheels as we drive over a slick manhole cover. I can make out every individual sound and movement, as if the car has no walls, or I am the car.

'I have done exactly what we agree,' Felipe says loudly. 'You send me text, remember? Before your plane has landed. *Have my usual drink waiting*, you say. *I'm desperate for pick-me-up. It's been too long, kiss, kiss, ciao, ciao.* And I know Gianfranco he is always searching for the tablets, for the needles. So I make sure a bottle is in the minibar, ready. I mix it myself. Gianfranco does not think to search the car. There is no reason for him to know that we have met before, many times — in Madrid, in Berlin, Paris. It's good, no? Powerful. Exactly what you wanted. I give you what you want, now you give me what I want …'

It feels as if I'm having a heart attack. Everything's hurting me — the light, the air on my skin, even the sound of Felipe's voice is grating and unpleasant. My jaws are clenched so tightly together that I can't open my mouth to speak.

I've never known if it's truly possible for me to die in a body I've soul-jacked, but this may be it.

Together, Irina and I seem to be bursting into flame, and none of the Eight is here to witness it. There's no one here to save me, because the Eight are under attack themselves — a thing so unthinkable, so brazen, I can still scarcely believe it. And K'el, my watcher, had walked away as if he never wanted to see me again.

My vision is blurring, growing dark at the edges, and I close my eyes.

I hear a male voice complain lightly: 'I wish you'd just enjoy the ride. You have access to wealth, material things, experiences that no ordinary human being could ever hope for. You should be revelling in everything that's on offer. The ability simply to *be*, to abandon oneself to human pleasure, is something our kind could learn from. In a way, I envy you. I really do. I find the act of possession too ... messy. I leave that to others. But it does mean that I ... miss out.'

I open my eyes with difficulty to see Luc seated opposite me, his elbows resting on the armrests, his long fingers steepled together. I'm hit by a freak wave of shock and longing. When I see him like this, there *are* no doubts. He is the one. No one could ever compare. How could anyone look at him and not love him?

But I can't speak, can't even move. Everything I'm feeling is in my eyes. Adoration, terror, pain.

Luc sees me watching him and smiles, saying softly, 'Hello, my love.'

And I think that maybe I *have* died. And this is my reward.

His ruffled golden hair is shorter than I remember it, and there's a sexy hint of stubble along his jawline. He's wearing a sharp, narrow-cut, single-breasted, three-piece navy suit with a thin navy pinstripe running through the weave, which emphasises his snake-hipped, broad-shouldered, long and lean form. He's paired it with a snowy-white shirt with French cuffs, two large and faceted sapphires set in gold for cufflinks, one at each wrist. At his neck is a Windsor-knotted striped tie in iridescent colours, like the sheen on a dragonfly's wings. Socks in a discreet grey-on-grey herringbone pattern; black leather lace-up brogues. There's a folded pair of aviator sunglasses with reflective lenses in the top pocket of his jacket. He couldn't look more perfect in his pitch-perfect human clothes.

Beyond him, I see that Felipe is turning to say something else to me, but I can't hear the words. It's obvious that he doesn't see Luc, because as he throws out his left hand, it seems to pass straight through Luc's left shoulder.

'H … ' I gag.

I'm trying to say: *How?* But also, I think: *Help me.*

Because Irina's body is spinning out of control. There's too much light, too much heat inside the car, inside us. I'm going blind. I'm a house of cards on the brink of tumbling down. Everything inside her, inside me, is simultaneously speeding up and shutting down.

It's a horrible way to die. And I wonder if she can feel it, if she knows. If she's frightened the way that I'm frightened.

Irina collapses across the back seat and I go down, too, powerless to stop it; the two of us so inextricably entwined in the throes of some terrible opiate I don't even have a name for.

Luc's pale eyes narrow as he studies us sprawled here, but he doesn't reach out, and I'm pierced by a sorrow so intense that a dull ache, a remembered pain, begins to build in the fingers of my left hand, the hand that last held his.

Luc is *here*. K'el wasn't lying. But why won't Luc touch me?

'It's only taken you by surprise because it's such a pure and concentrated dose. You need to *focus*,'

Luc says, and his voice is curiously urgent though his body language is still detached, distant. 'You should be doing more to control the outcome. Just because it's synthetic doesn't mean it must simply be surrendered to. Science is there to be countered. We were here before it, we'll be here long after it's gone. You need to pull away from her. You know how to do it. I know you do.'

How ... Wide-eyed and stricken, I can't even finish the thought.

'This is no dream,' Luc replies, and I hear a strange tension in his voice. 'You're in that waking state of paralysis between death and life that mimics the conditions of sleep. I can see you, even speak with you, across time, across great distance, but I can't help you because I'm not really here. I'm just an expectation, a forward projection, if you like. I'm not going to reach you soon enough to salvage that body you're in. If Irina's idiot driver spiked her drink with enough liquid meth to stop her heart, it's up to *you* to bring the girl back. I've shown you how it's done in your dreams. And I know that you've done it before — how else did you escape Paul Stenborg? When, if you'd stayed, I would've found you. We would already be together.'

I frown, trying to make sense of all he's saying.

'You need to stop looking to other people for answers,' he snaps. 'Be assured that your "confinement" will soon be over — I'll see to it. And I'll personally *destroy* every one of our kind that has ever had a hand in keeping you from me, that's a promise.'

The terrible anger I see in his eyes only seems to make him burn brighter, make his beauty even more piercing. And it reminds me how *alive* he always made me feel. Around him, everything always seemed hyper-bright, hyper-real, better than it actually was.

'I'll move Heaven and earth for you,' Luc insists harshly. 'But you have to keep Irina alive. Then I'll take over. With you by my side, everything becomes possible again. I expect you to be in Milan, waiting for me. If she dies, I lose you again. *Don't let me lose you again.* Not now, when everything is in readiness for you, my queen.' He leans forward, his gaze fever-bright. 'Do you think you can do what I ask? It's such a simple thing, *Mercy*.'

When he says the word, the false name I have given myself, his defences come down for a moment, and I'm stung by what I see in his eyes. Sure, there's affection there, even love. But nothing like it used to be; there's no *heat*.

There's doubt, too, and fury. Exasperation, desperation, disappointment, a dark and voracious need. And I can't reconcile any of it before Luc's gaze grows unreadable again.

His voice is low and insistent. 'When you see me again, when I am actually before you, you must fly to my side. *Come to me.* Only then will you be safe. Flee the Eight and their legion at whatever cost. But if I should somehow fail,' his beautiful mouth tightens ominously, 'then locate that human boy and return with him to the place where he lives, to *Paradise.*' He spits the word. 'He, too, will play a part in the final reckoning, when all debts due and owing to me shall be met in full and repaid in blood.'

There's a jump-cut moment — like a break in transmission — where I imagine for a moment that Luc's outline wavers. Then he abruptly dissolves out of being, and it's Felipe behind the wheel, chuckling almost to himself.

'So, *chica*, what are you going to give me, eh? What will you give me to keep the channels open?'

Irina's body goes rigid, and I know I should be working out how to fix her, fix *us*. But all I feel is a paralysing fear. Luc called me my love, as he always has, but something rang false. His mouth had said one thing, but his eyes …

It's the same kind of fear that used to strike me when we lay alone together in the secret garden he'd conjured for me out of thin air, out of wishes and longing. As I'd watched him sleep, I used to think: *What if, one day, he discovers I'm not good enough, that he doesn't want me any more?* I've survived so many things. But I couldn't survive that.

Irina's body convulses again, and I wonder dazedly how it is that she can sense my pain.

CHAPTER 8

A man's voice suddenly emerges from a speaker set into the dashboard of the car, drawing me back to the present against my will.

'How far?' snaps the voice in Italian-accented English.

With an oath, Felipe picks up a small handset and joins the chorus of disembodied voices discussing ETAs and alternative routes in every accent under the sun while the hard rain drives down, turning suddenly into hailstones the size of golf balls. The car slows to a virtual crawl and I let their words wash over me, let myself drift out like the tide.

I don't know what Luc meant by countering science, but I know I have to try if I ever want to see him again; if I want to be free; if I want him to love me the way that he used to.

I dive down, following the strands of myself inwards, following the linkages and switchbacks and false trails, the broken pattern that I have somehow been cast into. It seems easier this time, this process of atomisation, of unbecoming. I know what to do now, what I'm capable of. There's no pain, no resistance, no panic, as I cleave away from the flesh, shiver into a billion pieces behind Irina's eyes.

I am light now, I'm pure energy, as I flow through the canals of Irina's lymphatic and cardiovascular systems, her connective tissue, her muscles, the nerve endings and sinews, wet matter and bone of which she is made. As liquid as that poison I'm seeking. I chase it down. And where I find it — foreign, lethal, so concentrated it's a wonder Irina's not already dead — I break it down, molecule by molecule, atom by atom. Counter its dark science by turning it to vapour within my vaporous self, though it tastes to me like gall, like venom. I subtract it from Irina's blood, Irina's flesh, so that she's left clean and whole.

Even though Irina's soul is locked away, out of reach, I know that at some deep, animal level she'll remember this feeling of burning, of purging, of healing. And she won't be tempted to use again. My touch is electric. I have placed a mark upon her that cannot be seen by mortal eyes.

Abruptly, the weird sensation of unbecoming reverses, as if I've done all I can do. I'm pulled back, coalescing again inside Irina's skin, behind her eyes, as if I am her, and she is me, and there's no gap, none at all, between us.

I brace myself against the armrest with my elbows, feeling my temperature, my heart rate, fall. My sight grows clear again. The light, the air, no longer hurt me.

I'm on the point of sitting back up in my seat when I hear Felipe place the radio handset back in its cradle and murmur, '*Usted es una estúpida, una drogadicta, una puta. ¿Ve que fácil es poseer a otro ser humano? Ahora la poseo. ¿Desea que continúe? La primera cosa que haremos será deshacernos de esta perra curiosa Basso.*'

You stupid, junkie whore. You see how easy it is to own another human being? Now I own you. You want me to keep it coming? The first thing we're going to do, is get rid of that nosy bitch Basso.

He laughs, and I know he doesn't care if I hear him, because he thinks that by the time I come down I won't remember.

I sit up suddenly, tucking Irina's long hair back behind her small and perfect ears. Felipe catches sight of the movement, then my expression, in the driver's mirror. Something he sees there makes his own eyes widen in shock.

The car swerves abruptly to the right, hitting the raised edge of a stone kerb. The limo mounts the footpath momentarily before Felipe swings the wheel hard left, over-correcting so that the entire car skids with a squeal of tyres through a slow-motion arc, throwing up a huge plume of water and sleet. A car coming the other way swerves wildly to miss us with a long blare of its horn. There's the sound of rending metal as we take out the side of a parked car, before coming to a jerky stop hard up against a lamppost on the wrong side of the street, facing back the way we came from.

The hail keeps coming down. And that's all I hear in the car for a long while. That, and the sound of Felipe's chokey breathing.

'Creo en Dios, Padre todopoderoso, Creador del cielo y de la tierra. Creo en Jesucristo, Su único Hijo ...' he murmurs, looking curiously shrunken, his face in his hands. I realise that he's praying.

The radio erupts with voices. I hear fingers

scrabbling at the back doors of the limo and realise that the central locking is still on. The scrabbling turns to pounding, on the sides of the car, on the roof.

'Irina!' I hear someone roar. 'Irina!'

I'm getting so sick of that name.

Felipe looks up and around almost fearfully before releasing the central-locking mechanism. He does not look at me.

My passenger side door is wrenched open. Jürgen's standing there holding a large black umbrella, melting sleet streaking his overcoat. Then Carlo materialises out of the grey atmosphere and beckons me forward. Both men are soaked through and look very pale. Their eyes scan the inside of the car quickly and thoroughly, before homing in on Felipe's hunched figure behind the wheel, then flick back to me, raking me up and down.

Satisfied with what he sees, Carlo says, 'You all right, miss?' in a gentle voice, the way you'd address a frightened child. 'Please, come with us. Felipe, he will handle this.'

When he looks back at Felipe for confirmation, something Carlo sees in the other man's face makes his mouth harden. His voice is icy as he says, 'Gianfranco wants to talk to you after you are finished here.'

I hear the splash of many footsteps converging on us, hear urgent shouts in Italian, an approaching siren. There's the reflected glow of flashing lights through the open car door. The hail comes down as if it will never, ever stop. And I wonder why each life I'm being forced to live seems ever more unquiet than the last.

I gather up my hat, overcoat and handbag and hand them to Carlo as I prepare to step out of the car. Before I do, I turn to Felipe again, but he will not turn his head to meet my eyes. His cowardice causes a hot anger to rise in me like a rattlesnake striking.

'Deal's off,' I hiss. 'The product's lousy. Stay away from Irina, you piece of shit, or I'll track you down and force-feed you the same stuff you just gave a mentally unstable nineteen year old. *¿Comprende?*'

Outside the car, Carlo and Jürgen are huddled beneath the umbrella, talking loudly, while they hold onto Irina's things. They do not wonder at the strangeness of my words because they did not hear them.

But the sound of the hail and of the sirens also masks Felipe's reply. '*¡Demonio!*' he shrieks, making the sign of the cross in my face, his eyes wild, the whites showing.

Demon.

He's still screaming '¡*Demonio!*' at me as I shut the door.

Jürgen holds the umbrella over us all as he, Carlo and I run for the cover of the third limo. Gia throws the door open and holds her arms out for Irina's bundle of wet possessions. I clamber into the seat opposite hers and she leans across and slams the door closed behind me. But not before there's a couple of bright flashes outside. Cameras. Someone's taking photos.

Through the streaming windows, I see Carlo and Jürgen making a beeline for the nearest policeman in full wet-weather gear.

I stiffen as Gia grabs me by the upper arms, and turn warily. She doesn't let go of my arms, just leans forward and stares into my face.

'I thought you were going to die,' she says sombrely. 'I really did. I thought that the bad luck you carry around with you and sprinkle all over people like a bad fairy had turned on you this time. We saw Felipe suddenly accelerate and I thought he was going to flip the car. You couldn't get any traction. You must have been so *scared*.'

I shrug. Time had seemed to slow while the car had carved imperfect circles through the sleet on the road. But it hadn't been nearly as terrifying as anything I'd seen and experienced while I was Carmen, while I was Lela. And it hadn't been nearly as frightening as my dreams can be. But I don't tell her that.

Gia's laugh is shaky as she finally lets go of me and sits back. 'All I could think was — it's the drugs that are supposed to kill you. I hadn't even seen this coming.'

One of the passenger doors across from us is wrenched open and Carlo gets in, smelling of wet wool and leather, followed by Jürgen and the streaming umbrella. The interior of the outsized car suddenly seems too small to hold us all, and I shrink back against the door on my side so I won't inadvertently touch someone's bare skin and invite in the unwanted. I don't want to know what's running through their minds, I don't want a potted history of their lives. I have enough going on in my head.

'Drive!' Carlo roars at the dark-haired man in the driver's seat whose name I don't know. 'Drive!' Then he levels an apologetic gaze at me. 'One of the *Agence Habituelle* photographers got your picture. I'm sorry, but it begins.'

The limo weaves slowly out of the gathering crowd of emergency personnel and onlookers. Past

Felipe, who is standing beside the wreckage of the black car gesturing wildly at a policeman. Only he and I know the truth, and he won't be sharing it with anyone. Something he saw in my face scared him so much, he lost control of the car.

Gia nudges me and points out the back window and I see a helmeted man in a rain slicker, with camera equipment slung around his neck, following us doggedly through the rain on a navy blue scooter. A few moments later, a couple of men on a bright blue and white Kawasaki motorcycle swerve up alongside the windows, tapping on the tinted glass. 'Irina!' they call. 'Irina! Any words for us?'

'Just ignore them,' Gia says disgustedly. 'It's Felipe's fault everything's gone to hell. No one will even be looking at Natasha in the decoy car. What a monumental waste of time and money.'

The hail's getting heavier as we turn into a narrow one-way street lined with three- and four-storey stone buildings that stand shoulder to shoulder, some with balconies, some flying the Italian tricolour flag. There are parked cars, scooters and bicycles packed in tightly on both sides of the road, and one of the buildings bears a sign reading: Via Borgonuovo. We cruise up to the grand front entrance of a four-storey, honey-coloured building with iron grillework covering each of the tall, deep windows.

The already narrow street is pretty much impassable now that we're here, because an armada of scooters, motorbikes, Fiats and Mini Coopers is following us. Further up the road, Vladimir's car is already double-parked and blocking traffic with more scooters and motorbikes and cars banked up behind it. A sea of onlookers under umbrellas is lining the footpath on both sides of the street, despite the hail.

It's pandemonium as the limo comes to a stop. People seem to surge forward from everywhere, surrounding the car. None of the car doors are open, but already flashes are going off and it's suddenly as bright as noon outside the car's tinted windows. We could be trapped in a field of falling stars, of fireflies.

Gia sees the expression on my face and laughs softly. 'It's not as if you've never seen this before!' she says, shaking her head. 'Get ready to hustle. Just make for that portico with the sliding glass doors — Vladimir and our guys will try to clear a path and flank you. Don't stop, don't turn around. Once you reach the sliding doors, you're home free. I'll see you on the inside.'

Jürgen and Carlo exchange glances, then Jürgen opens his door, battering the milling group of men and women with his black umbrella. People are screaming in his face, tearing at his clothes, pushing him aside, trying to get their hand-held mics and camera equipment, video-enabled mobile phones and camcorders, in around the half-open limo door. They indiscriminately fire off shot after shot as Gia tries to shield me with her body.

'Is bad, today, very bad,' Carlo mutters before launching himself after Jürgen and slamming the door closed. Outside the car, he signals frantically over his head for help.

People fall back in surprise for an instant, before coming forward again like a wave with their questions, their cameras. The air is filled with voices shrieking, 'Irina! Irina!'

Abruptly, the hail ceases. People look up, then at each other for a moment, then the questions begin again.

'What do you have to say about today's hair-raising near miss?' I hear a female voice shout through the tinted glass.

'Is it true that your absence from the Palliardi show last year was due to involuntary admission to the Abbey for psychiatric and addiction disorders?' a man bellows.

'Who are you seeing, now that you've very publicly dumped Félix de Haviland and Will Reyne in close succession?' roars a third voice, also male.

'Don't listen to them,' Gia says forcefully. 'Just take a deep breath, and when the guys say *go*, you go. Head up, chin held high. It's all bullshit and lies, okay?'

I turn in shock as a stocky young man with wet ginger hair pulls open the door on our side of the car and thrusts a micro recorder in Gia's face, in mine. 'What do you have to say about the fact that you're cursed?' he yells. 'That you leave a trail of broken hearts and property damage wherever you go?'

Gia's trying with all her might to shoulder the young man out again, and screaming at me to help her, but I'm paralysed with shock. K'el's standing across the street between two parked cars, just beyond the wall of faces and bodies crowded around the limo. He makes no move to join the throng, to push in amongst them. He's just there, in his hyper-ordinary clothes, hands in the pockets of his broken-in blue jeans, watching me with his steady, unblinking gaze. Just watching. Because he has to. Because he can't help himself.

Vladimir's face suddenly comes between us for a moment, his burly, wise-guy hands pulling the ginger-haired journo out of the way while Angelo grabs hold of the car door and kicks out at the people still holding it open.

The circus around the car suddenly seems to be happening in slow motion, to somebody else. I don't hear the sounds of scuffling, of shouting, because my eyes are fixed on K'el's face.

It's unmistakeably him, although he's like a scaled-down version of his usual self. And I realise that others can see him, too, because people are pushing past him saying '*prego, prego*,' the way Italians ask a fellow human being to make way. Except that he's not human, he's faking it.

I hadn't imagined it before: when he'd walked away from me, he subtly shifted the way he looks. His eyes and hair seem darker, his skin paler, almost matte, like human skin. That light that usually accompanies our kind, that comes from within, is no longer visible to ordinary eyes, although I still see a faint glimmer of it in the skin of his face and hands.

And I wonder what the trick is to blending in, to making yourself look like a pitch-perfect human being. I wonder if I could do it — if I ever get free of Irina. Could I shift the way I look? Shift the way people perceive me?

What do you have to say about the fact that you're cursed? That you leave a trail of broken hearts and property damage wherever you go?

I shudder. The questions could have come from K'el's own lips.

Without realising I'm speaking out loud, I say, 'I *am* cursed. And you were right: it's all my fault. But how could I have known that it would lead to this?'

'I'll quote you on that!' a young woman crows triumphantly as she whips a recording device out of my face and pushes her way back through the baying crowd.

Gia lets out a loud 'Oooooh!' and kicks out with her booted feet, scrambling to pull shut the door from the inside as Angelo pushes on it from the outside. The central locking slams into place.

She turns to me. 'What did you say that for?' she wails. 'It'll go viral in ten minutes: *World-famous Russian beauty admits she's cursed*. God, you have no sense. Don't give them stuff they can use against you.'

Through the tinted car windows, I can still see K'el. His eyes never leave mine, even though by rights he shouldn't be able to see me through the dark glass.

I hear his voice in my head: *Don't try to leave Milan before the six get here, because I'll find you.*

Vladimir reappears at one of the windows and knocks on it with his scarred knuckles. There's some kind of cordon forming out there now: two rows of men in black suits, each built like a gorilla, pushing back at the crowd on both sides to form a clear area. People are shrieking and slipping over in the slush, and going down like skittles, as a path is cleared for the bitch queen from hell.

'Finally,' Gia snaps. 'Leave your coat and the bag — they're ruined anyway. I'll bring them. Oh, and give me that stupid hat.'

She twists it in her hands, punching at the crown, before she places it carefully back on top of my head. Almost tenderly, she arranges the ends of my hair upon my shoulders and grabs a small, gleaming gold cylinder from her capacious backpack. 'Trout pout,' she says, making a silly face at me, her lips pushed forward like a fish. I mirror her expression and she slicks the fiery red lipstick on me. Grabs a pencil with a brush on the end of it out of her bag and marks my eyebrows with quick, confident strokes. 'Strong brows, strong lips and you're good to go. It'll reproduce nicely, whatever the medium. Now remember what I said: Don't stop, don't turn around. Head held high. Just get inside. You're golden. You're a superstar.'

The limo driver releases the central locking on a signal from Vladimir and Gia pushes me out the door. I do as she says. Step out of the car as gracefully as I can manage in the teetering heels. With Vladimir on my right and Carlo on my left, I keep moving, chin up, head held high, letting the questions about my love life, whether I'm a binger or a purger, whether I wear any underwear to sleep, wash over me.

Though I keep moving as ordered, towards the grand portico, the sliding glass doors etched discreetly with the words *Via Borgonuovo, 22* that represent sanctuary, I can't help turning my head to scan the opposite side of the street, beyond my abandoned limo. K'el's gone. All I see in his place is the figure of a young woman in ordinary street clothes: a pale blue puffy down jacket, blue jeans, snow boots, a Fair Isle knitted cap jammed down low over the long, wavy dark hair that frames her sweet-looking face. She's a little above average height, and slender. I wonder if she knows that she's standing right where an archangel had been.

But then I look more closely at the skin of her face. To someone with eyesight like mine, there's something just the faintest bit 'wrong' about it. It's *almost* matte, like a human's. Almost, but there's a faint surface sheen to it, as if light is seeping out slowly through her pores, can't fully be disguised.

And I know that I've seen her before, and I feel Irina's heart kick into high gear with sudden, fearful wonder. My eyes fly wide in my pale face. The archangel Nuriel. My next watcher. She's already here.

It's who Justine Hennessy had reminded me of, when I was Lela. I'd seen Justine walking towards me in the stark, bright, noonday sun of an Australian summer dressed all in white, her long, dark, wavy hair unbound against the light and I'd thought then that I was looking at ... Nuriel, I realise now. Nuriel.

Our eyes meet across the chaos in the street and I recall that we were friends once, the best of friends. She always had my back. Although that day — when Luc and I faced the Eight — she sided with Them, not with me. It had been the biggest betrayal, the biggest shock, of my entire life. The Eight — They took her away from me, too. It's just one more thing to hold Them to account for.

Nuriel mouths: *Keep moving*, and gives me a heartbreakingly familiar smile as she suddenly vanishes, unnoticed by the crowd.

K'el had said that Nuriel had been assigned to watch over me in my next life, the one after this one. I start shaking as I realise that Nuriel's here for a reason. Those that remain of the Eight are going to try and shift me again. *Before* Luc gets here.

CHAPTER 9

Vladimir and Carlo each put a supportive hand beneath one of my elbows as I stumble beneath the graceful, rectangular portico, through those discreet sliding glass doors.

We stand there for a few seconds, looking up into the lens of a camera trained on us from above, while security runs some kind of visual check on us from inside the building. Beyond us is a second set of doors exactly the same as the first. Finally, these slide open to allow us into the reception area of Atelier Re.

I'm standing in a light-drenched, music-filled atrium that is completely at odds with the blunt neo-classical stone facade of the building's exterior. An intricately patterned mosaic floor stretches away from me in all directions, its thumbnail-sized tiles laid out in soothing sea greens and luminous blues, shades of ochre, white and black.

It could be the world seen from above. And I imagine the six that remain — Michael, Uriel, Gabriel, Jeremiel, Jegudiel, Barachiel — speeding here from all points across it, or maybe even the universe. To get to me. It could happen any moment. I might blink now and wake up somewhere else, as someone else, and have to start all over again.

K'el is ready to let me go. Nuriel's ready to receive me into her care. How else to explain her presence here?

Then I frown, remembering that though it takes the might of many to place me into a new human form, it takes only one of them to draw me out of a mortal body. The six should be gathering where my new host is going about her daily business, oblivious to the fact that she's about to experience a kind of spiritual lockdown. So why are they all coming *here* first?

Is it because there's no time? I don't think I'm mistaken in thinking that things seem to be speeding up; that the length of time between each soul-jacking seems to be shortening.

And why place me inside a new host whose life so closely intersects with Irina's? My last five lives were all so different. In age, in circumstance, physical location, culture, everything. Why put me into a new life that has two, maybe three degrees of separation, at most, from Irina's?

'We'll be on standby, Irina,' Carlo murmurs in my ear. 'If you need us, have them call.'

I nod distractedly.

At the peripheries of my sight, I see Carlo rejoin Vladimir, Angelo and Jürgen, and they exit back through the two sets of sliding doors, making for the limos, shoving a few of the remaining paps on the way, just for fun. For a moment, I'm on my own, listening to the music. It's an operatic duet of thrilling beauty: two female voices, two *soprani*. The melody seems familiar, but I can't place the language the voices are singing in.

I scan the atrium absently, ignoring the stares and whispers that form part of just being Irina. It's space age meets art deco on the ground floor of Atelier Re. Everywhere I look, there's an interesting interplay between mirrored glass and polished, curvilinear stone, rich-toned wood and black bakelite and chrome. Many of the polished, flowing surfaces seem to reflect the light that's spilling from massive, organic-looking, many-branched light sculptures that hang from the ceiling. Though the space seems uncluttered, almost under-furnished, there are groups of pretty people in beautiful clothes conducting meetings at small, pod-like break-out areas, or taking calls at ingeniously designed workstations that are miraculously free of wiring, dust or knick-knackery. Even the computer screens seem embedded into the smooth lines of the tabletops.

It's all breathtakingly elegant, and I'm still staring up at the small constellations of light bulbs, mesmerised, when someone calls out 'Irina!' and I lower my gaze to see an elderly man — maybe seventy? seventy-five? — standing in front of me.

He's almost the same height I am in my killer heels, with a full head of artfully dyed, dark brown hair that's slicked back in a retro, yet ageless style. He's clean-shaven, olive-skinned, and his bright blue eyes are framed by quirkily rounded tortoiseshell spectacles. He's a little paunchy now — his cleverly cut, Nehru-collared black suit can't hide that — but he would've had a rangy, athletic frame in his youth; he would've been handsome. And there's still great strength in his soft, wrinkled old man's hands as he grabs hold of mine, taking me by surprise.

I look down sharply at Irina's fingers gripped tightly in his and know that it would be rude to pull away. But

I feel something like panic as my left hand begins to ache dully. It's too late, the old man's grip is too strong. There's that sensation of a building pressure behind my eyes, then we flame into contact, and I see —

— Irina Zhivanevskaya as a sixteen year old, through the old man's eyes. She has dyed-black, punky hair, wild eyes and ripped clothes; an even filthier attitude. I see her slouching into the room towards him, feel the sudden leap of his interest, see her deliberately bump into a tall, slender, blonde girl who's just stepped down gracefully from a catwalk set up in the centre of the room under harsh lights, so that the girl stumbles and almost falls, then runs from the room in tears.

Then I see a woman with a pale, severe face and snow-white hair in a sleek chignon, all in black, sitting beside him. I hear her tell Irina to stand up straight, hear Irina snarl, 'Go to hell!' in her smoky voice, without missing a beat.

The woman turns and says angrily, 'She's no good, this one, send her away.'

But the man's voice says kindly, 'Walk, child, walk.' And his hand indicates the catwalk.

Irina mounts the stairs and transforms into someone else altogether as she storms along the narrow white platform, head up, eyes wide, shoulders back, hands swinging freely by her sides, hips thrust forward, her freakily long legs easily covering the short distance before she pauses, stares, pivots, and stalks back the other way. And I see what the old man saw that day — a certain look, a feline, haughty walk. Together with her wide-set eyes and narrow everything, that *go-to-hell* stare, Irina is unforgettable.

That's all I want to see, and I gently pull my hands free of the old man's. The ache in my left hand, behind my eyes, fades away.

'I feel a little bit ... responsible, you know?' he says with an apologetic lift of his shoulders. 'For all the craziness. You walked for me, and then nothing in your life was ever the same again.'

I shrug. 'In the end, we're responsible for ourselves, for our actions,' and I'm speaking for myself as much as for Irina. It's something I think I've only just begun to appreciate.

The old man gestures at one of the pretty people standing at a workstation across the room. 'Gudrun,' he calls. 'My cane?'

'Right away, Mastro Re,' calls out a beautiful ice-blonde in a high-collared red blouse, an artfully tailored navy peplum jacket and matching wasp-waisted pencil skirt.

Mastro. It's a very old word, archaic now, rarely used. And it means *artisan*.

The woman detaches herself from the two men she's talking with and heads our way, holding an elegant wooden cane with a bright gold handle in the shape of a resting lion. She's of medium height, with sapphire-coloured eyes and blood-red lips, her hair pulled into a sleek and immaculate French roll. Somehow, she manages to look enviably businesslike and blonde-bombshell at the same time.

As she reaches us, she says in a neutral, Swiss-finishing-school, pan-European accent, 'Irina, you're looking well. All things considered.'

Her voice and eyes are friendly, but I draw back a little from her, as Giovanni Re takes the cane the young woman's proffering and leans on it heavily. It's not my imagination. She's *gleaming*, the way K'el was, and Nuriel, even after they'd modified themselves in order to pass as ordinary humans.

Light seems to be seeping out of Gudrun's flawless, porcelain skin. And I know it's not illuminising powder that's causing it.

'Do I *know* you?' I whisper.

Her face isn't familiar, but she's an archangel, too, I'm sure of it. The woman I'm looking at right now is probably only a pale approximation of what Gudrun really looks like. She must be glorious in her angelic form.

'No,' she smiles, 'you don't know me. Though, of course, everyone knows who you are. I'm new here, though I do believe we have a few ... friends in common. Mastro Re's last executive assistant very sadly ... died. Heart failure, I understand. She was only thirty-three.'

Giovanni Re takes one of Gudrun's shapely hands in his. I see that her nails are long and painted the same glossy blood red as her lips.

'Gudrun's been invaluable,' he says gruffly. 'When Ainsley left us so suddenly' — there's a sudden sheen in his eyes, an echo of shock and grief — 'I was going to cancel the show, the documentary, the retrospective, everything. Ainsley had all the details of the set, the layout, the play list, the results of the castings, in her head. Luckily for me, Gudrun came along to sort out the mess. She convinced me it was possible to go on.'

Gudrun meets the old man's eyes and smiles sunnily. 'It's been marvellous working for you.' She's suddenly so radiant to my eyes that I wonder how it is that no one else in the room can see how much she seems to shine. 'It's been like a holiday,' she adds. 'I *am* going to miss you when all this craziness is over.' She gives the old man's hand a squeeze then turns to walk away.

'A holiday!' he exclaims. 'She's priceless,' he says to me. 'Priceless.'

Gudrun's eyes flick back to mine wryly. 'That's what they all say,' she replies, 'when they want something. Now, I'm here to keep an eye on you, Irina, so anything you need, just give a shout. Someone will know where I am in this warren.'

I watch her walk away. She must be one of Michael's reinforcements, like K'el, like Nuriel. Maybe they're all here because they're afraid of Luc in some way. Or they wish to stop him, and force is needed.

With a chill, I recall Gabriel's words to me as Lela lay dying in his arms. He'd said that I was fully justified in bringing Luc to the Eight to have him *dealt with*. That I was well within my rights to *slay him myself*. I feel the blood drain out of my face at the memory.

Even now, I can't understand what Luc could have done to justify punishment, even death, at my hands. I feel a dull ache begin behind my eyes. There's something I'm missing here. What are they all keeping from me?

But now I know why a power of archangels is headed this way. They're going to use me as bait. And if they don't manage to catch Luc — or kill him? — they'll shift me anyway, to preserve the *status quo*, to keep Hell and the *daemonium* at bay.

The old man's voice breaks into my troubled thoughts. 'Gudrun was right,' he says. 'You *are* looking well, all things considered. Sometimes the stories about you are so terrible, I don't know what to believe. But when I saw you at the rehearsal yesterday, you looked even better than I dared to imagine. You will make my final show so much more memorable. I was right to insist. There's something different about you today, I think? You seem calmer, more beautiful even than I remember. There's a glow about you, eh? Am I right? Is it love?'

'I wouldn't know about any of that, Mastro Re,' I reply carefully.

And it's true. I don't know how to catch hold of love, or to keep it. Luc used to love me more than life itself. But something's changed. I close my eyes briefly in anguish.

'Call me Giovanni, please,' the old man says softly. 'We've known each other too long to stand on such formality.'

His gaze and voice become suddenly distant. 'Seeing you now reminds me of a dream I had, though I cannot think why.' He leans heavily on his cane. 'The most beautiful youth came to me, Irina. He took my hand and said he would lead me to Marco, that Marco was waiting and we would be together again, very soon. It's been twenty-one years, did you know? Since Marco … Well, longer than you have been alive, my dear. The youth was tall, very tall. Dressed all in black, with eyes that were so blue they were like the sea. But though his face was the face of a young man, his hair — it was pure silver. Like moonlight.'

I go cold at his words. Giovanni has just described Azraeil, whom I last saw at the bedside of Karen Neill. *Azraeil.* The archangel of death.

'You're certain he took your hand?' I mutter.

Giovanni nods, his gaze still clouded by thoughts of his dream.

There's only one way to know for sure, and I steel myself resignedly before reaching out and taking Giovanni lightly by the wrist, searching for some specific information.

It *is* getting easier; I'm not imagining that either. Though Giovanni and I are both standing here, in this busy space full of busy people, he's not really here and neither am I. As we flame into contact, I feel myself loosen, feel myself dissolve *into* him somehow. There's pain, of course. But there's always pain.

I surf through it, through the pressure in my head, and reach down into his mind, into his flesh, to interpret what has been left there for my kind to read.

A moment later, I release my grip on his wrist.

'You're dying, Giovanni,' I murmur in Irina's husky voice. 'The show, the retrospective, all of it — you don't need to do them. There's nothing you need to prove to anyone any more.'

Giovanni struggles to hide his shock. 'Is it so obvious? Very few realise that I am ... "retiring" for reasons beyond my control. You must tell me who let the cat from the bag?'

'I've always had a ... sense about these things,' I reply quietly, which isn't strictly a lie.

'This illness — it is not something I could hide forever.' Giovanni's eyes are both amused and sad. 'But what a way to go, eh?' He chuckles. 'And they all warned me about you! You are like the lamb today, the dove. There were the strongest objections. Anna Maria — you remember Anna Maria?'

In my head, I see that stern older woman with the colourless face and hair who'd told Giovanni to send Irina away.

I nod. 'Of course. She never liked me.'

Giovanni chuckles again, placing his free hand beneath my left elbow as we begin to walk slowly out of the atrium.

'Anna Maria said that if I used you to open and close my final haute couture show, no one would insure me, I would be the laughing stock. But when she sees you in the dresses I have made with only you in mind, I think she will understand that I was right to insist. All my favourite girls will be here, all my muses across the years. I saw your potential when no one else could see it. And that makes you the most singular, the most beautiful, of them all.'

He stumbles a little and digs his cane into the ground to keep from falling, and I pretend not to notice any of it.

We enter a wide central corridor that runs the length of the building. The brilliant mosaic tiling peters out, like the foam that a receding wave might leave upon the shore, and I find myself walking upon burnished concrete. There are many brightly lit workrooms leading off it, filled with seamstresses and mannequins, house models and stylists, clients and buyers, and racks and racks of beautiful, iridescent evening gowns and sharply tailored work wear, all colour-coded. Interspersed with these spaces are offices full of handsomely attired administrative staff. Many of the rooms have sliding glass doors or large feature windows, to allow what's happening inside them to be observed, to give the impression that there are no secrets in this place.

We make a left turn into a quiet corridor at the far end of the central thoroughfare. It, too, has several doors facing onto it, but these doors are made of timber, burnished to a high sheen, and all are closed. Each door is numbered, three on each side of the corridor, with a pair of double doors at its far end. Seven rooms in all.

Giovanni's sharp blue eyes are intent. 'There are twenty-nine couture dresses to be shown. Thousands of hours by many, many pairs of hands dedicated solely to *me*, to this atelier, have gone into every creation. The audience of four hundred — by invitation only, of course — will contain many of your harshest critics. Disapproving fashion editors cheek-by-jowl with the women's wear buyers, the young aristocracy, old friends, old clients, of-the-moment actresses and singers to bring me global coverage in every medium I could wish for. They ring and ring! Asking for better seats. Asking: "Where are the bloggers to be placed?", "Where is Suzie to be? Anna? Isabella?" *Put me here, put me there.* I am almost glad it will be the last one. Rise above them all, my dear. I know you will make me very proud.'

He's about to say something else when I hear someone calling my name in an angry voice. Both of us turn to see Gia making her way up the corridor towards us, my heavy overcoat and large handbag jammed awkwardly under one arm. Her expression is tight-lipped, her hair's mussed and her eye make-up's smudged. She hoists her own bag higher on her shoulder and extends that small, flat, black device towards me.

I feel Irina's brow pleat. What do I want with it?

'Those bastards always follow after you and leave me to deal with the psychos on my own,' she snarls. 'I didn't think I was going to make it in here alive. Jürgen was assigned to *me*, not to you, but that's the story of my life, isn't it? You're like a bloody man magnet.'

A look of horror passes swiftly across her face as she takes in who's standing beside me. 'Mastro Re,' she adds with an embarrassed nod, jamming the black device into a back pocket of her skinny jeans and extending a small hand to him. 'Please excuse my language.'

He gives her hand a brief squeeze and laughs, though his face is pale beneath his tan and his other hand is gripping his cane very tightly now. 'The world has gone mad when such a slight creature as Irina can command so much time and so much interest.'

He turns back to me. 'Tommy will be with you shortly to take you through the three outfits again and the way he wants you to move in them. Valentina will supervise any last-minute alterations. And I should warn you ...' his blue eyes are suddenly evasive, '... one of my best couture clients is in town for the show and has seen the look book we put together for those wanting to order after the parade. She wants a private showing of several key pieces. She specifically requested that *you* model them, Irina. So it will be a long day, my child. Your iron will should come in handy today, eh? Don't let me down ...'

He waves the back of his hand at me and moves stiffly away, down the hall.

Gia glances at the double doors and says with satisfaction, 'I see he's given you the legendary Studio 4. Anja and Carly will be eating their hearts out right now — if they have hearts. They're crammed together in Studio 6 and word is they're *not* happy.'

She walks up to the double doors of Studio 4 and tries both handles. They're locked.

'It's only sensible, I suppose,' she mutters. 'What's in there is worth gazillions. Though I'd love to be able to put all your crap down somewhere. It weighs a tonne.'

She looks at me pointedly, and I reluctantly take back Irina's damp overcoat and the handbag that could house a medium-sized dog.

'Oh! I forgot.' Gia digs the black device out of her back pocket with a free hand. 'Might as well take it,' she says, waving it in my face. 'Tommy's got his hands full with Orla in Studio 1 — she's having a meltdown because she's just found out you're the opening act *and* you've got one more outfit than she does. Wait till she finds out it's the fantasy bridal gown at the end of the entire show!'

I take the device she's waving at me — a phone, I realise — and turn it over. My heart nearly stops when I see a bored-looking young man staring out at me from its screen. I almost drop the phone.

I'd know him anywhere.

It's Ryan.

CHAPTER 10

'I was wondering when you'd get around to remembering me,' Ryan says dryly, then his eyes widen as he focuses, really focuses, on my face.

'Can you see me as clearly as I can see you?' I say softly, angling my body away from Gia, waving at her to move back down the hall and give me some privacy.

He doesn't answer; he just stares at me. He's got an expression on his face like he's seen a ghost. Which, in a way, I suppose he has.

Ryan's the spitting image of Luc, save mortal, with dark hair and dark eyes. I'd forgotten, you see, about the resemblance. They could be brothers. It's uncanny.

Sometimes when I look at Ryan, I feel like I conjured him up out of my lonely subconscious, that he can't be real. That somehow, because I couldn't have Luc, I went and created a replacement.

I see movement behind his shoulder and focus on his surroundings. He's in a room with pale yellow walls and white wainscoting, and behind him is a door that leads out to a hallway. I realise with a jolt that I know that room. I've been inside it before. It's Lela's bedroom. He's in Lela's house.

He's still half a world away from me, and there are whole continents and oceans between us.

'Ryan?' My voice is uncertain. 'It's me, Mercy. Say something? Please?'

There's that flutter of movement behind his shoulder again and I see a white shape enter the bedroom through the doorway behind him.

'What are you doing?' It's a woman's voice, broad, laconic, the accent so different from Ryan's. 'Who are you talking to? Want me to handle it this time?'

I see a face lean in behind his shoulder, loom into the screen, her cheek close beside *his*, only an inch separating them, and get another shock when I realise that it's Justine Hennessy.

I'll always consider Justine a friend and remember her fondly. But I feel a shot of pure jealous *rage*. I can't help it. They're together, in Lela's house. In Lela's bedroom.

'What is *she* doing there with you?' I yell into the screen, and my anger seems to galvanise Ryan into a white-hot answering fury.

He shouts, 'Remember how I watched you die yesterday? Well, she's helping me *bury* you, *Mercy*.'

Justine looks at Ryan with confusion, then squints into the screen. Her eyes widen.

She turns to Ryan and says, 'Do you have any idea who you're talking to? Wait here!' she yells excitedly. 'Wait here.' She leaves the room in a flurry of white and bare limbs.

Ryan glares at me. 'You left her Lela's house, remember?' he snarls. 'It hasn't been finalised yet, but it was pretty cut and dried thanks to that piece of paper you had Dmitri witness. The police found it when they went through Lela's bag. The house isn't a crime scene, so Justine had every reason to return here. And I had nowhere else to go, because you lured me all the way to freakin' *Australia* and then left me again. Happy?'

Even though I already know all of this at some deep, subconscious level, it feels better hearing him justify things, hearing his blazing anger. I read subtext better than most people, and the fury in his voice tells me — clearer than words — that there's zero chance anything's going on between them, even though Justine's beautiful in that earthy, hourglass way that guys love. Still, my jealousy is leaving me light-headed; I'm actually struggling to breathe. I lean over the screen, my eyes drinking in every line of Ryan's face.

'Don't die on me again, damn you,' he says, his voice low and strained. 'Justine didn't find me for hours afterwards — hours in which I thought you'd been destroyed, that you were gone for good. That is, if people like you *can* be destroyed. I still don't know what you are. You've never given me a proper explanation for anything. You *owe* me.' There's devastation and fury in his words, in equal measure.

'I know,' I reply softly. 'I had no way of telling you I'd make it. They shift me in and take me out, and I have no control over any of it. I was gone before Lela was gone. And I found myself here. Looking like this.'

He smiles suddenly, though his face and eyes still look tired and haunted, and I quit breathing altogether, just for a moment.

'You get more and more beautiful every time I see you, do you know that?' he says.

I feel a pang of sadness, and my words come out more harshly than I intend. 'Don't go getting used to this face. She looks nothing like me. I'm no supermodel.'

Ryan smiles again, and this time it reaches his eyes and he's heart-stopping. 'It doesn't matter. *She* doesn't matter. I know what you look like, remember? I carry that sketch of you with me wherever I go. You look like the Delphic Sybil — remember we talked about it? — except your eyes are brown.' He grins. 'I could definitely get used to your new voice, though. I'd have no objections waking up to that every morning.'

He looks down suddenly, embarrassed, and I'm glad he doesn't see my face flame in answer to his last remark, see my free hand fly up to my mouth.

No crime against wishing; no crime against dreaming, right? How is it that love and desire can feel so much like physical *pain*?

There's movement behind him and I see him turn as Justine thrusts something into his hands off screen. I study his profile greedily, smiling as his fringe of dark hair falls into his eyes and he shoves it back.

'There!' Justine says, turning the pages of something noisily. Ryan holds it up to the screen. It's a glossy magazine.

'You're talking to her!' I hear Justine hiss. '*Irina!* She's the one who dumped Félix de Haviland — one of the heirs to the multibillion-dollar d'Haviland construction dynasty. She actually stole him off his fiancée, then left him for Will Reyne, the singer from Machine. Dumped him, too.'

Ryan looks at me, raising his eyebrows, and I have to stifle a giggle at his wicked expression. 'You've been busy,' he murmurs.

I grin at him and he grins back. And for a minute, it's like we're back in his crummy, rusting four-wheel drive, scoring pot shots off each other for the pure hell of it.

'Look!' Justine exclaims, pulling the magazine out of his hands and turning it over before handing it back. 'See this? It's her, too! She's everywhere.'

He angles the magazine at me again, and I see that he's looking at a full-page image of a woman's face. She's laughing and leaning on her hand. On her wrist is a large, diamond-encrusted watch.

'Irina's choice,' Ryan reads aloud, in the kind of stuck-up voice a newsreader would use. I laugh out loud, in genuine delight.

'She's not seeing anyone at the moment,' Justine goes on. 'You might have a shot if you play your cards right. Though she's hardcore, Ryan, she's trouble …'

'Don't need to tell me that,' he says, winking down the screen at me.

I see Justine peer over his shoulder briefly, eyes round with disbelief. 'Oh my God, I can't believe you know each other. Wait till I tell the others,' she says, so breathlessly that her words run together.

Before I can say, 'Hey, Juz,' the way I used to when I was Lela, Justine pulls her magazine out of Ryan's hand and slips out of the room.

Ryan frowns. He's always been able to read my mind. 'Don't,' he says quietly. 'Just leave it alone. Don't mess with her head. She was hysterical after Lela died. From what Dmitri told me about her, she's been through a really rough time lately. She doesn't need to know about you. It wouldn't change anything — it would just mess up the memories she has of Lela. We've already talked about this — the less people that know about you, the better. It's hard enough on the people who *do* understand.' His laughter sounds forced.

'Who chooses the … bodies?' he asks when I don't say anything. 'Who determines where you go, who you're supposed to be?'

I don't reply and he adds uncertainly, 'Irina's a little … left field, isn't she? A bit out there? She's nothing like Carmen, or Lela. You know … quiet. Uh … ordinary.' His voice is apologetic.

'So you've noticed, too?' I say, sidestepping his other questions. 'I'll take "ordinary" any day. It's insane here. I can't go anywhere without a battery of people following me around, or trying to slip me things. And that's just Irina's staff! You should've seen it when I showed up for work this morning — it was a bloodbath.'

'So when can I come out?' Ryan says suddenly, brushing that agonisingly familiar fall of dark hair out of his eyes with his long fingers. My breathing stills again. 'When Gia called, I'd just hung up from the funeral home. The timing was freaky. Total rollercoaster.'

I don't ask him whether he wept when Lela died, because I know he did. It's in his voice. And a sudden wave of love and regret and longing threatens to send me to my knees. He's so … sweet. So very human.

He adds quietly, 'Karen and Lela will be buried side by side as soon as Lela's body's released by the coroner. Should be Monday at the latest.'

Grief roughens my voice. 'They'd like that.'

'You speak as if they're still with us,' Ryan replies.

'They are,' I say, as a door is pushed open further back along the corridor I'm standing in. A young woman shrieks, 'Tell him to take his clichéd silver evening gown and —'

'Now, now, Orla,' interrupts a light, male voice coaxingly. His accent sounds a little like Ryan's. 'You know it'll make *all* the covers — it's easily the most stunning evening gown in the entire collection. Your face will be everywhere.'

I don't hear the woman's reply because there's the sound of a door slamming shut, then a loud exhalation. And that light, male voice exclaims behind me, 'Gia, darling. At last, a sane person. Orla's on the warpath. Hates both the dresses she's been allocated. Barely got out alive. Love the boots. So *fierce*.'

'Mercy?' says Ryan. 'What happens n— '

'Irina!' Gia's voice cuts in.

I turn my head to see her standing some distance away, outside the door marked *Studio 1*. There's a slender young man beside her, with a narrow grey fedora pushed back on his head of short, dark blonde hair. He's the latest word in street fashion, with his skin-tight, distressed indigo jeans bristling with hardware, his narrow, buttoned-up, hound's-tooth waistcoat over a faded grey, long-sleeved tee with a slogan on it I can't make out, sharp-looking shoes, wrapped leather bracelets encircling both wrists, bristling with studs. He's very pale and looks very young. He gives a little wave, blows me a kiss.

'Showtime,' Gia says to me apologetically. 'Wrap it up. You can pick it up again later.'

The young man scans me critically, up and down. 'Lookin' fly, Irina,' he calls out, head on one side, one hand cupping his cheek. 'Ready to get your freak on, babe? Loads to get through.'

'Mercy?' Ryan's voice issues loudly from the phone in my hand. I look back down at his face. 'Justine can take it from here,' he says insistently. 'She doesn't need me any more. You just tell me where and I'll be there. *I'll be there.*'

I close my eyes for a second, imagining that world — where Ryan could step onto a plane and I'd be there waiting for him, and we could be together for always, with no complications.

'Irina?' Gia says again sharply, and I turn and see a beautifully groomed, middle-aged Italian woman, her dark hair in a sleek, low knot, a measuring tape around her neck, entering the corridor. She's wearing a gorgeously tailored black suit and low-heeled shoes, and she looks at me, then at Tommy and Gia for a second, before saying, 'I can start with Miss Sebsebe in Studio 3 …?'

Tommy shakes his head. 'Irina's our number one priority now that Giovanni's gone and arranged a private showing straight after her fitting. We need to get a move on, people.'

'Give me a minute?' I plead as my imagined world slips quietly from view.

Gia holds up one hand, five fingers outstretched, to show me that those are all the minutes I'm getting. I turn my back on them, stare into Ryan's dark, electronically mediated eyes. My own eyes are stinging fiercely. I can't cry. I don't do tears. I'm not human. *I'm not human.*

'Merce?' Ryan says tenderly, from out of the palm of my hand, from so far away.

He could be Luc's brother, he could be his twin. Save that he is mortal, and gentle; dark to Luc's light, night to Luc's day — or is it the other way around? I wonder when those things started to become qualities and things that I revere. They're both so different. But they look so alike. Just another riddle without an answer in my fogbound, floating life.

'Where, Mercy?' Ryan insists. 'I'm already on my way.'

As is Luc, reminds that small voice inside me gravely, always one beat ahead of my waking self. *He'll be here soon. He'll love you again, the way he used to. You don't need Ryan any more. And Luc can brook no competition. You know that.*

I get instant goose bumps. It's a law of physics, isn't it? That two solid objects can't occupy the same place at the same time. There's only room for one of them in my life. One of them has to give. As K'el had to give; as Raphael did, in his turn.

Unlike Gabriel, Uriel and all the rest of my erstwhile brethren, I don't believe that things are pre-ordained, that they will always collapse towards a fixed point like a doomed star. In my view, fate is there to be meddled with. And that will always be the difference between the Eight and me. Why then, does having the right to choose, the simple act of making a choice feel so much like a punishment?

It's better this way, I tell myself. *You've only been putting off the inevitable.*

Something hard seems to crystallise in me, something sharp. As if my cold heart has been pierced through and is splintering, a piece of it breaking away.

I think I always knew that it would have to end like this; that one day I'd run out of excuses and options. The real world, the unseen world — I've felt them converging, drawing tight around me like a shark net, for a long time now. Ever since the day I woke as Ezra after her husband almost beat her to death, and I realised I could do something about it. That I could change her life forever.

Maybe there's never been the possibility of another outcome, only the illusion.

It may be the last time I ever see Ryan. Grief once more enfolds me in its wings, grasps my borrowed heart in its black talons so hard that I fear it will burst inside Irina's narrow chest.

I run my fingertip gently down Ryan's face on the screen. See him frown at the gesture.

How weak must I seem to him?

I remind myself forcefully that feelings are for humans, even though my eyes are stinging and the screen is blurring and Ryan's leaning forward and saying, 'Mercy? Mercy? It won't be long — just tell me where, and I'll find you. I'm already on the way.'

'There's no *where*, Ryan, no *when*,' I reply harshly as my eyes fill, and spill over, and a tear hits his face on the screen. 'Not for us. That's past. We've had our time.'

'What do you mean?' he says fiercely. 'Are you *crying*? Why are you crying?'

There's no answer to a question like that. So I tell him the first thing that comes into my head, because some part of me is still trying to shield him from the truth of Luc's existence. Ryan doesn't need to be hurt any more, and especially not by me.

'Those ... people I told you about once?' I sob, and I hate how I sound. 'The people that did this to me? They're coming here. And they're bringing reinforcements. You know what they can do — you've seen it for yourself.'

I see confusion on his face and I shout, 'Remember Scotland? That "man" who walked on water?'

Ryan's eyes widen in understanding and I say more quietly, 'He'll be here soon — and others just as powerful as he is. They're coming for me, to move me ...'

'We'll run,' he replies breathlessly. 'I'll hide you. I'll do whatever it takes to keep you from them, to keep us together. We'll use the darkness — hang out at gaming parlours and cafés, hotels and nightclubs, all-night service stations, diners — crowded places, dark places, places where no one wants to know your name, your business or your history. We'll keep on the move, keep to ourselves. We'll change the way you look ... if that's even possible for ... people like you. Power and invisibility are mutually exclusive, right?'

'Not in my experience,' I sob.

'You can't let them just take you!' Ryan yells, fear in his eyes and his voice. 'The Mercy *I* know would never allow that. Don't give up on us.'

'It would never be over!' I cry. 'And that's no kind of life for someone like you. You don't deserve any more disruption, any more grief or fear. Not after what you went through with Lauren. Can't you see that's the thing I'd never allow? I'm not worth it, Ryan.'

'To me you are,' he says violently. '*Please.* We have to try. Once I met you, my old life was over anyway. Without you, everything's just grey. It's pointless. I've only known you for a few weeks, but you're in here,' he taps at his chest, 'and here.' He places one hand against his head. 'You didn't just free Lauren. You freed *me.* It's like you're part of me now.'

His sweet words just make my tears flow faster. 'I'm *immortal*, Ryan,' I say brokenly. I see the look of stark rejection on his face, feel my heart splinter a little further.

As he shakes his head in denial, I weep. 'What else did you expect me to say? Met any other girls lately who can take over the bodies of total strangers? *I cannot be killed by bullets, I cannot be killed by weaponry. Our kind may only kill and be killed by each other.* Being with me would be like a death sentence for you; you would have no choice but to run, or to die. It would *never* be over. I would never want that for you.'

Ryan's eyes are so dark in his pale, strained face.

'What would it mean, "being" with me, anyway?' I plead. 'You're a son of man. I'm one of the *elohim*, the high ones. Go look that up on your search engines, your internet. We were here before your kind was even a passing whim in the mind of our creator. Even if I were free of this body, I don't know if you could kiss me, or hold me, or take me to the movies, like you would a "regular" girl. I'm strong enough to kill you. I'm both matter and anti-matter. I was created to govern and to wreak destruction in equal measure. You and me together equals *pain*.'

I can barely see the screen for my tears. But through them, I see Ryan hang his head for a moment, looking away from me, and that's how I finally work up the courage to snarl, 'You can't come here. I forbid it. Don't go looking for me in my next life, because I *won't* be looking for you.'

'No!' Ryan yells, raising his head. His dark eyes seem to blaze out at me from the screen, because he can read me like I can read him and he knows that I'm lying. In my heart, I will always be looking for him. And a little piece of me will always be wishing and dreaming and wondering.

I hang up on him then, and the screen goes black.

So this is what it feels like to have your heart removed from you while it's still beating. Now, now I understand.

I wrap my arms tightly around myself to hold in the hurt, but it is impossible. I cry and cry, only dimly sensing the others hurrying towards me, Gia lifting the phone out of my nerveless hands and placing an arm around my shaking shoulders.

I tell myself fiercely there's no point, none whatsoever, to my tears. I'm crying for something that could never have been. But I can't stop the tears falling.

My cowardice disgusts me. I couldn't bring myself to tell Ryan how I feel about him, or the truth about

Luc. About what Luc would do to him if he caught him here, with that look in his eyes — of love, for me. Luc would *destroy* him. In a heartbeat.

In the end, maybe it's not really a question of what I want, or what Ryan wants. It's a straightforward question of Ryan's survival. I would never forgive myself if something happened to him. I have enough blood on my hands.

So it's better this way.

Better to have a world with Ryan in it, than no Ryan at all.

CHAPTER 11

Gia slips her phone back into a pocket of her leather jacket and gives me a gentle squeeze.

With Valentina following us discreetly, she leads me towards the locked double doors at the end of the corridor, which Tommy now opens with a key he produces from a pocket of his distressed, skinny jeans.

Studio 4 is in total darkness. But before anyone flicks on the lights, I can already make out the layout of the room and what's waiting for me at the far end of it. Surprise stems the flow of my tears.

There are three clothed human forms standing there in the darkness, all unnaturally still.

The bank of fluorescent lighting above our heads flares into life, giving shape to the large, neutral space that's dominated by two long wooden work tables holding sewing machines and open wooden boxes filled with notions, ribbon, lace and fabric. Shelving runs along one long wall, containing drawer after drawer, each one bearing a neat typed label in Italian. There's a spacious area on the far side of the room with a raised square podium, or pedestal, in the middle of it. Grouped around the pedestal, two to the left and one to the right, are three life-sized mannequins with blank and featureless faces, hair moulded into a stylised beehive. Each form is clothed in a spectacular gown, and each gown is strikingly different from the next.

The first is devastatingly simple in silhouette: long and lean, with a plunging V-neckline, narrow through the bodice, waist, hips and thighs, but flaring gently from just above the knee so that by the time the gown reaches the ankles it pools in gentle folds upon the floor. The sleeves are long and cuffed tightly at the wrists, and mirror the line of the dress. They begin narrow and fitted at the upper arms, then bell out gently, before the fabric pools a little around each cuff. What makes the gown extraordinary is that it's covered entirely in square, gold-coloured, metal paillettes, every single one painstakingly hand-stitched on, I'm guessing. From a distance, it's almost as if the dress is made of molten gold. But up close, the surface of the gown resembles chain mail, or armour.

Gia walks up to it, awe-struck, followed by Tommy. Valentina hangs back, smiling a little with pride.

Numbly, I position myself next to Tommy as he muses aloud, 'Hair down for this one, maybe with a messy wave through the ends? And a wreath in the hair, or a crown of thorns. Bare feet. A bit Joan of Arc meets Jesus meets lunatic asylum, I'm thinking?'

Gia gives him a sharp, quelling look and Tommy clears his throat and mutters, 'Let's move right along to look number two.'

'Look number two' is a strapless dress with a tight-fitting black bodice featuring a plunging, heart-shaped neckline that's highlighted by a central, heart-shaped panel across the front entirely covered in tiny black crystals that catch the light. The skirt is an explosion of swagged black silk. There's some sort of crinoline underneath it that gives the dress a life of its own. Valentina steps forward and lifts one edge of the voluminous skirt proudly and we see that it's faced with hot-pink silk. It's a show stopper, although I don't see how the heavily beaded, shockingly indiscreet bodice would stay up if I actually went anywhere in it.

'We'll go with a black tricorn hat with a face veil,' Tommy murmurs. 'A bit American Revolution meets Bette Davis. Maybe some shoe-boots that are part dressage, part bondage. I'll get Juliana's team to put something together.'

We come to a stop before the last gown. The fantasy bridal gown Gia spoke of earlier. It has the same killer-chic aesthetic that informs the other two dresses, but it's a romantic confection this time: tight-fitting lace and intricately beaded chiffon, tight, long sleeves, a high and modest neckline. The upper half of the dress seems both concealing and revealing at the same time; but the skirt is something else altogether. It's tulip-shaped; layers and layers of hand-draped and swagged chiffon and silk gazar that end at a point just below the knee. It's a completely unexpected combination of shapes, but it somehow works. I don't understand fashion in the slightest, but I can see that the wedding dress before us is something quite unique.

'A simple topknot,' Tommy breathes. 'With a miniature tiara sitting just above the hairline.'

As the four of us stand silently in front of the remarkable dress, Gia's phone rings. She draws it out of her jacket pocket and glances at the screen.

'I have to take this,' she says apologetically.

She turns to leave the room and I say, sounding strangely tentative even to my ears, 'You'll come back? You'll stay with me today? However long it takes?'

I don't think I could bear to be alone right now, in the company of strangers. However kindly they might be.

Gia's eyes seem to soften as she replies, 'Your humanity is showing again, Irina. Of course I'll come back. It's just management as usual, checking up on you — checking up on me. Be right back.'

As Gia closes the door behind her, Tommy turns to me and places a hand beneath my chin, studying my face for a moment. 'Who's this impostor we've got here?' he says gently. 'Where's my bulletproof ultra-bitch gone?'

There's laughter in his light voice; it's impossible to be offended.

'*Tommy*,' clucks Valentina disapprovingly as she begins carefully removing the first of the couture gowns off the mannequin, the one that resembles golden armour.

When I find myself smiling back mistily at the slight young man before me, he whispers, 'Now, that's more like it. Time to play dress-ups, my darling.'

The golden dress has to weigh at least seventy pounds on its own. It's lucky that I'm strong, and that I no longer really care what I'm doing here. I just listlessly do as I'm told. If the real Irina were here, I'm sure she would've thrown at least one bitch-slapping tantrum already *and* orchestrated a walkout. Despite the so-called stratospheric glamour-quotient of Irina's life, hers has to be the most unbelievably tedious job I can ever remember experiencing. Even worse than cleaning the toilets or taking out the rubbish at the Green Lantern café, because at least then I'd had autonomy. All I seem to be here is a collection of flawed body parts, and it's just a never-ending round of requests to *stand still*.

I've been poised on the raised podium for almost two hours as Valentina and two assistants have poked and prodded me from every angle, worrying at the hem of the dress, tugging at the cuffs, reworking the gown's back fastenings because I've inexplicably put on a half-inch around the waist since yesterday morning and a seam somewhere is puckering.

I address Gia over the heads of the reproachful

seamstresses. 'That would be because I actually ate a decent breakfast!'

'Just ignore them,' she says, looking up at me from the stool she's found from somewhere. All morning I've watched her playing with her little black phone, heading out into the corridor occasionally to take a call. 'You're doing surprisingly ... great,' she says encouragingly. 'This has to be your best effort *ever*. You haven't thrown a single thing. No one can quite believe it — I know, because I've been eavesdropping.'

The left-hand door opens and Tommy comes sailing in with a plump, smiling woman at his side, in her late twenties or early thirties. Unlike all the other glamazons in the building who are wearing top-to-toe Giovanni Rè suits, she's fearlessly dressed in a heavy, aubergine-coloured wool dress of a striking design with a forties-meets-seventies vibe, heavy wool ribbed tights in burnt orange, and vintage-looking dark and lime green Mary-Janes. Her straggly, shoulder-length hair has dark roots and bright yellow ends. I like how comfortable she seems in her own skin, and I like her face. It's plain, but strong. There's a fierce intelligence in her bright blue gaze that seems to take in everything around her.

'This is Juliana,' Tommy says. 'Resident "special effects" guru. She's Giovanni's secret weapon — every show she's put together for him since she left design school has been a sensation. We've been talking, and my Jesus-meets-Druid headwear idea for this gown was so, so off the mark. I'd completely forgotten that Giovanni's had Juliana and her crew whip up something a little extra special for the show.'

He crosses back to the doorway and undoes the floor and ceiling bolts holding the right-hand door closed. 'Ta dah!' he sings, and opens the door with a flourish.

On my raised pedestal, above all their heads, I freeze in horror as I see what's being wheeled up the hallway towards us, suspended by hooks on a steel clothing rack: three pairs of wings hanging like meat for sale at a butcher's shop. One gold, one black, one white, their end feathers trailing upon the concrete floor.

They're so lifelike, it's as if they've been cut from some mythical creature. I almost expect to see blood dripping from them onto the concrete floor.

For a moment, that hateful sensation returns — of being balanced on razor wire over the shrieking abyss.

I feel so dizzy, so sick with dread, that the world seems to telescope, or the world is in me, and I lose any sense of up, of down, and fall off the pedestal onto the hard concrete floor, as if I have fainted. I stare, shaken, at the fluorescent lights above that give out such a cold, cold light, as if channelled from a distant galaxy.

'Irina!' Gia yells, dropping her phone and scrambling off her stool towards me as the black-clad seamstresses, as Tommy and Juliana flock around, lifting me into a sitting position.

'I'm all right,' I say gruffly, holding my pounding head. 'It's just vertigo.'

'Vertigo?' Gia says incredulously. 'The podium's about a foot off the ground! What are you talking about?'

But it *is* vertigo, which is as crazy as it sounds. It overcame me when I saw those things being wheeled towards us. I can't take my eyes off them, though they both repel and fascinate.

Juliana follows the line of my sight and says haltingly, in heavily accented English, 'You don't … *like* them?'

I swallow hard, feeling nausea as the wings reach the doorway of the studio. I hear Juliana's two assistants — one male, one female — squabbling a little in Italian as they try to manoeuvre the rack through the door without upsetting its cargo.

'They're so beautiful,' I whisper, 'that they look *real*.'

'As if I have reached up and plucked them myself from the backs of angels?' Juliana says happily. 'That is what I hoped to achieve! Giovanni said I was mad to make them all — and all different. But when I see his designs, I could think of nothing else but the wings.'

'You should see Juliana's workroom,' interjects Tommy with a grin. 'It's like a flock of angels moulted in there.'

'A power,' I say absently. 'A power of angels.'

I want to look away from them, but I can't. When I look at those wings, in my mind's eye I see *elohim* with flaming swords upraised, engaged in combat, slaying their enemies with holy fire. And I don't know if these are real memories — *my* memories — or whether they are things I have witnessed through touching another's skin. All I know is that when we are angered, when we are called to do battle, when we are of a mind to *kill*, then and only then do we show our wings.

Like furies. Like harpies. Like birds of prey.

No, that's not quite right.

We don't need wings to propel ourselves from the ground, because we can materialise anywhere we wish — any height, any depth — so long as we know where, so long as we can see it in our mind's eye. Will it, and it is done.

No, we use our wings to strike fear into the hearts of our enemies. Like a cobra's hood, a scorpion's tail, they are a symbol of power, a portent. They serve as a warning of the terror to come.

We angels are misconceived in the human world. People perceive us as kindly and bountiful, when, in truth, we are about as fluffy, as gentle, as yielding, as rattlesnakes.

As I stare at Juliana's wings, I realise where the sensation of vertigo came from. It's something I keep buried, something I try not to think about too much, because I can't reconcile this phobia of mine with what I used to be. I have a terrible fear of heights.

Fear doesn't even begin to describe how terrified I become when I even visualise myself being any great distance off the ground. When I think about the actual mechanics, even the bare concept, of flying, I break out in a cold sweat and my left hand burns with pain.

I look at the circle of concerned faces and, refusing all offers of assistance, climb unsteadily to my feet. Juliana takes down the first set of wings — every feather on the balsawood frame handcrafted from a light, brittle kind of metal and painted gold — and guides my arms through the leather straps of the harness. The wings are a perfect fit; they're lighter even than the dress. They could *be* my wings; although, in truth, the wings of the *elohim*, our weaponry, our glowing raiment, all these are fashioned out of our own energy. We don't carry them around with us. They're part of us. When we need them, they're simply there.

Tommy arranges my unbound hair upon my shoulders then says triumphantly, '*Voilà!*'

Everyone in the room takes a small step away from me, their hands clasped together, their eyes welded upon me. And, to a man, to a woman, they all sigh.

The wings are taller than I am. They're like the wings from a painted religious icon made real. And every second they are on my back, I shudder.

Tommy tilts his head and cups the side of his face in his hand as he studies me. 'You were right, Juliana. Nothing else is needed. Just the wings. They're enough.'

He walks around me a couple more times with Juliana and Valentina following anxiously in his wake. I wonder if they can see me shaking.

'Perfection,' Tommy finally pronounces, and I almost collapse again — with relief, this time — as Juliana finally removes the wings from my shoulders.

It's after 5 pm when I'm allowed at last to leave Studio 4, bound for another part of the building where the moneyed haute couture clients have their private showings. Gia and Juliana chat in rapidfire Italian like old friends as they lead me back through Atelier Re. I see that the building is steadily emptying of its fashionable occupants. In small groups, they leave their seamless workstations, their pattern-cutting tables, bead boxes, rolls of fabric and hat blocks, meeting rooms and endlessly curated collections of elegant clothing, grouped by season, for the front exit, where Giovanni's security team looks into each person's face and bids them farewell by name.

Someone has turned off the sound system and the building is quiet, but I'm still haunted by that aria that was playing when I entered the building, so many hours ago. The melody keeps tugging at me, and I realise that, like the ability to recognise certain languages, the ability to recognise snatches of music is beginning to return in me, too.

I'm back in the leather pants and simple cashmere tunic that Gia picked out earlier today, but I've had her throw the high-shine, high-heeled, torture-device shoes into Irina's holdall. I stalk the cold, brushed-concrete floors in my long, bare feet, still wearing the heavy, mask-like make-up that Tommy and his team of stylists came up with for the fourteen models taking part in the anniversary parade. I catch sight of my reflection in a glass window as I pass by: eyes ringed in smoky black kohl, lids filled in right up to the brow line with a glittering grey eye shadow, the inner and outer corners of my eyes illuminated in gold. My lips and nails are the same blood red that I first saw on Gudrun — *rosso Re*, my manicurist had confided as she'd filled in the nails of my hand, Giovanni Re's signature shade of red, his trademark colour. The make-up artists had finished by dusting my cheek and brow bones with a fine, gold powder. I don't think I've ever looked so truly alien.

As I walk barefoot through the emptying building — almost weaving with exhaustion — I rip off my false eyelashes and let them flutter to the ground like butterflies. Shake out the sleek topknot Tommy insisted on for the bridal look and run my fingers down through the wavy strands of Irina's hair. There's so much pressure inside my skull that it feels as if it's about to split open. The heavy pounding of Irina's heart forms the soundtrack to my progress.

Gia takes my elbow as we cross the now quiet atrium. Juliana is leading us towards a spiral concrete ramp at the far side of the building, and I realise it's the main staircase connecting all four floors of Atelier Re. I study the elegant spiral that rises and twists so far above us.

'How far up are we going?' I say through gritted teeth.

Two storeys I can handle. Four might kind of be pushing it, for me.

Three lives back, when I'd woken as a single mother called Lucy who lived in a filthy, high-rise apartment in a virtual ghetto of government-owned tenements, I'd had to make sure that I never looked out the windows. Every time I stepped out of the lift that had stunk of vomit on the twenty-second floor, I'd stayed clear of the balcony that ran parallel to the apartment entrances on that level. Each time I'd been forced to return to Lucy's flat — because it was nightfall, because there was nowhere else safe to go — I'd hugged the inner wall, inching painfully towards

Lucy's front door, her listless, malnourished baby on my hip, almost overcome with vertigo and a strange sense of shame. Back then, I hadn't understood why. But I do now, because it's somehow linked to the reason I'm even here on earth at all.

'Second floor,' Gia replies, shooting me a glance. 'You didn't go back to sleep this morning, did you? After that … nightmare you had. Your eyes are practically burning holes in your head.'

'I couldn't sleep,' I reply simply. 'And it didn't help that Felipe offered me a morning heart-starter of vodka mixed with pure liquid meth.'

'He *what*?' Gia says, turning to me in disbelief.

'No biggie,' I say wearily, the way Ryan would, forgetting how strange it might sound in Irina's Moscow-via-Novosibirsk accent until I've said the words. 'I handled it.'

The thought of Ryan fires off more starbursts of pain somewhere in the region of Irina's neural cortex and I clutch at my head momentarily, hearing that achingly familiar voice crying into the border between sleep and wakefulness: *Mercy, where are you?*

Gia pulls her mobile phone out of her leather jacket. 'Management have got to be told. I knew there was a reason I hate that guy.'

206

'It doesn't matter,' I say. 'Just drop it. He won't be troubling Irina again. I made sure of that.'

I'm still not quite sure how, but it doesn't matter now.

Gia gives me a weird look and replaces her phone in her pocket uncertainly.

I look neither left nor right as we ascend the ramp to the second storey of Atelier Re, the knuckles of my left hand white upon the smooth, concrete banister, my right gripped tightly around the handles of Irina's handbag, as if it is a life jacket.

The corridors on the second floor are softened by lush, honey-coloured carpets, and the high, art deco-style ceilings are punctuated by enormous modernist chandeliers, white, like floating clouds. It's a different world up here: timber-panelled walls and traditional-looking wall sconces, antique furniture mixed in effortlessly with modernist pieces in a way I've come to recognise as quintessentially Giovanni. We move past a private lift and a couple of life-sized ceramic sculptures that seem almost two-dimensional, like freestanding paintings. On the flat surface of one sculpture there's a boy playing a pipe, painted in strong and hasty brushstrokes. On the other, a warped caricature of a female figure — eyes in the wrong places; crazy, funfair colours.

'Picassos,' Gia says, without stopping, and I crane my head to look back at them, at the strange energy in the lines.

Juliana stops outside a door, knocks on it gently.

'*Entra!*' a male voice calls out.

Juliana opens the door. Giovanni is framed in the doorway, seated at a colossal writing desk and surrounded by bookcases and shelving, undoubtedly priceless art and memorabilia, figurines, awards, framed photographs of himself with people who must be notable in some way. The only source of light in the room is a desk lamp upon the table.

He puts down the pen he is holding and takes off his tortoiseshell frames for a moment, rubbing at his eyes.

'All finished?' he says wearily in English. 'Good, good.'

He gets up from the desk, but his hand slips off the edge and he almost falls, and just catches himself on the way down. He stands there a moment, head bowed, breathing hard.

Juliana rushes across the room to steady him. 'You need rest, *Zio*,' she chides, almost tearfully.

Zio, she called him. *Uncle*. I didn't see the resemblance before, but now, looking at them both together, I notice it around the eyes and nose.

Giovanni pats her hand. 'Soon, soon, *cara*. But first, I must thank Irina for her hard work today, and apologise that there is one more thing she must attend to before she leaves us.'

Juliana hands her uncle his lion-handled walking cane and he struggles towards me across the priceless, hand-knotted silk carpet with the name of its maker, and his god, woven into the borders of the pattern. 'Please, follow me,' he says.

I don't need to touch him to sense his strange and feverish anxiety.

'There's no need to exert yourself, Giovanni,' I reply. 'I can find my way with Juliana's help.'

He shakes his head and the feeling of anxiety that hangs about him seems to deepen. Maybe he's worried that I'll screw up and upset his best client.

'I must make the introductions,' he says tightly. 'It is only … right.'

'I'll behave,' I say reassuringly.

'I'm sure you will,' he says distantly, patting my arm briefly. 'But will *she*?'

He ushers me out of the room towards a wide corridor opposite his office that has several doorways leading off it. Gia and Juliana fall into step behind us, suddenly quiet, sensing something in Giovanni's mood. He limps towards a door marked with the number three in Roman numerals and turns the handle.

In the strange way I sometimes have of seeing too much, all at once, I see that the room is decorated in a soothing palette of blonde wood and navy and ivory furnishings. It's very brightly lit by an enormous crystal chandelier, and every wall is covered in a floor-to-ceiling mirror that reflects the room's only occupant — a young girl sitting, with her back to us, in a cream-coloured leather tub armchair. There's a doorway opposite the girl that leads to a large dressing room — also brilliantly lit — that's partially obscured by a navy velvet curtain.

I see all of this before the girl even turns and looks at us directly with her pale blue eyes. I'm surprised by how young she is. I'd been expecting someone far older, because if I've learnt one thing today — only seriously rich people can afford Giovanni Re. The girl has an oval face and dark, arched brows, light olive skin, waist-length, unbound, dark glossy hair and a slim build, narrow hands and feet. From the expression on her face, I realise that she's actually older than she looks — maybe mid to late twenties. She's in an effortlessly chic tweed jacket, in a weave of reds, whites and blues with gilt buttons, a red silk blouse with a self-tie neck, and slim, indigo blue jeans, vertiginous red heels. Beside her chair, there's a velvet ottoman, and on it sits a handbag of navy quilted leather with gilt hardware.

The young woman looks poised, serene and beautiful, so I'm shocked when her eyes fly to my face and flare with an antagonism so strong that it's like a presence in the room.

I don't need to touch her to feel it. She *hates* Irina. Would happily scratch her eyes out.

I'm instantly wary. Out of the corner of my eye, I see Gia and Juliana look at each other uneasily. Evidently, Giovanni hadn't told them whom we were meeting.

'Bianca!' he says warmly, spreading his arms in welcome.

The young woman rises and places a kiss on each of his cheeks. 'Giovanni,' she replies, smiling. 'So good of you to make time for me in your punishing schedule.'

'You will treat her ... gently?' he says.

She gives him a reassuring smile and I realise suddenly that this is some kind of set-up. Who is this girl to Irina? Not a friend, clearly.

'All I'm going to do, Mastro Re,' she says laughingly in a European accent that's hard to pin down, as if she's been schooled in many places, 'is give my credit card a severe workout. When I heard Irina would be here today, I thought to myself: *Who better to showcase your designs than the incomparable Irina?* It's high time we met properly.' Her eyes are suddenly hard as they flick to me. 'We'll have a cozy little ... chat, won't we, Irina? We have plenty to catch up on. Lots of mutual acquaintances to chew the fat over. It's so rare that our schedules line up in this way.'

Giovanni's eyes skitter nervously across my face before returning to Bianca. 'Then you won't mind if I leave you in the hands of my niece, Juliana?' he says, almost relieved. 'I think you know each other? And Irina's assistant, Gia.'

Bianca inclines her head graciously towards Juliana. 'Signora Agnelli-Re,' she says. 'So good to see you again.' She ignores Gia altogether.

'With your leave, Mastro,' she continues smoothly, 'we're old enough friends that you might just leave me with Irina today? I'm sure Signora Agnelli-Re has better things to do than listen to Irina and me … gossip.'

Giovanni starts to reply, but Bianca holds up one slim hand. 'I'm well aware that the looks I've asked you to set aside for me form part of the anniversary collection and are worth in the vicinity of a quarter of a million pounds. I shall treat the gowns with the utmost reverence.'

I note that she makes no such promise where I'm concerned.

Giovanni looks helplessly at his niece, who gives him the faintest frown in return that seems to say: *What have you done?*

'Very well,' he says reluctantly. 'Juliana will return shortly to see how you are both … getting on.'

'What the bloody hell are you playing at? This wasn't part of the —' Gia's protests are cut off as Giovanni and his niece bundle her out of the room, shutting the door firmly behind them.

CHAPTER 12

Bianca weighs me up with her cool, blue eyes before snapping, 'Our schedules have never lined up, *bitch*, because you've been deliberately avoiding me.'

I tell myself wearily to duck and weave until I can figure out what the hell she's talking about.

I dump Irina's heavy handbag by the door. 'Which dress do you want me to start with?' I say calmly as I head into the dressing room.

Five separate evening gowns are laid out across a button-backed, ivory leather *chaise longue*. There's a futuristic-looking, ankle-length black gown with wicked, sequined, pagoda shoulders, a plunging V-neck and daring front split. Beside it, a slim, one-shouldered sleeveless dress in Giovanni's signature shade of *rosso Re*, with a complicated neckline, plunging back and small train. Alongside that is a wasp-waisted, Victorian-inspired, ankle-length gown in hand-dyed silks of gradated purples and pinks, with enormous puffed sleeves and a neat bustle. And beside it, a breathtaking, strapless, 1930s-inspired sequined silver gown that I'm guessing must be Orla's. Lastly, a slim, floor-length gown that seems entirely made from feathers, hand-painted to resemble the wings of butterflies.

As I begin to shrug out of my cashmere jumper resignedly Bianca holds up a hand to stop me, saying sarcastically, 'For a model, you make a great actress. Let's cut to the chase. I'm not here for the clothes, clearly.' Her voice starts to shake. 'I just wanted to see, with my own eyes, the *slut* Félix left me for. And to let you know, personally, that I'm going to derail your sad, pathetic life even more than you derailed mine. I'll recover, but you *never* will.'

I frown, rummaging through the disorder in my head for the names Félix and Bianca, getting no immediate hits. Irina's not an over-analyser. She doesn't keep a journal in that oversized bag of hers that I'm forced to lug around.

'Do you have any idea who you've messed with?' Bianca says. 'What I could do to you?'

I shake my head, genuinely perplexed, which only seems to upset Bianca more.

'The chairman of Mondial Publishing and my father are old business partners, and the editor-at-large of the Costa International Group is a longstanding family friend,' she says threateningly, moving forward so that I'm forced to step back hurriedly to avoid her touching me.

I find the backs of my legs pressed up against the *chaise longue*. One of the heavy beaded dresses slithers to the floor.

'Point being?' I snap. 'To me they're just names, just words without context or weight.'

Bianca's face is contorted, almost ugly, as she spits, 'I'll be lobbying to ensure that none of the fashion magazines published by those organisations ever use you again in an editorial spread. And I'll also be suggesting that any advertising campaigns you feature in are permanently postponed in their pages until you're dropped by the companies you represent.' She jabs me just below the collarbone for emphasis. 'We're talking a complete blackout in publications across France, Italy, Russia, China, the Americas, Great Britain, Germany, Spain and the entire Asia-Pacific region. I know for a fact that your management company is thinking of letting you go because you're more trouble than you're worth. One tiny push and your so-called career and "A-list" life? Will be over. I'm going to ruin you. Try and take me to court, and the financial might of the St Alban Group will bury you!'

She's shouting now, and I'm reminded of that red-faced reporter screaming at me earlier: *Who are you seeing now that you've very publicly dumped Félix de Haviland and Will Reyne?*

'You'll be lucky if you can get hand-modelling work for your local discount chain!' Bianca yells. 'That is, if the drugs don't get you first and you end up a very minor postscript in the Obituaries section of the *New York Times*.'

I hear Justine's voice telling Ryan: *She's the one who dumped Félix de Haviland ... She actually stole him off his fiancée.* And something goes *click* in my head.

'What do you have to say about that?' Bianca shrieks, knotting her hands into the front of my sweater, tears in her eyes.

'You're the fiancée?' I blurt out.

Bianca goes off. '*The fiancée?*' she shrieks, gripping me by the upper arms and shaking me like a rag doll.

'Don't. Touch. Me,' I warn and she lets go of me abruptly, covering her mouth with both hands, weeping as if something inside her is irreparably broken.

'The future I thought I'd be living just *vanished*. It's *gone*,' she wails. 'Everything I loved about Félix — his family, his friends, the places we used to go, the things we used to do, his stupid, disgusting dogs, the apartment we shared, the *life* we shared — you took them all from me. Everything they say about you is true — you contaminate everything you touch. Destroyer. *Destroyer!*'

I'm so stunned at her words that for a moment I think she's talking about *me*. Then I remember that we don't know each other, that she's a stranger to me and all of her anger is for Irina.

I gaze at her with compassion. Before, I would have had trouble recognising the emotion; it would have seemed an abstract concept, a human construct. But that was before. A lot of things have happened since then. I've suffered my own losses.

'You really loved him, didn't you?' I say quietly, and I am wholly unprepared when Bianca looks up sharply at my words and slaps me hard across the face.

We both freeze. And I feel something dangerous leap inside me. I have to stop myself from retaliating in kind, because the way I'm feeling, I could *kill* her.

Bianca stares at me wide-eyed, sucking in a hurt breath as she massages the fingers of her right hand. I can see her wondering why the force of the blow didn't make me fall down, break down, or even flinch.

'You're like a heartless *stone*,' she gasps. 'You don't feel anything for anyone, do you?'

'How dare you?' I find myself roaring. 'You're the one with no idea. *All I have left are feelings.* How dare you judge me?'

I can see from her frightened gaze that she doesn't understand what I'm saying. She begins, almost imperceptibly, to back away from me, like a cornered animal.

'What do you want me to say?' I snarl, my voice rising as I follow her across the room. 'Sorry? Well, I *am* sorry. Sorry the pretty, shiny life with the rich husband didn't work out, didn't even get off the ground. But don't expect me to empathise with you, or feel scared, belittled or even ashamed, because *you don't know me*, you will never know me. Never know that there are worse things in life than a broken engagement. You can't know what I'm feeling inside, what it's been like for me. You're right. People like you *always* recover, because you *can*.'

Bianca glances back through the velvet-curtained doorway towards the outer door with genuine fear in her eyes, and something seems to take hold of me as I yell, '*Be grateful* that you'll never be forced into an arranged marriage with a husband that beats you. *Be grateful* that you'll never have to live hand to mouth at the mercy of a drug-dealing de facto. *Be grateful* that your fate isn't to be locked in a homemade dungeon while someone you once trusted keeps you chained like a dog in the darkness and does unspeakable things to you against your will. *Be grateful* that you are not *me*.'

I raise my burning left hand, struggling to stifle that impulse to lash out, to wound. I'm so sick of all the hatred, all the haters, all the people whose fears and motivations and vengeances and cruelties I will *never* understand.

Then I hear: *Mercy*.

I look around wildly, though his voice is only inside my head.

Don't, he says quietly, as if he has appointed himself my conscience. *You don't need to do this. You're frightening her, and you're better than that. It will soon be over, one way or another.*

Then I see him — looking at me from out of the flat surface of the mirror to the right of the velvet-curtained doorway in which Bianca cowers, oblivious to his presence.

'K'el?' I say.

I look around the room for him, but he's only visible in the reflected world, not the real one that I'm standing in. 'K'el?' I say again, stumbling with outstretched hands towards his reflection that is no reflection.

He's so hyper-real, so hyper-beautiful, with his gleaming olive skin, his dark gold hair, his tawny wide-set eyes — like the eyes of a young lion. And in his face is that unspoken longing and self-loathing he seems unable to hide when he's around me. He's watching me because he has to, and because he can't help himself.

'*Now?*' I plead. 'Is it to be now?'

Because maybe if They move me again, I'll stop feeling so numb. And maybe this time, those of the Eight that remain will be merciful and will do the job properly and somehow make me forget Ryan Daley forever. I don't want to have to find him and then lose him all over again.

I walk towards K'el's gleaming form so that he and Irina and I seem to converge for an instant, before he walks away from me into the next pane of silvered glass. And the next and the next — his tall frame crossing smoothly from one mirror to another, as if such a thing could even be possible. Until he's circumnavigated the entire room and is standing, facing me again, in the last mirror to the left of the velvet-curtained doorway.

I see him shake his head in negation, in warning. I hear his voice in my mind like a breath of fire.

Soon, he says. *Be ready.*

Then the looking glass is suddenly empty of his image. Only Irina and I are left there, staring, ashen-faced.

It's a long time before I realise that Bianca's made it all the way to the outer room, her eyes wide, her face drained of all colour.

'Who are you?' she says shakily. 'You're not Irina.'

I move out of the dressing room towards her and she places the leather tub chair and ottoman between us, for safety.

'Who do you want me to be?' I say wearily, bypassing her entirely and heading for the outer door. I feel her surprise more than see it. 'You've said what you came to say,' I mutter. 'Go ahead and ruin Irina's life. I'm not going to stop you. Not today. I'm tired. There are too many of you to guard against, to guard, to save. Maybe Gabriel was right, maybe I should've just kept my head down all along and done nothing. Let life tear each of my fragile charges, my flawed vessels, to pieces, while I simply stood by, watching. It's what my kind does best, after all. *Watch*.' My voice is bitter. I hope K'el hears it.

I place a hand upon the outer door, heartsore and on edge. I know it must seem crazy that Irina's talking about herself as if she isn't even in the room, but I'm tired of pretending. I'm never going to see this girl again, so what's a burning bridge or two?

'I've got enough going on in my own messed-up existence,' I add quietly, 'without having to deal with people like you coming at me for things I don't even remember doing. Félix is a cheater. He showed you his true colours. You got lucky that it happened now, and not twenty years after the happy day. Be grateful and move on. That's the best advice I can give you.'

Bianca cries, 'Wait!'

Though I shouldn't be able to hear them through the soundproofed wood, I can discern Gia's voice and Juliana's, in the hallway outside, as they talk to each other in low voices, in Italian.

And it's spooky, but as I listen to them, their words seem to meld together in my mind and reform, growing comprehensible to my ears.

'*Dopo un anno? Forse ...*' Gia says. *After another year, perhaps.*

'Then maybe I'll come and work for you, eh?'

'You should,' Juliana replies earnestly. 'Tommy has only the best things to say about you. We could use your skills very much at Atelier Re. You would be the perfect fit, in talent, in personality.'

Hour by hour, minute by minute. Everything's slowly coming back to me except the one thing I so desperately crave. Freedom.

'Wait!' Bianca says again behind me, so forcefully that I turn and regard her with surprise. What she sees in my face makes her flinch, but she stands her ground bravely. 'I *saw* something.'

I growl in Irina's heavy Russian accent, 'And I'm telling you, I don't care what you saw — do your worst. Descend upon Irina like a plague. She's Teflon-coated anyway. She's got nine lives, maybe more. She'll survive anything. Now, since you've gotten everything you wanted to say off your chest, I'm going back to my hotel so that I can get up again in the morning and take my clothes off in front of more strangers, okay?'

'No, you don't understand,' Bianca whispers, and there's fear but also wonderment in her voice. 'I saw something. Back there, before you started talking to yourself. Just a flash. But I saw something. Someone. You don't even talk like Irina, do you know that? Oh, I mean you *sound* like her, you sound Russian. But she just complains and complains about everything. Nothing's ever good enough. And she hardly ever meets your eyes unless she wants something from you. She's a vicious mix of towering arrogance and total insecurity. But she's not even here, is she?'

My eyes fly back to Bianca's as I finally grasp what she's saying, and I feel Irina's heart skip a beat.

'If you say you saw something,' I challenge, mouth suddenly dry, 'describe it. Describe what you saw.'

'I saw a, a … young woman with brown hair that hangs down just past her shoulders and brown eyes. She was very pale and very tall, and I don't know how it's possible, because she was so faint, but I could kind of see her *within* you, or around you, like a … glow. She looked beautiful. And kind. And very, very sad.'

Tears spring suddenly to Irina's eyes, roll down her cheeks, her hands fly up to her wet face and all of these things are like reflex actions.

Kind? What would *I* know of kindness?

Now, sadness. Sadness is something I'm acquainted with.

Bianca could see *me*, if only for a moment? How would that even be possible?

Was that what Felipe meant when he screamed *¡Demonio!* in my face? Had he seen something of me, too? In the driver's mirror?

Crying is for humans, reminds that voice in my head, as I cry.

And what am I these days? I tell myself, dashing tears off my face with the back of my hands, *if not human?*

'It was just a waking dream,' I say aloud through the strange ache in Irina's throat, 'an hallucination.'

When what I want to tell Bianca is: *Yes, that's me. You've described me perfectly.*

I realise that the linkages between myself and Irina must be at breaking point if Bianca could somehow see me inside Irina's skin with her human eyes. Though I haven't felt a thing this time: no jarring shift, no sense of dislocation, of unlinking, nothing. It had just happened.

I close my eyes, willing myself to dissolve, to search out and test those invisible bonds that somehow anchor me to Irina.

The hard knot that binds me to her is still there; it still holds firm. Irina's still there, too, locked away. That part hasn't changed. And though I struggle and twist within her boundaries, I cannot draw away from her entirely, however desperately I might wish to. Then, abruptly, I feel myself pulled back, as if by a cord, or an elastic band.

Bianca moves a little closer, fascinated despite her dread. 'All I see and hear is Irina but I'm *getting* someone else completely.'

She walks around me, studying me from every angle in silence and I meet her gaze steadily. 'No ghosts, no evil spirits here,' I challenge quietly.

Bianca's eyes well again suddenly as if she might cry. And I know how she's feeling, because I'm feeling it, too. I move away from her and lean back against the door, crossing my arms tightly to try and ward off the hurt that always accompanies the thought of Ryan Daley being out there in the world without me. And then I see Luc's eyes again — that strange mixture of fury and dark need in place of the love that used to greet me — and the pain intensifies, making me lean forward and draw a quick, sharp breath. How much more must I be made to bear?

Bianca hesitates, picking up her designer bag and slinging it back over one narrow shoulder like a shield, 'Well ... Irina,' Bianca says with a small, sad smile, 'you've pulled off at least one miracle today. All I've wanted to do, ever since Félix decided he didn't want me any more, is murder you with my own hands. I did think about doing that today, but ... fate very kindly intervened.'

'Fate?' I murmur. 'Fate has nothing to do with any of this.'

I turn and open the door before Bianca can say anything more. Gia and Juliana look up immediately, then hurry towards me.

'You're still *alive*,' Gia says wonderingly.

'What of the dresses?' Juliana queries, shooting Gia a warning look.

I glance back at Bianca, and she returns my gaze steadily before she replies, 'The red and the silver, I think. Designs 13 and 28.'

She takes Juliana's arm in hers and the two women set off up the corridor ahead of us towards Giovanni's office. 'I'd like them sent to my villa in Lake Como — Giovanni knows where it is,' Bianca adds, her voice growing fainter as she reaches the end of the corridor. 'By the water in Moltrasio.'

Juliana knocks on Giovanni's office door. 'I know it,' she replies. 'The cream house with the dark green shutters. There's a guesthouse and private pier, right by the water's edge?'

Bianca nods. 'I'm staying in the guesthouse for the next couple of months while my apartment's put up for sale. Ask Valentina to bring them up and we can ...'

The two women enter Giovanni's office and close the door behind them.

CHAPTER 13

'What happened with Bianca St Alban?' Gia asks, taking my arm. 'I can't believe you're still here, still in one piece.'

I'm so tired I let her lead me. 'Still here,' I mutter. 'Where else would I be?'

She gives me a strange look as she turns us back towards the circular ramp that will take us back downstairs.

The nightwatchmen walk us across the mosaic-tiled foyer and into the enclosed portico that serves as the entrance to Atelier Re. Sensor lights go on and the electronic eye looks down upon us for the last time today.

As Gia and I wait for the second set of sleek glass

doors to open to let us out into the street, I see that it's snowing steadily.

It's also very dark, and I'm reminded of the time Ryan made sure I didn't stray out of the circle of light cast by the street lamp outside his house, so that his ex-girlfriend, Brenda, wouldn't see the skin of my face and hands glowing in the night air. He's still helping me navigate this life, even though he's not here.

I feel a wave of intense pain and turn to Gia and say more gruffly than I intend, 'Give me one of your scarves.'

She hands one across and watches me bemusedly as I pull the scarf over the top of my cloche hat and wrap it tightly about my face, then shove Irina's hands into her black leather gloves.

'Bag lady chic,' Gia exclaims. 'Now I've seen everything.'

The second set of glass doors finally glide open and we step out into the icy night. We pause on the footpath, surveying both ends of the narrow street. A light layer of snow lies over everything. Even covered as I am, I make sure I position myself behind Gia's left shoulder.

She looks up at the sky in wonderment. 'I've been here so many times, and I've never seen it snow before Christmas, ever.'

She pulls her remaining scarf up around her face, zips the collar of her leather jacket higher and turns back to me. I'm ready for her, so all she sees is the top of my covered head as she says apologetically, 'We had to give Natasha your overcoat to wear to the decoy limo, and it's kind of ruined anyway, the way it's been handled today. Andreas would be livid if he knew how we'd treated his gift.'

She starts to cross the footpath cautiously and I mince after her in my killer heels, kind of sideways, like a crab.

Her voice floats back to me. 'Natasha's the reason the street's so deserted. I arranged for her to flounce out of here in your overcoat, a bad wig and big sunglasses. Carlo just called to tell me that it's crazy where they are — they've brought the area around La Scala to a total standstill. They'll keep it up until I call to let him know you're safely back at the suite.'

Two black limos slide to a stop just as we reach the icy kerb outside Atelier Re. From beneath Irina's long lashes, I see Vladimir jump out of the first car and hold the two back doors open for Gia and me.

I shuffle past him, my head bowed inside my hastily rigged up camouflage. Gia helps me into the car and gets in after me. We take seats beside each other, placing our giant handbags down on the floor at almost exactly the same moment, sighing in unison, relieved that the day is finally over.

It's almost 10 pm and I'm starving. Since breakfast, I've been offered three cups of camomile tea and two rice cakes. Being Irina sucks.

The soft interior lights are all on and I surreptitiously check the half-inch of exposed bare skin between the cuff of my sweater and the edge of my glove for any giveaway signs before unwrapping Gia's scarf from around my face and head. I let it fall loosely about my shoulders. Then I take off the gloves and hat, laying them down beside me, and shake out Irina's long, toffee-coloured hair.

Gia slides down in her seat and puts her wicked boots up on the empty seat opposite.

Vladimir slams both doors on us, then returns to the front of our car, which dips a little at his weight. We don't see him get in, we don't even see the driver, because there's now an opaque glass window between us and the front of the car. It's meant to be some sort of privacy screen, I guess, but for some reason it's making me feel nervous. I'm finding it claustrophobic back here and I know it's because I can't get a sense of what lies ahead. And I know I'm being stupid, because all we're doing is heading back to our hotel, but having that screen in place has effectively given me a huge blind spot.

'Do we need that?' I ask as our limo eases out into the road, the driver deftly navigating the parked cars, the scooters and motorbikes under tarpaulins that are parked out from the kerb at crazy angles.

Gia follows the direction of my gaze and her tone is apologetic. 'Gianfranco blew his stack when he heard what Felipe did today. So the new policy is that someone always rides with you, and you don't get to know who's driving you between jobs. Window's got to stay up. I told Vladimir to sit up front. The way he glowers at everyone makes me uncomfortable.'

She crosses one leg over the other and frowns at me. 'What I can't understand is why you even told me about the stunt Felipe pulled. Gianfranco had no idea you guys had hooked up before and neither did I. When Felipe first introduced himself as your driver two days ago, he played it so cool I could've sworn you two had never met. Why didn't you just grab what was on offer? It would've been a sweet set-up for you. And for him. None of us would have found out for months, even years.'

'I did drink it,' I reply absently.

'You *did*?' Gia is shocked.

I add hastily, 'But I honestly didn't know there was anything in it besides vodka. It just never occurred to me that he'd put something else in there.'

Gia looks sceptical. 'But I spoke to you afterwards, and you were totally coherent. More coherent than usual, in fact. Felipe said the stuff he gave you was pure. It should have knocked you out.'

'Must've been a bad batch,' I lie, looking out at the falling snow. 'Didn't do a thing for me.'

Except damn near kill the body I'm in. But Gia doesn't need to know that.

Rain, hail, snow: all in one day. I wonder what tomorrow will bring; whether I'll even be here, even be Irina, tomorrow. I can feel the crosswinds of convergence blowing, and I don't know how to read the signs, read the skies. It's making me jumpy as hell.

I wonder who'll reach me first in the eternal game of tug o' war for my soul.

There's that sick feeling in my stomach again, of wanting to stay, but also of wanting to run and keep running.

Soon, K'el said. *Be ready.*

The feeling of disquiet intensifies and I hunch over in my seat, arms crossed protectively over my belly.

'You're quiet,' Gia says as I stare out the window.

I know it's rude, but I'm no good at small talk. I don't bother to respond, or even turn away from the darkened streetscape flying by, the strangely empty streets.

'That Ryan guy,' Gia says casually, and this time I *do* respond, turning to her in surprise, feeling my skin instantly prickle at the mention of Ryan's name.

'How'd you meet him?' she asks. 'I'm with you all the time, and you'd think I'd remember someone who looks like he does — I nearly died when he picked up. But I don't remember ever even seeing him before. Did you meet him at *Mahiki*? Or was it that time we hit *Tao* with the *Elite* models? Maybe he featured in some ad campaign. How do you know him? And why were you arguing with him after everything I'd done to find him for you?'

'We always argue. That's what we do,' I reply tonelessly. 'He's just someone I met way before I knew you. Lifetimes ago. I can't seem to leave him alone.'

Gia's mouth turns down in sympathy.

'He's worse than liquid meth,' I mutter. '*Boom*, straight to the heart. Like a bullet. Every time.'

I don't tell her that I know what that feels like,

too. That the ache I feel for Ryan right now resembles a mortal wound.

'That bad, huh?'

Gia's eyes are so kind, I can't bear it. I look out the window again so she won't see the hurt and confusion on my face. Irina and I might actually *be* the same person, the way we've trashed every relationship we've ever formed with anyone.

'The timing's always been lousy,' I mutter. 'We're never free to be with each other. Something always gets in the way. Like now.'

Something? More like everything. Every damned thing.

Why? I rail silently at the starless night sky. *Why must you always, always, show me the things I cannot have?*

'So he's seeing someone then?' Gia asks. I hear disappointment in her voice and turn on her, feeling something evil rise in me. 'Little young for you, isn't he?' I hiss. 'You've got to be, what, pushing thirty?'

'What do you care?' Gia challenges. 'You're the one who dated a sixty-year-old rocker has-been — *eeuugh*, I might add — for a few weeks just to see what it felt like. Besides, you told Ryan to get out of your life — I heard you. So he's fair game.'

I glower at her in silence.

'And why'd he call you "Mercy"?' she queries. 'You're about as merciful as the crocodile they murdered to make your handbag.'

'You wouldn't understand,' I reply tightly, kicking off Irina's high-heeled shoes and looking back out the window so she can't see my eyes shine with unshed tears.

'Try me,' Gia says. 'I'm actually in the mood to hear you talk, for a change.'

'Do you believe in angels?' I reply tightly.

Gia looks at me quizzically.

'Nope,' she says, unzipping her leather jacket and stretching. 'Biggest atheist out there. That new age stuff makes me want to laugh. Uncontrollably. What do angels have to do with — ' I don't let her finish.

'Everything. They have everything to do with it. They're the reason we're even here, talking together in this car.'

'Uh, okay.' Gia laughs uncomfortably. 'I didn't realise you were religious. Some of the stuff you've done — '

'It's not a question of religion,' I snap. 'Religion is what people call things they can't explain, imposing order where there is no order. Let's save the theology discussion for another day, okay? I'm tired.'

Gia sits back huffily, but there's no point even getting into it, because she can't help me. No one can.

So now it's just a waiting game, and I hate waiting almost as much as I hate heights.

There's a stony silence in the car for a few blocks, and the sense of panicky, edgy dread I'm feeling seems to be sucking all of the air out of the atmosphere.

I gesture at the smoky pane of glass between us and the driver. 'Can you talk to him? Tell him I need him to open the sunroof?'

'Irina, in case you haven't noticed, it's *snowing* outside,' Gia exclaims. 'Why on earth would you want to do that?'

'I'm homesick,' I say feverishly, when what I really want to scream is: *I'm suffocating in here.*

'You live in the Bahamas, when you're not working,' Gia reminds me incredulously.

I screw up my face in confusion and Gia sighs. 'It's *hot* there?'

'I want to feel the snow on my face, like I did when I was a child,' I plead.

'No shit?' Gia frowns, before knocking on the glass partition.

It descends an inch or two, just enough for us to see Vladimir's pale blue eyes, the top of his head.

'What is it? What do you want?' he says sharply.

'She wants the sunroof open,' Gia says, jerking her thumb in my direction. 'She's "homesick".'

Vladimir's pale blue eyes zero in on me for a second and I think he's going to say no, but then he nods tersely.

'We're almost there, I see no harm in it. Do it,' he says to the driver.

The opaque screen slides back into place. A moment later, the inner panel on the ceiling of the car shifts across and then the fibreglass sunroof itself slides away and the cold air outside comes rushing into the car. I feel small flakes of snow settle on my upturned face, then melt.

'Ugh.' Gia shivers beside me. 'You're mad.'

But she shifts across to allow me to stand up, and I wriggle my head and shoulders through the opening, placing my bare hands on the roof of the limo. They immediately begin glowing in the night air, as I'm sure my face and neck are doing, but there is no one to see it.

The wind is so strong that it causes Irina's long

hair to ripple out behind me, like a bright flag, a pennant. I bare my teeth to it, grateful for the relative solitude. The elements I can handle; human relations, not so much. I'm still an abject failure at those.

I turn briefly, catching the headlights of the second limo behind us. It's at least five car lengths back and falling away slightly, as if our driver's just been told to step on it. I look back at my hands on the roof of the car: the glow of my skin seems brighter tonight. Brighter even than stardust, than moonlight. Light seems to leak from me in faint wisps, in errant curls that blur and fade.

I look up as we turn into Via Victor Hugo and, at first, imagine that I must be seeing things.

There's a man standing in the centre of the road up ahead, his back to us. I feel my skin prickle in warning as his dark shape grows clearer the closer we get to him. Our limo driver isn't stopping, he's actually picking up speed. I don't think he's seen the man in the roadway because he doesn't have my eyes.

'Move!' I yell at the man, waving one arm. 'Get out of the way!'

'What is it, Irina?' I hear Gia calling from inside the car. 'What have you seen?' She tugs sharply on the hem of my sweater to get my attention.

The man's just standing there, looking down the road away from me, his arms loosely at his sides, posture straight, as if he was crossing and became lost in thought.

'Are you deaf, man?' I scream. 'Get out of the way!'

From inside the car, I hear Vladimir and Gia shouting, 'Irina! What is it?', 'Irina, what's the matter?' and I duck my head down a little and call through the opening, 'Tell the driver to slow down! There's a man in the road.'

'A what?' Gia yells.

'A MAN IN THE ROAD!' I roar.

But all our driver does is flick on his high beams so that I see the man turn, shielding his eyes against the light, his face full of fear as he registers, too late, the car bearing down on him, registers me looking down at him from the open sunroof, horrified, and in the instant his eyes fly wide, I see, I see —

Ryan.

It's Ryan on the road. In the same beat-up leather jacket he was wearing when I last saw him in Australia. Layered tees, one blue, one grey; indigo jeans, scuffed boots. He might have stepped straight out of my memory into this place. And all I can think as he turns his head away from the car, the car that's going to run him down, is: *Oh God, he came for me anyway*.

Ryan throws his arms up as if to shield himself from the impact. But it's too late, it's useless, he just goes under the front wheels.

I don't think, I don't even breathe, I just pull myself out onto the roof in one smooth action and somersault off the moving car and onto the road, screaming his name as I land on my bare feet — like a cat — looking around wildly.

CHAPTER 14

The others don't have my reflexes.

Our limo travels another hundred feet at least before the driver brakes suddenly, tyres squealing. The second limo almost runs me down where I'm standing, frozen and gaping, in the roadway. At the spot, the very spot, where Ryan was hit.

People explode out of both cars and slip and slide across the icy surface towards me. Five burly, dark-suited men, a couple with weapons drawn, and Gia, who's screaming in the way people do when they go beyond the point at which there are any words to express the horror they're feeling.

'What were you thinking?' she sobs, grabbing hold of my upper arms. The men circle me warily, as if I'm wired with explosives and might blow at any moment.

'You killed him,' I say dazedly, craning my head to look around them, over them. 'Didn't you see? Help me look for his body.'

But even as I say the words, I know that I just witnessed an illusion. Something a demon might send to taunt me, to make me question my sanity.

Vladimir shines a narrow, stainless-steel torch in my face, then plays it across the slick and uneven surface of the road around us, up the sides of nearby buildings and over parked cars. 'What body?' he drawls in his heavy Russian accent.

Gia's voice is shaky. 'Irina, what are you talking about? There's nothing here.'

'No blood?' I say tonelessly, already knowing the answer. 'No body?'

Six people shake their heads, shuffling uneasily, shooting each other covert looks.

But I saw him go down.

'The driver says he didn't see or … um … feel anything,' Gia adds softly.

I wheel about in the snow, and shake my fists at the sky, shrieking, 'What are you playing at? What are you waiting for? Come and get me!'

And I actually try to run. In my bare feet, I try to break free and run from the vision of Ryan being mown down by the very car I was travelling in, run from all the horror and devastation I'm feeling inside. What I told Bianca was true. *All I have left are feelings.*

I try to run from them all: from beings both seen and unseen; even from the watchful, lowering sky that, once, could never have mastered me.

'Come and get me!' I shriek, taking Angelo by surprise and shoving him out of the way so hard that he sprawls to the ground, his weapon clattering against the raised stone kerb. I dodge Vladimir's outstretched arms and scramble away up the road on my scratched and bruised bare feet, almost losing my balance, then recovering it as I stretch out Irina's long legs and *run.*

'Are you seeing this?' I shriek. 'Any of you? Come and get me! I dare you! Show yourselves!'

I've almost made it past the hotel driveway when I'm crash-tackled to the ground by someone at least three times Irina's body weight. Still facing down, the surface of the pavement moving past me in a blur, I'm carried at a run, under the arms, by the ankles, back through the emergency exit doors we came out of this morning, through the laundry room, the sound-deadened luxury lift, as if the day is being rewound all around me.

Someone throws open the door to my suite — every light inside blazing bright — and I'm set down, none too gently, on hands and knees on the floor. My damp hair hangs down stringily on either side of my face. I can feel that the soles of my feet are cut up and wet and filthy.

I look up to see a man in a suit standing over me, with a kind face and a courteous manner. He's stocky and paunchy and clean-shaven, with a leonine head of grey, wavy hair and a tie like a stockbroker, all the stripes running upwards.

'I've never seen you before,' I say, squinting at him as someone helps me to stand. 'Gianfranco?'

'No,' he says kindly in Italian-accented English. 'But Gianfranco *did* send for me. And if you're a good girl, you won't ever have to see me again.'

Moving quickly for someone so large, he adjusts something just out of my line of sight and I feel a small stab of pain in one arm.

And just like that, I'm gone.

There's the sensation of rapid movement, of leagues being eaten up in the space between two heartbeats. I'm flying, oh God, I think I'm flying. Something that's been denied me for so long.

In the instant I recognise what I'm doing, I feel an intense wave of almost paralysing fear, but, also, exhilaration. And the two emotions could not be more distinct.

I'm looking down at the distant snow, so far below, a dull white in this moonless night. The air whistling past me is colder than any mortal could stand, but I'm moving through it easily, as if I'm a bird. Or an angel. Soundlessly, with purpose.

Watching the great distances pass beneath me, I feel my gorge rise, as if I'm going to be sick. I'm suffused with fear, almost rigid with it, and yet I fly on, under cover of darkness: over snow, over standing stones, ravines and valleys, one mountainous pass after another on which ski lifts and cable cars stand idle, all the floodlights out for the night. There's no movement, no light, in the houses that I soar over unseen. The humans inside, they're asleep. They'll wake later, never knowing I was even here.

Am I ... hurt? There's a slight dragging pain in my side, as if I have a stitch, or I've been wounded. Not gravely; more of a flesh wound, a deep cut.

I'll live. But it's slowing me down, everything's getting in my way, and I'm suddenly pierced through by so much rage, so much frustration, that I turn my head to find a target for my fury. I see a double-storey house with a steeply pitched roof and quaint paintwork, empty flower boxes at all the windows, and a winding drive. There's a collection of outbuildings, built in the same style, gathered around it. Humans and animals all asleep within.

I narrow my eyes at them. That's all I do. *And set them all on fire.*

The buildings burst into flame simultaneously.

Will it and it is done.

The night air is suddenly rent with screaming, the bellows of trapped beasts, the sounds of breaking glass, but I fly on. Torching anything, everything, I see. Because I can; because I am of a mind to do it.

Snow-covered trees with bare, frozen limbs as hard as iron; byres, barns, farmhouses, cars, convenience stores and cathedrals — all gone in seconds. Roads, cobbled laneways, truck stops, turn-offs, flyovers — all these become rivers of flame, the asphalt turning liquid, like mud.

Things that should not even burn — I set fire to them all. And I laugh.

A ringing laugh. Masculine.

There's a sudden sensation of distance — as if I'm zooming out, refocusing, before zooming back in —

and I realise that it's not me doing this at all. Someone else is turning the world to fire and I'm just seeing it *through* his eyes. I'm somehow getting his feelings and mine, together. Unshakeable confidence versus sheer terror; triumph versus horror.

Of course, all the negative emotions I'm feeling are mine.

I know that laugh. Amusement tinged with cruelty.

How often did I hear it with my own ears when I was me, inhabiting my own body? How often have I heard it in my dreams?

Luc? I scream silently. *Desiste! Stop!*

But if Luc hears me, he gives no sign. Everything seems so real, it's as though I've been given a temporary line into his head, as if I've hijacked his senses, shrugged on his skin. But what I'm seeing is unspeakable. The night sky lit up with flames, with suffering. It can't be real, can it?

I'm hit by a sudden recollection. Of a time when the universe was young. Of Luc disrupting the settled orbits of planetary bodies, sending them careening into each other, displacing objects billions of times our size, mass and density, just because he could. Life had been an endless game to him, the universe his playground. But back then it had not teemed with the life it teems with now, and what he's doing at this moment screams *wrongness* to me.

Luc crosses a final peak and soars down the heavily populated flank on the other side of the mountain — house after house built in terraces down the steep incline. In the distance I see a large body of water, a handful of lights gleaming upon its banks.

As he flies unerringly towards the vast lake in the darkness, he picks out main streets, town squares, winding highways, clock towers, restaurants, cafés, villas, jetties, pontoons, sailboats and cruisers and casually sets fire to them all. The lakeside is soon surrounded by a wall of flames reaching high into the night sky and sirens quickly fill the air, the lights of emergency vehicles wind up the twisting roads into the foothills, people spill out into the streets, into the gardens of their homes, to see the skies lit such an unnatural, incandescent red. Red laced with a blue so pale it is almost white.

Holy fire.

Except it can't be holy fire because these people are not our enemies. They have done nothing to deserve our wrath. How could anyone even justify using it this way?

It's the dead-heart of winter, with everyone inside away from the cold. Maximum damage, minimum effort. The loss of life would be terrible, if this were not a dream.

Luc continues, following the main body of the waterway until it splits into two tributaries. He chooses the right fork, flames rising in his wake along the right bank.

Through his eyes, I look back at each town or village that has been claimed by fire, feeling both exultation and nausea, his emotions still weirdly entangled with mine. I can't understand how this is happening — how I can see what he sees, feel him, *be* him.

I know our connection is strongest while I lie sleeping, but this is something else altogether. Luc has always been so guarded, so unknowable. But tonight, I think I'm actually inside his mind, or what my sleeping self imagines his mind is like. And what I'm seeing there is utterly repellent.

When I knew him — when he and I lay entwined beneath the fragrant boughs in that hanging garden he created solely for me — I could never have imagined him capable of any of this.

This Luc? I don't even know.

I'm so busy looking backwards at the devastation Luc has wrought that I don't see her until she is upon me, *us*, with a rush of air, of silent fury. I am buffeted by her wings, the giant wings that are unfurled across her back like a warning of the terror to come.

I know those dark eyes, that wavy hair, that face that is as familiar to me — and as dear to me, I realise — as my own face. My true face. It's Nuriel.

She's moving so quickly that I only catch a glimpse of her. Her wide eyes are dark with anger as she cries in a voice to rend steel, to rend stone, 'You may go no further, Luc. No further.'

She seems to draw a flaming sword out of nowhere, out of thin air, it's suddenly just there in her hand, and she's suspended in the air before him — before me, the ghost in the machine — with contempt and righteous anger in her eyes.

She's more beautiful than the sun, and completely terrifying. Every part of her seems made of electricity, or lightning; the locks of her dark, wavy hair snake out around her face as if she has suddenly turned into that gorgon of myth, the Medusa. I can't reconcile the gentle, playful creature who was my friend with this vision of terror and beauty. She seems ready to slay Luc, or die trying.

Luc laughs again, hatred in his voice as he replies, 'I was the highest of you all. You were *nothing* before, never my match! Why dare hope that you could stop me now?'

'I'm only the first line of defence,' she tells him fiercely. 'Even if I am defeated, they gather to end your misrule.'

'If they believe *you* will buy them all enough time to reach Milan, their confidence is *misplaced*,' Luc sneers.

Suddenly, the air before him — before me — seems to displace with the heat of a thousand suns. The air itself bursts into flame and there's a flaming sword in Luc's hand — in mine — and there are giant wings flaring across his back — as if they are mine, too — and Luc rises into the air and falls upon Nuriel without warning, sword upraised.

I scream at her: *Fuge!* Flee!

But my cry is silent, and goes unheard, and Luc slashes down without hesitation, his burning blade driving at a point between her right earlobe and her jawline. He follows the blow swiftly with all his weight, as if he would strike Nuriel's head from her neck in one blow.

She was his friend once, too, a long time ago. But there's no glimmer of past affection. Certainly, no mercy.

It's true that her strength did not ever equal his, because I glimpse genuine fear in Nuriel's eyes as she brings up her own blade, clumsily, just in time, so that the two cutting surfaces meet with a crack of energy at impact, like a lightning strike. Her blade is caught at an awkward angle between their two bodies.

Luc and Nuriel grapple together, their blades locked for what seems an eternity, spinning and falling through the air in a dance both graceful and deadly. And the whole time, I'm completely disorientated, because it feels as if it's *me* fighting Nuriel.

The cold air whistles past us as we fall and tumble through the icy winter air, the whole world red with flame at the peripheries of my sight. Nuriel's eyes bore into mine with contempt, with barely concealed terror, and she bares her teeth against me, crying, *'Haereticum!'*

Heretic. The word causes a little catch in my breathing. What could she mean?

Luc drives down inexorably upon Nuriel's blade, pushing it in towards the sweet curve of her face. I sense her beginning to falter as he bears down upon her with all his ferocity.

'If they are all as weak as you,' he hisses, eye to burning eye, 'then your rule is truly over and mine? Begins now. I ascend even as you *fall*.'

He roars the last word, and the light of his blade seems to leach into the light of Nuriel's. His blade is beginning to cut through. In seconds, she will be dead, her energies scattered.

But I *know* Nuriel.

And even before my eye catches her doing it, I sense her flow away from the point of weakness, the breach, until almost the only thing left of her is her broken blade, and then that, too, unravels and dissolves. Nuriel has become a slipstream of particles so fine and luminescent, Luc can't hope to catch it or bend it to his will.

I watch as the particles disperse then re-form some distance away — like a swarm of bees coming together. And I see Nuriel again, in her customary form, her giant wings outspread, her hands empty of any weapon. Then she seems to somersault backwards, spiralling down gracefully, deliberately, with the velocity of a speeding arrow, towards the slick, dark surface of the lake far below.

Her feint has caught Luc by surprise, and she's already pulled herself into a low, tight, skimming trajectory just above the waterline — moving away quickly, faster than a mortal eye could follow — well before he subsumes his own burning weapon in the palm of his hand and turns to follow.

Nuriel streaks past a large estate by the water's edge — red light reflecting weirdly upon a small guesthouse and private pier on the lake's edge — well before Luc has even completed his own dive.

Nuriel is picking up speed ahead of us; she's now only a faint, luminous streak almost lost to sight in the reflected glow of red upon the water. Luc laughs again as he launches himself after her like a bird of prey, vengeance singing in his heart. The two of them are locked in pursuit, tearing over the water, weaving their way through and around islands both inhabited and uninhabited, exploding *through* outbuildings, ferry terminals, church towers, gateways, boundary walls, leaving only incandescence in their wake.

Luc goes after Nuriel without hesitation as she counted upon him doing. She's leading him somewhere. Somewhere with reinforcements. At least, she's trying to.

She may not be his equal in strength or ferocity, but when I knew her, there were few fleeter in mind, in spirit, than Nuriel.

And it hits me, that this isn't a dream.

This is real. It's happening. Happening right now.

Luc has reached the outskirts of the city. He's almost here.

CHAPTER 15

For a long time, I just drift. There are periods of dark, interspersed with periods of light, as if I am a rudderless boat on uncharted waters, a ghost ship.

I hear voices — both human and celestial, both real and remembered — and I know that real life is intruding upon memory, and memory upon real life. But that is the nature of my illness: that I must always straddle two worlds — the seen and the unseen. And also two ages, two epochs: the time when I was whole; and everything that came after that time.

But the pull of the light seems ... stronger, somehow.

And yet I can't seem to struggle back up into the light for an age.

The outline of the room I'm in finally starts to regain colour and detail, and I see Gia in her vintage pink and white blossom-covered kimono, curled up in an armchair she's pulled up right next to my bed, her pyjama-clad knees poking out beneath her wrap. It's like she's keeping vigil over me while she taps away on her mobile phone like she always does. The chandelier's dark, but all the lamps in the room are lit, suffusing the air with a soft, warm light.

My internal clock tells me it's almost 5 pm. How long have I been … out?

For a moment, I see entire Swiss-Italian border towns on fire, fire pouring down the mountainside like a flood and I go cold with horror.

'You've got to get out of Milan,' I rasp in Gia's direction before she even knows I'm awake.

I know I've given her a shock, because she jumps, visibly, dropping her phone down the side of her armchair.

'You've got to get away from me,' I insist, 'if you want to live.' My tongue and throat are so parched that they actually hurt.

Gia fishes her phone back up and taps something hurriedly into the screen, then tucks it beneath one knee. 'That's exactly what I tell myself all the time,' she says. 'That you're bad for my health, like staring into the sun. Welcome back.'

She gives me the ghost of a smile and I see that her eyes are shadowed and puffy, as if she's been crying steadily for many hours. *For me?* I didn't think she liked Irina enough to have tears to spare her.

'I know I'm not making much sense,' I croak, 'but you've got to leave. It's not safe any more around me.'

'I know,' she murmurs, shifting in her leather armchair.

I frown. 'If you know, then why are you still here?'

She doesn't answer; just uncurls her legs from beneath her and crosses the room to a fussy, bow-fronted, marble-topped armoire with gilt-trimmed legs and gilt handle pulls. She pours some water out of a covered silver jug into a glass tumbler and brings it over to me, carefully setting it down on the bedside table to my left.

'Want some help sitting up?' she says.

I shake my head, but just doing that seems to set off carillion bells behind my eyes. I roll over gingerly towards the wall to my right and lie with my back to Gia for a moment, unable to catch my breath, or see, for the terrible pounding inside my skull.

'I still don't know how you managed not to kill yourself going off the roof of the car like that,' she mutters as she sits on the edge of the bed behind me. 'Everyone thinks you're certifiable right now. Gianfranco had to call Giovanni Re just before midnight to give him the bad news that his star model just tried to throw herself from a moving car. Everyone's thinking of pulling the plug on you — Giovanni, even your management.'

Gia's voice is barely audible. 'I called Giovanni at noon to give him a progress report. He told me that if you woke, and you still wanted to do it — anchor his show — he'll have you. If not, he'll retire the three looks he made especially with you in mind. They'll be archived, and never again see the light of day. Orla will get her way and close the damned parade in her sparkly silver dress.'

I shut my eyes, unsure how to reply. If I don't 'walk' for Giovanni tomorrow, I'll be responsible for ruining one of the defining moments of his long and celebrated career. And Irina will go from global icon to global outcast. She'll probably never work again. But if I do … who knows what will happen?

There are so many variables, all of them beyond my control. The sudden blaze of intense irritation

I feel is enough to send shock waves down Irina's nerve endings. Immediately, I feel less sluggish, less weighted-down and sedated, more myself. I lean up on my elbows, with a feeling in my throat as if I have swallowed broken glass.

Gia sees me wince and brings the tumbler of water to my lips. I drain it in one go and gesture at her to get more.

She hurries to do so, then says, 'It's almost five thirty. We need to make a decision about whether you do the show. You've been asleep for almost eighteen hours. While you were … gone,' she hesitates and tears fill her eyes. 'Terrible things have happened. All these towns — Domaso, Gravedona, Rezzonico, Menaggio, Tremezzo, Argegno, Laglio, Urio — people are saying they're all gone. They've been swept away …'

She spins clumsily, before feeling around on the end of my bed for something.

'… by *fire*.'

My eyes widen as Gia puts her hand on the remote control for the in-room television and the screen flares into life.

People wail and shriek and stumble blindly around before us, through smoke, through walls of flame with strange colours at their heart — gold and silver and the palest, most luminescent blue. Trees burn, retaining walls, stone buildings, vehicles, shops, bus stops, car parks, street signs, infrastructure of every kind, all incinerated by a kind of fire that resists water, chemical retardants, every ingenuity known to man. They burn and burn until they simply burn out, and there's nothing left but an ash so fine it is borne away on the wind.

We watch in horrified silence as the news services on almost every station, in every major language in the world, show clip after clip caught by ordinary people on the ground who woke in the midst of Armageddon.

When the same clips and hysterical voices start to recur, Gia turns off the television, tightening the sash of her kimono as she walks back to her armchair to retrieve her phone. 'The fact Giovanni is going ahead with the parade is a highly sensitive issue. Half the world will be waking to the news of the incredible devastation that just fell out of nowhere on one of the most highly developed nations in the world. Oh yeah, and that's what people are saying — that fire *fell* out of the sky; flames, they're saying, came *down* through the trees.'

I have to wrap Irina's thin arms around her bony knees to stop myself falling over. Am I somehow to blame for unleashing my nightmares, for unleashing *Luc*, upon the physical world? Has he changed so much? Or have I?

Gia's voice is husky from crying. 'The dress rehearsal at the Galleria Vittorio Emanuele will start in one hour — we're already an hour late for hair and make-up,' she says quietly. 'It's a big, big deal, this parade. Giovanni managed to shut down the entire Galleria for more than twenty-four hours. Do you have any idea how hard that is to do?'

I shake my head numbly, still groping for some kind of connection between the Luc I fell in love with, and the force of absolute ruin I witnessed in my dreams.

Gia points her phone at me. 'Giovanni will need to know if you're still in. He's intending to donate all the proceeds from the documentary and the touring retrospective to the victims of the fires. Some will say that Giovanni Re is going on with his self-congratulatory fashion parade as if nothing has happened, but *we* will know that he's doing it to help, to celebrate life. Most of the models are donating their appearance fees to the rescue and rebuilding efforts. Your fee alone is something in the order of two hundred thousand Euros. Make it count. People always say that fashion doesn't matter, that it's all as disposable and meaningless as candy. But if we can use it to rebuild lives, rebuild concrete things? Then that has to be a good thing, right? A great thing.

'So I need to know if you're in,' she continues, her voice growing stronger, 'and then we need to get to work on a number of levels. You need to walk like you've never walked before. You can't be seen to be anything other than perfect, savage and indomitable. Now get up.' Her voice is suddenly harsh. 'And follow me.'

I trail Gia out of Irina's bedroom unsteadily, crossing the suite into the room that's been turned into an impromptu walk-in wardrobe. It's still a complete bombsite, and I don't know how Gia is able to locate the exact pair of shoes she's looking for amongst all the bags and cases.

She holds them up for me to inspect. They look like ordinary stilettos in a shocking red colour, except that the heels have to be eight inches high.

'That's it?' I say. 'You just want me to walk around in those and I'm good to go?'

'You were very unconvincing yesterday when you put the black Loubs on,' Gia says with a frown. 'I couldn't believe what I was seeing. It's like driving a truck — if you can reverse park one of those babies, driving any kind of car after that is a breeze. Walk in these, and the crazy-tall bondage boots Tommy's organised for you to wear with the black strapless number, and the heels he's paired with the bridal gown? Will be a cinch.'

Gia's face suddenly clouds over. 'It just occurred to me that you gashed your feet pretty badly last night on broken glass. They looked like raw meat while the doctor was cleaning you up — I was almost sick. You're probably bleeding into your dressings right now.' She points the shoes in her hand at me.

I look down to see that my feet are heavily bandaged. I hadn't registered the fact until now.

Gia sighs. 'Maybe you *will* have to pull out. You'll be lucky to manage a pair of kitten heels, *if* you can even walk for any extended period of time. Sit down on this case and let's look at the damage.'

She hunkers down on the ground, placing the red heels beside her, and carefully unwinds the bandages around one foot. She takes my heel gently in one hand, lifts it and studies the sole, before doing the same with the other foot. She rises, crosses her arms and just looks at me uncertainly, her face paper white.

'How bad are they?' I say.

'See for yourself,' she replies, and her voice is almost inaudible.

I lift up one foot, then the other: they're both pink-looking, healthy. There are black stitches up the instep of one foot, but no apparent reason for them to be there. The flesh around the surgeon's thread has already healed.

'You didn't see what I saw last night,' Gia says shakily. 'The doctor removed a shard of glass from one of your feet that was at least two inches long.'

She waves one hand wildly in the air. 'It's got something to do with *you*, hasn't it?'

I close my eyes briefly and see fire like liquid death overtaking everything in its path and that feeling of intense horror and shame returns. Did *I* do that? Did Luc?

Gia has my full and sudden attention as she says, 'They're all saying you've lost it, but I don't think you're crazy. You thought you saw someone on the road, and you tried to save him, right? I *saw* you dive past the window. I saw you *land*. You landed on your feet. And I think I'm the only one who caught that. Maybe it's me that's going crazy because it wasn't an accident, was it? You look like Irina, you even sound like Irina, but I've been listening, really listening to you speak, and the things you say? The words you use? You're someone else altogether. Something else. How is that possible? I want to know.'

She's right that I'm good with words. I find comfort in them, they hold no fear for me and I will use them like a weapon if I have to. Maybe it's a skill I've developed over time, maybe I've always had it. It's one thing I know I'm good at and I can't hide it, whoever I may be or become. In the end, I can't ever be anyone else except myself. It's both a strength and a weakness. I've always been too full of pride, too much of a smart-arse to just play nicely. For many years, maybe it was all I had in each new life I was forced to assume — the ability to talk my way out of a minefield.

Gia flinches only slightly when I raise my eyes to hers. She's a brave woman. I don't need to touch her to know that fear and fascination are at war in her right now.

'Why aren't you afraid of me?' I rasp, answering her questions with one of my own. 'You should be.'

Her eyes are huge in her small face. 'You just told me to save myself. If you were truly ... evil, wouldn't you have harmed me already?'

'I'm not evil,' I murmur. 'Well, not any more.'

Gia's eyes widen at my words.

'You have nothing to fear from me,' I say quietly. 'I'm just a creature who needs help and affection and understanding, like everyone else does. I'm trapped, and so is Irina, for her sins. And there are so many things that I want — but what I want more than anything, is to be free. And then things like love and vengeance and truth? I'll be able to work out for myself again. I'm sick of being acted upon. Of being judged. Of being at the ... mercy,' I feel my mouth twist, 'of others.'

Gia adds tentatively, 'You don't really have a brain disease, do you ... Mercy?'

I have to laugh, but when I do, the pounding in my head intensifies unbearably and I have to take quick, shallow breaths to get the pain back under control.

'In actual fact, I probably do,' I gasp. 'I can't remember things, important things, even simple things, about myself. This thing that's happened to Irina, it's happened before, I've "been" different people hundreds, maybe thousands, of times. And these "lives"? I think it used to be years between each one, but now the time frames are speeding up, getting shorter and shorter ...'

'*What are you?*' Gia breathes.

I glare at her and she takes a step back.

'Why must you people always ask?' I growl. 'Why must you always insist that your curiosity be satisfied? Be grateful that I do not wish to snap you in half like a twig.'

It's just an idle threat on my part, but Gia goes pale. The feeling of fear that hangs about her, like a presence, seems to ratchet up a notch.

I wave a hand at her to diffuse my words. 'I'm older than you are,' I say, 'for all the jibes I made earlier. And I'm tired. A tiredness that sleep cannot mend. I thirst, I hunger, for freedom. I do not thirst, or hunger, for your blood.' I laugh at the words, but it's a despairing sound.

She hovers beside me, uncertainly, and I say harshly, '*Go*, while you can. People, like me, are coming for me soon.'

Her unusual eyes, one blue, one brown, grow even wider, more fearful.

'When I … leave Irina,' I add more gently, 'it could get … messy. It has to happen sometime before Irina's scheduled to leave Milan. Maybe we *should* pull the plug on all this. I don't want to be responsible for anything happening to Giovanni or his final collection. This time it's me calling the bad luck down on everyone. It's not Irina's fault.'

'Don't you see?' Gia says. 'It doesn't matter what you decide, because the thing you're so afraid of is already here, it's already happening. You can't stop it. So you either give in to your fear, or just carry on. What other choices are there? You're just going to submit? Give up? That doesn't gel with what I ... know about you.'

We stare at each other for a long moment. 'I can't be responsible for you,' I warn. 'I couldn't bear it if you ...'

I look down at my hands, and for a moment I see Lela Neill's small, capable fingers and trim wrists. She's going to be buried on Monday. I hug myself tightly so that Gia will not see me shaking.

She reaches out and gives my shoulder a small squeeze. 'I can take care of myself,' she replies quietly. 'What do you think I've been doing all this time?'

'Now just put them on,' she says, pointing at the red shoes, and I hear some of the customary steel return to her voice. 'And start channelling Irina, wherever the hell she's gone. I'll work out something for you to wear.'

'No, no, no!' Gia shouts, throwing up her hands as I flounce towards her up the 'runway' she's cleared down the centre of the sitting room. 'More hips, more hair, more arms, less shoulder. Chin up, head back, bum in ... This is *hopeless.*'

Her mobile phone rings and she waves both hands frustratedly at me to stop.

She's speaking in rapid Italian but I understand every word she's saying to whoever's on the line. 'Another hour,' she pleads. 'Run through the other girls first without her, and as soon as we arrive do a final run-through with Irina's looks included, okay? No need for hair and make-up. There's no time. Yes, I know, but yesterday she could barely walk ...' She shoots me a look. 'Yes, yes, I understand, but her feet are still a little sore. We're just giving them a final assessment before we head over. No, she doesn't need more sedatives, it's the last thing she needs. She's just very stiff. We're just doing a few ... stretching exercises' — I have to stifle a laugh — 'and then we'll get down to the cars. I'll call you if there's any delay, okay? I appreciate your patience. *Ciao, bello.*'

She hangs up and glares at me. 'We have a serious problem. A five-year-old girl could do better "top model" than you can. The models Giovanni's assembled for this love fest are the best-of-the-best, and they're mostly humourless robots spliced with piranha — they will *eat you alive* then fight over your bones, and your clothes. You have to get this right or Irina's ruined anyway. Her new donkey walk might even push the Lake Como disaster off the front pages. As soon as everyone at the Galleria gets a load of the way you're moving right now? Pandemonium.'

I can't even visualise the things she's told me to incorporate into my walk, let alone put them all together.

'Could you have put me in jeans that are any tighter or longer than these?' I complain as I duck-walk past her. 'And what's with the chain mail shirt? The gold dress Giovanni made for me is lighter than this.'

'Oooh,' Gia snarls, 'I wish I could *show* you how Irina does it!'

I'm suddenly reminded of the memories I lifted straight out of Giovanni Re's head when I touched his skin that first time. Of how Irina had gotten up on that makeshift catwalk and transformed from a sixteen year old with bad hair, clothes and eye make-up, into a steely-eyed, ground-shaking Valkyrie.

'Is this how?' I say as I recreate how I saw Irina move in my mind's eye.

I pivot sharply at a point near the front door of the suite and stalk back the other way, pausing dramatically near the dining table Gia shoved to one side before angling my body first one way, then another, and pivoting again to stalk back down the cleared area towards her. To say there's a tearing pain in my arches, ankles and calves from trying to move quickly in the eight inch heels would be a giant understatement. Everything is simultaneously numb and on fire.

Gia's tight expression clears as I get nearer to her. 'Better,' she breathes. 'That's much closer to the way she walks — we can work with this. But straighten your head and neck — imagine a string pulling you up by the top of your scalp. Loosen your arms, but don't throw them out too wide; more weight on the ball of the foot, more length between the steps; and the eyes, give me knowing and sultry and — '

'Go to hell?' I finish for her.

I make subtle adjustments to Irina's posture, her speed, her stalk, and do the pause, angle, pause, angle

I picked up out of Giovanni's memory, then pivot and power back down the room away from Gia. When I get there, I place Irina's hands on her bony hips and look at Gia over my shoulder, shaking out Irina's mane of burnt caramel-coloured hair.

'Exactly,' Gia murmurs. 'You've got it. That *go-to-hell* stare of hers. It's perfect. Better than perfect. There's nothing robotic about you, you don't seem as jaded as Irina's been lately. She's been phoning it in. But you? It's like you're doing it for the first time.'

I burst out laughing at her words, and Gia — looking startled — can't help but join me a second later.

'I suppose you are,' she says.

But then her laughter dies and she doesn't say anything more for several minutes, she just twirls her fingers a few times, indicating that I should turn, keep moving, turn, keep moving.

The doorbell suddenly peals loudly and Gia claps her hands.

'You need *fuel*, right? That's what you called it the other day; it kind of stuck in my head when you said it, because Irina likes to pretend that food is entirely unnecessary to sustain life. Let's have a quick pit stop to get your story straight. We need to come up with something that will convince all the people it took to restrain you last night — physically and medically — that you're well enough to walk. And then we need to hustle. Everyone's waiting impatiently for the star to arrive.'

'Juice, toasted *panini* filled with roasted vegetables and goat's cheese, fruit salad,' Gia says as she lifts the silver domes off the food on the tray. 'Just eat. We can move all this furniture back later.'

We perch on armchairs close to each other as Gia fires questions at me.

'You thought you saw a …?'

'Dog,' I reply firmly, taking a bite of the still warm, golden-brown, crescent-shaped sandwich. 'A large dog. Standing in the road. Directly in front of the car.'

'O-kay,' Gia says with her mouth full, 'that could work. But why couldn't anyone else see it?'

I take another big bite of my *panini*, and lick a splodge of thyme-encrusted goat's cheese off my lower lip as I think. 'I had a reaction to the stuff Felipe put in my drink. It wasn't my fault. I didn't know the drink was spiked. Felipe's not around to contradict me, is he?'

Gia shakes her head. 'Won't wash. Giovanni's physician took a blood sample and it showed negative for traces of drugs or alcohol. You were stone-cold sober and drug-free when you saw that "dog". How do you explain that?'

I finish my sandwich, and drain the glass of pineapple juice Gia's placed in front of me in one hit before reaching for the bowl of fruit pieces and a fork. 'The way I tried to pass myself off to you as Irina,' I say, as I chew. 'I have a mental illness ...'

Gia's eyes widen and she puts her *panini* back down on the plate on her knees. 'And what Felipe gave you exacerbated some underlying condition you're too afraid to have checked out. It'll mean a stay in a rehab facility in the not-too-distant future, but even though you're feeling very fragile, you're physically well enough to do one last charity appearance ...' She crosses back to the trolley and puts her half-eaten *panini* back on it. 'Works for me.'

She takes a sip of her juice, then puts it down, lost in thought. I cross over to her and put my glass and plate down next to hers. I see her shoulders tense as she zeroes in on the backs of my hands. Is it my imagination, or is Irina's skin the tiniest bit ...

luminescent? When I stare harder at it, it just seems like ordinary skin to me.

I know Gia's biting back a million questions as she crosses over to the console table near the door and picks up the telephone receiver. She looks down and dials a number.

'I've always liked puzzles,' she mutters as she waits for someone to pick up. 'Who knew one day I'd end up working for one?'

CHAPTER 16

It's probably a ten-minute walk from my hotel to Galleria Vittorio Emanuele — the place where the parade's supposed to take place. But when you're Irina Zhivanevskaya you don't ever walk anywhere unless you're paid to do it. So we drive there, and it takes us twenty minutes to make it from my suite to the car. The whole time Vladimir watches me, stony-faced, with his wise-guy eyes, and says nothing. He doesn't even try to make nice, because at some subterranean level, he doesn't recognise who I am any more.

Gia watches him watching me and calls Gianfranco, feeding him the fake story we've worked out together, in fluent Italian. Then she calls Giovanni's head of security and tells him the same story, in the same language, and says we're on our way. Lastly, she calls someone at Irina's management company's head office in New York to let them know that Giovanni Re won't be suing for breach of contract now, because Irina's feeling much, much better.

It takes us another half-hour to reach the edges of the Piazza del Duomo, where paparazzi surround the car, shouting twenty questions in almost as many languages. Some of them even start banging on the outside of the limo. But the driver just keeps crawling forward at a snail's pace and, like an overcrowded life raft complete with clinging humanity, we edge closer towards a grand, triumphal arch at least one hundred feet high.

I realise as we get closer to the giant arch that it's the main entrance to the Victorian-era Galleria: a building with a wide frontage onto the Piazza del Duomo that's punctuated by graceful arched windows. The few people allowed to pass under the arch by the burly security guards standing on either side, look like ants.

Everybody seems to be focused on my car. Nobody's looking at the sky, which is filled with billowing grey storm clouds as high as mountain ranges. They look like the massed sails of a fleet of Spanish galleons setting out to war. Nuriel and Luc are out there in that, somewhere. If one of them hasn't already killed the other. The thought makes my stomach lurch.

Don't force me to choose sides, I think feverishly. *Please.*

Gia sees me shiver, and knocks on the glass screen between the three of us and the driver, telling him to turn up the heating.

As we draw up to the entrance of the Galleria, she points out the two giant banners hanging down either side of the high, open archway and murmurs, 'You see how much faith Giovanni placed in you? The gamble he took on you was huge.'

The left banner, at least one hundred feet tall, features a colour photograph of a model with strong eye make-up and a sky-high beehive wearing a stunning red, vintage-style evening gown, the kind that Gia herself would kill to own. I realise belatedly that the dress looks vintage because the photograph itself is from another time, maybe the 1960s. And it's in Giovanni's signature red, *rosso Re*. It's from the start of his career.

The right banner depicts a model whose small, symmetrical face is dominated by smoky, smouldering eyes; her long, caramel-coloured hair is tousled and unbound, and pulled forward over her shoulders. She's wearing a gown that looks as if it's made of chain mail created from molten gold. Her hands are wrapped around the bejewelled pommel of a golden sword, which she's holding point down before her, like a medieval knight in a painting or on a tombstone. The model's long, narrow feet are bare and she looks like a pagan warrior queen, a powerful sorceress.

The two images side by side are so stunning, and so unlike each other, that it takes me a moment to realise that the figure on the right is Irina. It's the opening look from the parade, without the wings.

'When was it taken?' I whisper, craning my head up to study the vast image through the tinted windscreen of the limo. I would have remembered the sword. It would have made me recoil even more than the wings.

'When *we* arrived three days ago,' Gia replies softly. 'But before ... *you* did.'

Vladimir startles us both by saying loudly, 'We're in position.'

The car door on my side is suddenly thrown open and I have to shield my eyes from the sudden glare of camera flashes. Giovanni's head of security leans in and Vladimir hands me out towards him.

'Well, if it isn't Little Miss Crackhead,' I hear someone say nastily as I make my way under the arch, blinking as my eyes adjust to the level of light inside the Galleria.

In the strange way I sometimes have of seeing too much almost at once, I see that the building — a kind of glorified shopping mall that's four storeys high — is cruciform in layout, shaped like a giant cross. That fact alone raises instant goose flesh on the backs of my arms. It's formed of two covered arcades at right angles to each other, each with a vaulted, arched ceiling built of struts of iron and thousands of panes of glass. Where the two arcades meet in the middle, there's an octagonal space, topped by a giant glass and iron dome that has to be over one hundred and sixty feet across. The floors of the Galleria are inlaid with mosaic tiles that form symbols and patterns of great beauty and rich colour, and there are colourful painted scenes upon the pendentives beneath the gigantic dome. It's all stunningly beautiful.

The arcade I'm facing down forms the north–south axis of the cross. A team of black-clad men and women are putting the finishing touches to a narrow white catwalk that runs down its dead centre, and laying out white chairs in rows on either side. The catwalk features a circular platform that's centred beneath the giant dome, and narrows again as you move away from the dome towards the northern end of the arcade. There it ends abruptly in a white, featureless 'wall' with a concealed opening, which is actually one wall set in front of another that runs back behind the first. The effect is such that the people I see coming and going through the narrow aperture seem to suddenly just appear or disappear.

More people are busy setting out white chairs around the central, circular platform, while others are standing at the iron railings of the third-floor balconies, carefully making final adjustments to the false wall of giant video screens that hides the shopfronts inside the Galleria from the audience. It's as if real life is not allowed to intrude on the spectacle Giovanni has planned. I realise suddenly that all these people are busy turning this glorious building into a kind of giant blank canvas on which his final vision is to be projected.

Gia takes me by the arm as Juliana materialises in front of us, surrounded by security men in dark suits. There's a worried crease between her strong, dark brows, but a smile lightens her expression when she meets my eyes.

'You are just in time,' she says to us both. 'While they test the sound and the light, we make you ready, yes? Come this way.'

We're absorbed into Juliana's security detail and move as a group towards the northern end of the catwalk, through a sea of stares and whispers and gestures.

Someone abruptly turns on the lightshow. My hands fly up to my face in awe as the entire space — the blank white of the catwalk, the video screen-covered walls, even the chairs — is suddenly transformed into a moving, changing panorama of the universe. Giovanni has brought the cosmos inside: everywhere I turn, I see comets, black holes, supernovae, strange fissures in time and space, twisting and curling overhead, all around. Along one side of the arcade, a solid wall of stars melds into the weird towering shapes of stellar spires — so much like reaching fingers, the expelled breath of the universe itself. On the other, the remnants of supernovae morph into the surface of distant Io, then Saturn's rings, then the boiling fury of the sun. Celestial bodies wheel and turn all about us, in every colour, in every hue, as if painted by an artist's hand. And almost every person inside the Galleria stops what they're doing to witness these acts of creation and death, time itself, unfolding all around us, moving across our skin, our faces.

As we walk beneath the giant dome, it comes to life, dripping with a cobweb of tiny, sparkling blue lights. A blue so pale and luminescent it's almost the colour of holy fire.

And the music that suddenly bursts forth from the speakers is the operatic duet that was playing when I walked through the atrium of Atelier Re yesterday. Two voices, two *soprani*, singing a piercing melody so haunting, and so familiar, that I screw up my face in pain, trying to remember where I've heard it before, how I know it.

'It's the closing song,' Juliana bellows cheerfully. '*Your* song. You appear in the white bride's dress, the wings and *boom* — the voices, like the angels. The end. Happiness.'

Happiness?

It's too much for me to process. I feel as if I'm spinning weightlessly, out of control, through space as those disembodied *soprani* sing:

Sous le dôme épais
Où le blanc jasmin
Ah! Descendons
Ensemble!

It's French. Someone told me that once. From Léo
Delibes' *Lakmé*. The Flower Duet. And it means:
Under the thick dome where the white jasmine ... Ah!
We descend, together!

Lauren Daley and Jennifer Appleton sang that
duet together one night, at an inter-school concert in
the tiny town of Paradise. After that, their lives were
never the same again.

I don't believe in fate. I believe in coincidence,
that's how I'm wired. But when I hear the words Paul
Stenborg uttered in another life, in Carmen's life,
coming at me from the surround-sound system at a
volume loud enough to split my head open, I actually
swoon. I fall to the ground.

And the uncaring universe that swirls and turns
and changes above me, that reminds me so much of
home, goes dark for a little while.

✎

'Irina?'

'It's a gigantic publicity stunt, I tell you.' It's a woman's voice, malicious. Hint of an Irish accent. 'The gold dress should've been mine, anyway. Couldn't you just see it with my hair? I told Giovanni it was a mistake to cast her, from the word *go*.'

'Irina?'

'*Was ist los?*' Another woman, speaking German, sounding curious.

Voices are coming at me from everywhere, in languages I don't ever recall knowing or speaking — Japanese, Dutch, Korean, Chinese, Italian, Spanish, Sudanese — almost all asking: *What's wrong with Irina? What's she on? What's she playing at? What's her game?*

I open my eyes to find that I'm backstage. I've been carried behind that blank white wall at the northern end of the building. I'm slumped untidily in a raised armchair before a mirror surrounded by light bulbs. It's a make-up chair, I realise, as I see, on either side of me, models having their faces touched up or painted, all craning their swanlike necks, trying to get a look at me between brushstrokes. There are people everywhere, crammed into this narrow area alongside racks and racks of mind-blowingly beautiful, intricately detailed gowns. Some are in various states of undress, curlers piled high atop their heads; others clutch the weapons of beauty in their hands: brushes, dryers, tongs. A parade of elongated, idiosyncratic beauties passes behind my chair constantly, all wearing that fearsome demon facepaint Tommy devised: smoky eyes touched with gold, strong brows, and blood-red lips and nails.

I see Irina's face in the mirror. Free of any make-up.

Giovanni's, Juliana's, Gudrun's, Gia's and Tommy's faces are reflected there, too, crowded around Irina, all looking concerned.

And my own face is reflected there, though visible only to me and to Gudrun. She meets my eyes, knowingly, in the mirror and I wonder again why she always wears modest, high-necked, old lady's blouses when she has such killer curves.

'Say something,' Tommy pleads in his light, silvery voice. 'Don't tell me you fractured that multimillion-dollar skull of yours when you went down.'

'You say she has the trouble with her *feet*,' Juliana murmurs to Gia. 'Not the balance. Feet and balance together — that's very bad. How can she walk?'

I see Gudrun — her skin faintly gleaming, but only

to my eyes — wrap one of Giovanni's arms in hers. She pats him on the hand reassuringly, her blood-red nails glistening.

'It's too late to change the banner now,' Giovanni confides to her worriedly. 'It must remain. But Orla will have her way. We must end with the silver gown.'

A woman with flaming red hair, dressed in a heavily beaded, blue-green bustier, blue jeans and bare feet, gives an excited little clap at the periphery of my sight.

'Over my dead body,' I say, refocusing the attention of everyone gathered around me. 'And, clearly, I'm not dead.'

The redhead's expression congeals as Tommy calls, 'Let's do this, people! In ten. From the top.'

I place my hands upon the padded armrests of my chair and hoist myself upright, then lift my arms resignedly as a phalanx of complete strangers rushes at me, shouting at me to take my clothes off and *for heaven's sake, be quick about it.*

When we return to the hotel suite around midnight, I'm in no mood to talk.

'Get some rest,' Gia says at the door to my bedroom. 'You were unbelievable today — I had shivers down my spine every time you appeared. And when Orla stepped on the hem of her silver dress and fell out of it *and* her shoes right before you came out in the fantasy bridal gown, I nearly died laughing.'

'Just one more day ... Mercy,' she says my name hesitantly, 'then maybe you'll get to go ... home.'

I don't reply. I just lock myself inside the ensuite bathroom and stare at my reflection, at Irina's, and shed her clothing as if it is contaminated.

Then I sit on the floor of the marble shower stall and just let the water pound down on me for a while.

When I fall asleep, it's as if I slide into a black and formless pit.

It's out of habit that I reach for Luc in my dreams, search for that slender thread that continues to bind us together, even though I still can't reconcile the horrors I witnessed through his eyes, through the news footage, with the Luc I love and remember.

Instead, I find myself in a blank, black void, deprived of every sense. It's never happened before, and I can't even call out Luc's name because nothing's working.

I can't feel him out there.

It's as if I've been shut down, or shut out.

It's as if the connection between us — that's always been there, always — has been severed.

When I wake suddenly and turn my head to look at the clock on the bedside table, it's already 10.05 in the morning. My cheeks are wet with tears. Because that feeling of absolute disconnect can only mean that Luc's badly injured, even ... dead.

I sit bolt upright and have to stop myself from letting loose a scream to shake this building to its foundations. Gia doesn't need to see Irina, me, *us*, caving in.

He's been my only true friend, my constant companion. How do I make you understand what this sense of absence ... feels like?

There's a roaring in my ears, darkness in my eyes. It feels as if I've lost my hold on the physical world. My mind is suddenly crowded with memories: of the two of us in our sacred garden, our perfect place; of Luc laughing, his golden head of hair thrown back, revealing the sinuous line of his throat; of Luc dazzling me, almost scaring me, with his feats of grand magic; of Luc placing my happiness first in all things, disregarding everyone and everything else around us.

He'd said he existed to amuse me. He'd said he existed to prove what love *could* be.

And he'd said:

You are the best and most loved thing in my life — let nothing ever be possible, or complete, if you are not with me. And may the elements witness my vow in all their silent glory.

I can't help it, I let out a wail that has sharp edges to it — a sound of such terrible grief and loss and mourning, that Gia bursts through the door of my bedroom at a run.

From inside the cavernous, black limo, I stare up, numbly, at the hundred foot image of Irina that stands guard at the entryway to the Galleria.

I don't even know if Luc's alive.

I feel emptied out, incapable of feeling anything right now.

Maybe I don't know who he is any more, and maybe I won't like what he's become since we've been physically apart, but I can't imagine a life, any sort of life, without Luc.

It's something that will take major adjusting to, and right now I have no time. I can feel it getting away from me again, reeling out of my hands like an angler's line.

I just hope They do it properly this time when they shift me — so that I forget everything. It was almost simpler when I didn't remember, because I had no concept of what it was possible to lose.

CHAPTER 17

'It's just gone noon,' Gia says gently, casting me her thousandth sideways glance of concern for the day, 'and the parade's set for four with cocktails at six, dinner for the chosen ones at eight then the afterparty from midnight onwards. As soon as the parade finishes, I'll meet you backstage, but before then, you're on your own. Juliana doesn't want any extra bodies back there — it's already a tight squeeze. She's somehow managed to wangle a front-row seat for me beneath the dome. Just do what you did yesterday, okay? And you'll be helping Giovanni, Irina and all those poor people ...'

We look at each other sombrely, recalling how we'd watched the world burn from our six-star hotel room.

The limo's door is opened from the outside and Vladimir hands me out onto the red carpet that's already been laid from the Piazza straight into the Galleria's arched entryway. There's the usual wall of noise and faces and camera flashes, but it's all being kept at one remove by the golden ropes cordoning off the red carpet. I look neither left nor right as I hurry towards the entrance, Vladimir's unyielding hand at my back.

Gia gives my elbow a squeeze from behind as we walk under the giant arch. When I look back, she's nowhere to be seen, but Giovanni's pretty people are everywhere: counting chairs, consulting lists, consulting together, pointing, shifting name plates, placing a gift bound with signature red ribbon upon each seat. Black-clad technicians, wearing headphones and security cards strung on lanyards, are doing sound, mic and lighting checks all over the building.

The dome is already lit palely blue as Vladimir and I hurry beneath it towards the backstage area, and I shiver, recalling the sound that Luc's sword made when it struck Nuriel's, the way the blades crackled when they came together, the way Luc had casually turned the fire of his wrath upon the sleeping innocent. Or maybe I'd done that. I shake my head, unable to get those images of a burning world out of my mind, unable to suppress the terrible feeling that it was somehow all my fault.

Vladimir melts away as soon as I'm seated for hair and make-up.

'This is it then,' an Englishwoman I don't recognise says cheerfully as she grabs my long hair and twists it into a rough topknot. She rubs something abrasive into my face and I have to close my eyes.

'If only it were,' I murmur in Irina's thick accent, wishing They would take me now.

'Carefully! *Carefully*,' Juliana gripes as two people wrestle the golden wings onto my shoulders and tighten the leather straps of the harness. I can't help the chill that ripples across my skin when they all step back, satisfied.

'No shoes,' Tommy interrupts from the side. 'Ditch the flats, they're so wrong. I've changed my mind. She can carry it off in bare feet. Just like in the banner. Look at her. Perfection.'

I glance at the full-length mirror someone has positioned alongside me and think the heavy shadow ringing my eyes, my unbound, teased up, matted, madwoman hair and glistening, blood-red mouth make me look sick. My eyes skitter away from the reflection of the golden wings that rise from Irina's narrow shoulders. I can't bear to look at them for too long; just seeing them makes me dizzy.

'Half an hour!' a woman in headphones yells as she moves through the chaos backstage. 'Half an hour! Positions, people. Places.'

We line up in a snaking line: fourteen flat-chested, freakishly tall women of varying ages in garish make-up and fourteen very different looks, each accessorised with a pair of wings. Some, like mine, are so large that their end feathers trail upon the floor; some are so small and diaphanous they're barely noticeable. When I look at any of them, I get a sick feeling in my stomach and have to swallow hard.

What are you waiting for? I rail silently at the six who remain. *Shift me now, damn you. Why make me participate in this inglorious farce?*

'Break a leg, my beauties!' Tommy calls out as he moves up the line towards me with Juliana and Giovanni in tow. He runs his eyes across each of us, adjusting a wing span here, a neckline there.

When the three of them reach me, Juliana and Tommy step back behind Giovanni respectfully as he raises my hands, kissing them before releasing them.

'My dear,' he says, 'you and I — we have come a long way, yes? When you look like this, it makes it possible to forget how much is wrong with this world. I thank you — for putting aside your pain, your demons; for putting me first.'

I see his eyes grow shiny with emotion and look down hurriedly, feeling my eyes sting in answer. My pain is always with me, it can never be put aside, it has made me who I am.

And my demons? My own personal demons? They have not yet arrived to drive my soul into another body. And so I wait, going through the motions of Irina's bizarre, high-octane life while They tarry, doing who knows what?

I raise my head as the classical music they've had playing on a loop during the lightshow winds down to its last few bars.

Tommy says, 'Shake the floor, Irina! Like the giant you are. Bring the house down.'

And I walk out of there, the way K'el told me to. Without looking back.

The pounding techno opening track bursts out of the loudspeakers and the awe-inspiring lightshow universe immediately winks out.

I emerge onto the catwalk as if by black magic, and the spotlights go up, white hot, so it's impossible to make out the features of the audience members in the darkness beyond the front row.

The entire room seems to give a collective gasp as I stand there motionless for a full minute — the way I've been told to — the light striking off the surface of the golden paillettes that cover my gown, like armour deflecting arrow strike. All down the arcade, the giant video screens show images of me from every angle. There must be cameras positioned everywhere. I know I'm dazzling. I may not be able to make out most of the audience immediately, but I can feel every eye on me as I stand, holding my pose, arms loosely at my sides, golden feathers cascading down my back and trailing onto the floor behind my bare feet.

As the track segues into something even louder, faster, fiercer, I look down the bright white line of the catwalk. *All that exists*, I tell myself, *is this present. Don't think about what could happen. You have no past, and no future. It's all been erased. Or it's about to be. And you'll have to start again, like you always do.*

That's how it has to be from now on. Without the things that have always anchored me, without Luc, without Ryan, it will always and forever be about living in the moment. I feel a surge of pain that almost makes me crumple. Almost.

Just breathe, says my inner demon again, through my anguish. *Just walk. Don't screw it up.*

Then I begin to stalk down the runway, my tousled, mussed-up, centre-parted hair flying back behind me and tangling with the beaten-metal feathers of my golden wings. As I walk, the video screen shows a magnified image of my form in side profile, the three of us moving fluidly down the runway at the same pace.

I'm walking so quickly, so surely, that I swiftly cover the distance to the circular platform beneath the overarching dome. I pause there and stare down at the expectant faces that are turned up towards me, my eyes searching for Gia in the front row as I place my hands on my hips and angle my body aggressively to the right and glare the way I remember Irina does, to remind people she's the main event. My eyes move along the curve of the front-row patrons seated below and I catch sight of Gia's familiar glossy, China-girl hair, her down bent head as she puts something in the handbag tucked beneath her feet.

Why isn't she even looking at me? I think, irritated, as she turns to say something to the young man seated beside her.

The world seems to telescope weirdly as I take in his dark eyes that look almost black in the harsh light, the dark shadows beneath them, his pale face, the hectic spots of colour high on his high cheekbones. Gia may be murmuring in his ear, but she can't hold his attention. When he pushes a familiar lock of dark hair out of his eyes, I think my confident stance falters, and he immediately stretches out one hand to me, as if he's afraid that I might fall.

I almost bend down and take his hand.

Ryan, I think dazedly. *What are you doing here?*

I hadn't thought we'd ever meet again. In any life. I feel a surge of joy that's immediately subsumed by an intense sorrow.

Not for you, Gabriel had told me. Twice now, I've been forced to leave Ryan, against my will. If I'm forced to leave him again — and I know it's coming; there's nothing more certain — I don't know what it would do to him. Or to me.

Gia catches my eye, and grins when she sees all the longing in my gaze, my eyes moving possessively over his face. *Surprise*, she mouths.

I forget where I am and actually smile at her, in thanks for this small thing of beauty she's wrought for me.

And that smile lights up Irina's bored-looking, haughty, high-fashion little face. I know, because I see it reflected back on all the video screens, the smile shining out of her dark eyes. People actually whistle and stamp their feet, shouting their approval.

Some of the cameras pick up Ryan's face and project us both along the video wall. My face, then his, mine, then his, all down the length of the building on both sides.

Ryan looks down, embarrassed, and the cameras catch that, too. People laugh in sympathy, murmuring at his beauty.

Later, Gia mouths, gesturing with her hands. *Keep moving.*

I suddenly remember where I am and force myself to stand straighter, making subtle adjustments to my stance, the muscles of my face. *Glower, smoulder, pout. Check.*

It's almost physically painful to rip my eyes away from Ryan and cross the circular platform towards the front-row patrons seated on the other side, but I promised Gia and Giovanni, Juliana and Tommy, that I could do this, that Irina would meet all her obligations. So that is what I do, even though every bone in my body is telling me to grab that boy and run. Flee. Before They find me and shift me again.

But it's impossible, what I want. Somewhere in this building is my watcher, K'el. I'll never be able to flee the gathered *elohim*. It's just a silly pipe dream. So somehow I do it: I walk away from Ryan.

I'm right in the middle of Irina's signature *pause, angle, pause, angle* manoeuvre when a golden-haired couple sitting just beneath me catch my eye. They're so handsome together that they seem to cast the people on either side of them into a dull light. Even in the hyper-bright glare, the golden-haired couple seem to gleam faintly to my eyes.

And I recognise the woman as Giovanni's executive assistant, Gudrun. The tall, handsome man seated beside her, with reflective, rock-star aviator sunglasses on, wind-ruffled hair and the barest hint of golden stubble along his jawline, takes me a second longer to place.

When I do, I feel my blood freeze.

I recognise his clothes before I recognise him, because I hadn't been expecting to see him here, or maybe ever again. He's in a sharp, narrow-cut, single-breasted, three-piece navy suit with a thin navy pinstripe running through the weave, a Windsor-knotted tie in iridescent colours like the sheen on a dragonfly's wings. The whole ensemble only emphasises his snake-hipped, broad-shouldered, long and lean form. He lifts one hand to remove his sunglasses and light glances off the giant faceted sapphire he's using as a cufflink. As he tucks the glasses into the top pocket of his suit, his pale blue eyes — like broken water, like living ice — burn into mine. And he makes a gun of the fingers of his right hand, the muzzle pointed in my direction, before he laughs and runs the hand through his golden hair.

Luc! I cry, for his ears alone. *You're alive!*

Did you expect anything else, my love? he replies in my head, laughter in his warm, rich voice. *When you've always been the prize?*

I don't know what I'm feeling. Hope? Love? Anger? Confusion?

And I can't help my gaze from flying from Luc back to Ryan, from Ryan to Luc. Many in the front-row seats on both sides of the catwalk catch my movements, and a small murmur starts up around me that seems to spread out into the crowd like wildfire. People point and stare.

The video cameras pick up both men's faces for the benefit of those further back in the audience, projecting them onto the banks of video screens — and the room bursts into an open speculation that's audible above the volume of the music. Though Luc and Ryan couldn't be more differently dressed, and one is so fair, the other so dark, it's clear that they could be twins, so physically similar are they.

Gia's eyes widen in shock as she looks across the circular platform at Luc. The look is mirrored on Gudrun's face as she studies Ryan's features with her enormous, sapphire-blue eyes.

Seeing them together like this, in a way I never thought would happen, it's a shock to me, too, that I so evidently have a 'type'. That out of all the mortals in this teeming world I could have fallen for, I had to go and find someone who is the spitting image of Luc.

Only a few feet separate Ryan and Gia from Luc and Gudrun. And the antagonism Luc and Ryan are radiating at each other is so strong I can feel it from where I'm standing, caught in the middle. It's like a poisonous cloud hanging over all of us, so strong I can almost see it.

The tension doesn't go unnoticed, and camera flashes go off in the press gallery located at the end of the catwalk as photographers strain forward for shots of both men. I can see the headlines now. Luc will show up as a smear of bright, white light, if they're lucky. If he shows up at all.

'Irina!' Gia hisses as the jarring techno track makes way for a smoky jazz standard that has nothing to do with the dress I'm wearing and everything to do with look number two.

I look down at her dazedly.

'Keep walking,' she says. '*Time*. Time's getting away from you. We'll sort this mess out later. *Move*.'

Her words send my heart into overdrive and I tear my gaze away from Luc, away from Ryan, and lurch up the catwalk in my dress of molten gold. I stare down the barrel of all the lenses of the world's fashion press with my haunted, fearful eyes, then sweep back up the catwalk and behind the blank white wall at the catwalk's end, without pausing.

Juliana grips my sleeves tightly and says fiercely, 'Tommy's waiting, go, *go*. Lila and Kirsten can make up the time — I will send them together. *Go*.'

I stumble into Tommy's waiting arms, and feel hands reach out to strip me of my golden armour, because I can't seem to make myself move any more.

When I emerge onto the catwalk in my second look — the jaunty, black tricorn hat and face veil atop that sinful black dress with the barely there bodice and full skirt lined in shocking pink, those black wings — I look at no one and nothing but the bright white line of the catwalk, clutching the black leather horse whip they've placed under one arm like it's a life belt. I pass beneath the dome and I don't look around and I don't stop walking.

They're both still there, I can feel it. That, and my building terror.

I pause for the delectation of the world's press, then pivot sharply and head back up the catwalk towards the dome.

All I can think about is Luc's plan, back before he somehow managed to get a lock on my position in Milan. Luc had said: find the boy, give the Eight the slip, get back to Paradise and wait it out for him.

But Ryan isn't needed any more, because Luc's found me. Somehow he got away from Nuriel. Luc's here.

Ryan's here, too. And Luc's seen him.

My kind think people like Ryan are disposable.

Luc has the power to crush Ryan like an insect.

The thought makes me falter, visibly, and I have to pause on the circular platform beneath the twinkling dome.

The moment I do, thunder loud enough to shake the glass and iron roof of the Galleria suddenly booms in the sky above us, drowning out the driving soundtrack. It's quickly followed by lightning so bright that the glassed-in roof — in the shape of a vast cross — turns an eye-searing white for an instant.

Talk immediately ripples through the well-heeled audience, and continues as I stagger back into the marshalling area.

They don't know, you see, that the storm that was promised, that storm for the ages, it's here. It's finally come.

Just as Luc has.

First fire, then flood. He never does things in small measures.

Juliana squeezes my forearms and says in her thick Italian accent, '*Magnifico*. Now you must think the happy thoughts, the thoughts of the bride, okay? Think of light, of love. It is almost finished.'

Love?

As first the wings then the black dress are taken off me, piece by complicated piece, and hands tug the lacy, fitted white bodice of the bridal gown down over my head, I think: It is almost over.

And when the last of the players arrive, there will be fear and pain, reprisals and death. An accounting.

CHAPTER 18

Orla takes her time coming off the catwalk in her strapless, silver screen-siren dress, and bumps into me deliberately as I stand in the wings clutching a bouquet of gardenia, white rose and lily, a small sparkling tiara set forward on my crown, my long, toffee-coloured hair wrapped into a smooth and complicated topknot. *The happy bride.* That's what I'm supposed to be.

Orla just ends up hurting herself, because I do not yield. She just glances off me — a moving force hitting an immovable object — and almost loses her balance, coming down out of one shoe again. 'Bitch!' she shouts, rubbing her bare shoulder, her usually pale complexion almost as violent a red as her dyed hair. There's a large bruise already forming upon her skin where we made contact.

She limps away, holding one shoe, and I walk out of the wings with my head held high.

Think light and love. Right.

Then *that song* bursts forth out of the speakers and I begin to tremble.

The Flower Duet, impossibly lovely, so moving that people immediately begin to clap and whistle when they see me. Some rise to their feet.

I curtsy gracefully — the way I was taught to do, like a dancer — and begin to walk slowly down the runway, holding my bouquet lightly in my clasped and shaking hands, looking straight ahead despite my tension and the weight of the white snowy wings upon my shoulders.

I don't look at my golden beloved, who has finally run me to ground after all these years.

I don't look at Ryan, whose life may now be counted in minutes, in mere seconds.

I hear K'el's voice in my head again, saying: *Not for us, that 'lifelong partnership' that's said to unite mortal woman and mortal man in heart, in mind, in body. We are elohim, Mercy.*

Not for me, then, the fate of the happy bride.

I suddenly spot something in the back row, to my right. A cloud of light building about the head and neck of a short, paunchy, balding human male. The light seems to grow in density, it begins to coalesce. And K'el seems to step backwards out of the body in which he'd been disguised, the human slumping forward suddenly in his chair, as if he's asleep.

K'el takes up position in front of one of the giant video screens, as five others, all over the room, do the same — pull themselves free of the human hosts they'd hidden themselves in, coalescing and assuming their customary forms. All of them are male and, to my eyes, all are luminescent.

They position themselves equidistantly, three behind Luc, three behind Ryan. Six archangels. All lethal, all familiar, all beautiful.

It begins.

The humans in this vast space are so busy looking at me that they haven't registered the six of them faintly silhouetted against the chaotic wall of ever-changing video screens. From beneath my downswept lashes I recognise Gabriel, Uriel and Barachiel on Ryan's side of the room; Jeremiel, K'el and Michael on Luc's side.

Something seems to leap in me when I see them all, gathered together. My people, my brethren, once like brothers to me.

I can actually see them. I am permitted to gaze upon them. For now, I am part of their world again.

Gabriel inclines his head at me in greeting, while Uriel scowls — exactly the way I would. Barachiel's face is expressionless, as I knew it would be given our history together; we were always too alike for comfort. Jeremiel regards me steadily with his silver gaze. K'el looks down, away from me, and Michael's black gaze seems to burn holes in the very air between us.

But something's wrong. Raphael and Selaphiel I knew to be missing, but where is Jegudiel?

K'el is a stand-in for the missing, I realise suddenly, but he's nowhere near as powerful as any of the Eight.

And Nuriel?

What has Luc done to her?

As I sweep onto the platform, into that space between them all, time stands still. Time, and the world, and everything in it.

'You're too late,' Luc says smoothly, standing suddenly and turning towards Michael behind him.

Gudrun rises with him. Her hand is on his arm, his hand over hers protectively. My eyes narrow as I see something that hadn't been apparent to me until now. They're a couple. They're actually *together*.

That roaring returns, that darkness rises in me, and for a moment I feel again as if I've lost my hold on the physical world. I have no place, no centre, no anchor. I am rage, I am pain. I'm freefalling.

I step towards Luc, swept by a sudden, incandescent fury at his betrayal. I throw the corny bridal bouquet at the back of his head and it disappears, turned to ash as it touches him. It's such a mortal, puny gesture. I have no weaponry. I'm defenceless against my anguish.

'How could you?' I shriek, and he turns. 'You just ... replaced me? When? When did this happen? Recently? Or the second I was *exiled*?'

I don't catch them moving, but Jeremiel, K'el and Michael are suddenly closer to us, moving through the still forms of all the humans now frozen, mid-whistle, mid-applause, like mannequins themselves. I'm sure that, behind me, Gabriel, Uriel and Barachiel have done the same, started closing that shark net in which I am the live bait.

They were never going to shift me first, I realise suddenly. They were always going to wait until they'd drawn Luc here. That, too, makes me furious — to be used in such a way.

Something dangerous flashes in his ice-blue eyes. 'I don't need to explain myself to *you*,' Luc snarls at me. 'When you left, you took everything from me; you ruined my life in that instant. *Everything* changed. Because of you, I've been trapped on this earth, caged like an animal, for centuries. Gudrun has made the intervening *age*,' he spits the word, 'significantly less of a trial.'

Gudrun looks up at me with open hostility in her bright, sapphire eyes and I recoil as Luc pulls her closer. They're so obviously made for each other, such a matched set, that I wonder how he ever could have thought I was *the one*. Does he love and desire her the way he claimed to have loved and desired *me*?

For a moment, I'm so disoriented I stumble and almost fall.

I look nothing like her. I have none of the easy charm she displays around people. She's my opposite in almost every way. Compliant. Womanly. So clearly not Luc's equal, and nor does she strive to be.

And she's no archangel, I realise suddenly, despite her luminous beauty. She might have been, once. But no longer. Not for a long time. But what is she now?

Gudrun places one hand on the fussy silk bow at the throat of her high-necked blouse and actually growls at me. Like a panther. I rock back on my heels, my horror etched on my face.

'I warned you,' Gabriel interjects, his voice steely. 'You have little idea of how much your "beloved" has changed. He is not the one you remember. Stand aside, Mercy. Let it all end here. Let *us* deal with Luc as he should be dealt with. And when it is done, you will be free to go where you wish, be who you wish. We will no longer have any claim over you and you will no longer pose a threat to the order of anything, anywhere.'

When I stand there, still transfixed with shame and fury and envy by the sight of Luc with the bombshell he replaced me with, Gabriel says more gently, '*Soror.*' Sister. I look down at him.

'Turn away. Cover your eyes. And when we are done and gone, get that boy safely home.'

Gabriel raises his hand and I turn to follow it, and see Ryan, his seated, frozen form, his eyes fixed on the empty air where I'd been standing only seconds before. There's that look in his eyes. Of love. For me. Captured there for all to witness.

Horror rises up in me again. Gabriel's right. Ryan will always be vulnerable to those of our kind who wish him harm. I need to get him out of here.

I nod to show that I've understood, and back away from Luc's achingly familiar, achingly beautiful form, all my dreams of him, of home, of our secret garden, like ashes now, too.

'That's it?' Luc throws back his head and laughs. 'You think I'm afraid of you *six*? K'el is no substitute for the great Raphael — who was not easy to subdue, I'll admit. He's no substitute even for that weakling Selaphiel. As for Nuriel? We have her, and we'll keep her for as long as we deem it necessary. She's not particularly … comfortable, but she's still alive. If barely.'

I see Gabriel and Uriel exchange worried glances.

Luc laughs again, and his voice has a ringing, grating edge to it that makes me want to clap my hands over my ears in pain. 'Which means you stay exactly where you are, *Mercy*. You and I are nowhere near finished.'

I can't summon any words of defiance. Truly, all I have left are feelings. While I somehow manage to find the strength to hold Luc's gaze, I am being slowly torn apart inside, as if by wolves.

I feel Gabriel leap lightly onto the platform beside me. He places a strong hand upon my back, and from it flows the strength to defy the one whom I would have died for. Years ago, aeons.

'We *are* finished,' I tell Luc bitterly. 'I don't recognise you, and I don't want to know who you've become. I've wasted enough time holding out hope that we'd be together again, the way we used to be. This is the point where I get out of the frame, at long last. You *disgust* me.'

I'm turning away from him, from them all, when Luc suddenly calls out my name. My true name. And I wrap my arms around my head in agony.

It's like I'm the only still point in a spinning, screaming world, and I fall to my knees, sweating and shaking, my own name a weapon of absolute control.

As I fall forward onto the runway — deaf and blind to everything except the shattering noises in my head — the entire room comes alive around us.

It only takes seconds for people to register the eight shining beings gathered around my prone form on the catwalk, growing in stature right before our eyes, becoming giants until they tower over everyone present. Become less and less human. More and more luminous, more beautiful. Grow *wings*.

Then swords of pure flame ignite in their hands, crackling with energy, and the air around me begins to superheat as six move to contain two.

People begin to shriek and scramble backwards, away from us. I sit up slowly on the runway, head pounding, eyes watering.

Luc raises one hand casually and the vast space is suddenly plunged into a terrible darkness in which the only visible things are the eight beings surrounding me.

One by one the video screens go up in flames along the length of the arcade, so that those who have not already made it to the southern exit turn and flee for the east–west axis of the cross-shaped building, screaming in terror, trampling others in their desperation to flee the flames.

The darkness is lit by fire, by the screens of mobile phones, by eerie flashes of lightning from above. Around us is utter chaos; the theory of that man Darwin in motion.

'Mercy!' I hear Ryan shouting somewhere behind me. 'Mercy! Where are you?'

I turn to look for him, but all the chairs have been swept aside. There are bodies everywhere, people pushing and buffeting each other. The smell of burning plastic and circuitry is intense and acrid.

'We have no quarrel with you,' I hear Barachiel say to Gudrun as she edges towards me, as if for safety. 'Stand aside from him and you get to live.'

K'el, Jeremiel, Uriel and Gabriel close in around Luc's golden, watchful form.

Michael turns his head of short, black curls in my direction, fury in his black eyes and raises his blazing blade. '*Flee*,' he roars at me, at Gudrun. 'You will have little stomach for what we are about to do to the one you each call your *beloved*.'

'Kneel,' he bellows at Luc, judgment in his bell-like voice. 'Submit. There is no one left to pray to. He turned from you when you turned from Him. I should have finished you properly the first time.'

The six close their circle around Luc, intending to sacrifice him here, before us all.

Through the screams of the injured and terrified, I hear Ryan again. 'Mercy! *Mercy!* Tell me you're still here.'

I swing my head in his direction, shouting, 'Ryan! Yes, I'm here. *I'm still here*. Don't move — I'm —'

Then Luc does it again. He roars my name and I'm as good as dead. Bent double in agony, I can't hear, can't see, can't speak. All because Raphael once thought it a good idea to hide the memory of my name inside me, so deep that I can't recognise it, or bear to hear it, without going haywire.

Gudrun seizes me by the throat then, lifting my mortal form easily off the ground.

Michael frowns; the other five exchange glances. But their watchful stances never vary. They are here for Luc first and foremost.

'Let her die,' Michael says dismissively, turning away from Gudrun, from me. 'At heart, she's one of *you* anyway. Do your worst, demon.'

Demon? Is that what she is?

Is that what Michael and the others really think of me?

I am filled with so much rage and shock and hurt, that my clenched left fist begins to blaze in agony and I kick out, almost breaking free of Gudrun's imprisoning hold. She digs the fingers of her right hand harder into the flesh of Irina's throat as Michael and Luc circle around us slowly, blades raised and rippling with a pale blue luminescence.

As I struggle to get air into Irina's lungs, to stay conscious, Michael's black eyes clash briefly with mine before they slide away. My shock deepens when I realise that he's doing this deliberately. He's actually trying to provoke me, and somehow, just for a moment, I could divine his intent. Anger can be used; it can be channelled, his gaze seemed to say. There must be no surrender. The realisation only makes me struggle harder, though my eyes are failing, and my movements are growing feeble and unfocused.

Luc's voice is amused. 'Still haven't worked it all out yet, my love? You didn't used to be so *slow*.'

Lightning splits the sky above the Galleria again and I see Ryan gripping the edge of the catwalk about ten feet away to my left, people pushing and shoving past him like a living tide. His own eyes widen in shock when he sees Irina dangling like a doll in a bride's dress and crumpled wings at the end of Gudrun's arm.

The others don't see Ryan vault up onto the runway, staying low. And I can't warn him to keep away, not to try anything heroic, because Gudrun's crushing my windpipe in her right hand, the nails blood red.

Flames suddenly burst up the sides of the runway and Ryan dives out of view. At the edges of my sight, I see the hysteria worsen as people are hemmed in by flames on all sides. They change direction multiple times, like a stampeding herd. People go down and stay down, lie still.

'Don't you understand?' Luc says calmly, facing down the tip of Michael's flaming broadsword without flinching. 'My trap is sprung within yours. It has already closed around you all — *most holy, most high*.' He throws his golden head back and laughs.

'It is you who must kneel. I have a special vengeance reserved for all of you; but for you, Michael, I have something truly exceptional in mind.'

Luc raises his blazing blade aloft and light seeps up out of the mosaic floor in multiple locations, twines swiftly around the ankles of all the people pushing desperately for the exits, slides over the still bodies of the prone, before coalescing into shining shapes that move rapidly towards the catwalk and rise unscathed through fire. They gather upon the catwalk, a shining army, a score of them at least. All beautiful, all tall, all lethal. They must be part of Luc's personal guard; the most fearsome of his legion: his *daemonium*.

They are winged as the archangels are — for that is what they once must have been. And they are still indistinguishable from us, save that most are in shining raiment that is high-necked or long-sleeved. Not for them, the glowing, sleeveless raiment of the six archangels they now surround. They are truly our opposite, in attitude and appetite.

Swords ignite in their hands as they fall upon Michael, upon Barachiel, Jeremiel, Gabriel, Uriel, until their shining forms are engulfed. I hear the sizzle as blade meets blade, and the air is a whirl of limbs, wings, ambient light.

K'el, the weakest of the six, is engaged by five of Luc's forces at once, and immediately takes to the air, trying to shake them off. Uriel, too, suddenly ascends — as if he would protect K'el — parrying the blades of the two beings that harry him, one from each side.

People scream and point upwards as they flee.

I kick and twist within the grip of Gudrun's crushing fist but she is like a creature of legend, a stone giantess. Darkness invades my sight once more as Irina's body begins to suffocate, to die.

Luc turns to Gudrun and gives her the kind of smile that once would have brought me to my knees with love.

'Give her to me,' he says. 'Alive or dead, I still have use for her. The moment is upon us, my dear. It begins tonight.'

Gudrun throws me down onto the catwalk, and I suck greedily at the tainted air, searching through the smoke and flames and darkness for Ryan. But he's nowhere to be seen.

Luc's sword vanishes into the palm of his hand and he crosses the short distance to me, looks down upon my bowed, human head.

'I told you something once — in a fit of love-struck madness,' he says. 'Do you remember it?'

I close my eyes briefly and nod, remembering the two of us entwined in our secret garden, the air heavy with the scent of a thousand different blooms that no human hand could possibly have put together.

You are the best and most loved thing in my life — let nothing ever be possible, or complete, if you are not with me. And may the elements witness my vow in all their silent glory.

My eyes sting in remembrance. How happy I'd been then. I hadn't known that happiness would be denied me, all the years thereafter.

'That was my undoing,' he whispers. 'My vow *was* witnessed, and it has dogged me all of my days upon this earth. It is the supreme irony that without you, I am nothing. I have power, but only so much; a kingdom, but such a poor, mean kingdom with no hope of expansion or conquest. Until now. Now, your soul is mine again. And it shall free me.'

I recoil at his words as if I've been spat upon. He speaks of kingdoms and conquests when all the universe was once ours to play in. What happened to us?

Luc raises me up with one gleaming hand, and I am forced to look into his eyes, so far above me, that are so pale, so glorious, and yet contain so much darkness. I never saw that darkness when he appeared to me in my dreams. He is indeed a liar of talent, the best there ever was.

'Tonight,' he murmurs, 'I begin the reclamation of what I have lost. And you shall witness me bring the kingdoms of earth and of Heaven to their knees, so that I may be God at last, over all.'

He places the heel of one shining hand upon my forehead and I am transfixed by his touch, as if by a live current. I can neither breathe nor struggle, though my mouth is stretched wide in a silent scream.

My left hand ignites. It bursts into a searing white flame that is as coruscating as it is beautiful.

And all around me, I see an answering flame — shining from Luc, from Gudrun, from all of his winged warriors, his *daemonium*.

Each of them bears a glowing wound that is suddenly visible beneath the long-sleeved, high-necked raiment that they wear. Some bear scars at the base of the throat — as Gudrun does — some upon the shoulder, the centre of the back. Many are scarred upon their forearms, or their upper arms. Some bear one scar, others two.

Even Luc bears a glowing scar right in the centre of his broad chest, visible beneath the human clothing he has assumed. The size of an archangel's handprint.

They are all marked, as I am.

In some way, they are all exiles, too.

But there is no time to ponder the mystery. The pain of Luc's touch is excruciating — it's as if my soul is being destroyed, or transfigured.

His touch reaches down into Irina's skull, into her flesh and bones, the very matter of which she's made. He's drawing me out, coil by resistant coil. He's following the switchbacks and false trails, the broken pattern that I've somehow been cast into. He is irradiating me with his fire, seeking to remake me, remould me.

And I see, I see —

— that final, fatal moment in which Luc and I were the epicentre of something vast, a conflagration waiting to happen, an ache in time, a breath suspended. The Eight arrayed against us, weapons of power raised, a shining multitude gathered behind them. Behind Luc and me, another shining multitude. Two halves of a people that had once been whole and united.

I remember Luc's words: 'Then, as an act of faith — of *goodwill*, shall we call it — take that which is most precious to me.' His tone is final, without emotion, as he says, 'I permit it.'

And I remember that searing pain in my left hand, feel it now. But this time the world does not go blank and white. This time, I do not block what happened from my mind.

This time, when I relive that moment, the moment when my left hand sustained the wound that begot all wounds thereafter, my memories do not twist and shatter like glass. I live them as if that time is now, not some long ago yesterday.

My left hand was grasped so tightly in Luc's that when he pushed me with every ounce of his indomitable strength, I was unprepared. His act of betrayal seared me forever.

He *sacrificed* me.

And I'd fallen through the canopy of Heaven itself, fallen through the night sky, screaming just one word.

Mercy!

CHAPTER 19

All the horror of those days is mirrored in my eyes.

Luc curses as he meets some final point of resistance in my unravelling. There's something caught in me, like a locked box, a hard knot. My name; my name is bound in there. My name is the anchor point. Raphael called it the last defence, but he did it for my protection, unwittingly creating a weapon to be used against me. None would be able to draw my name from me willingly, but what if my name were already known?

Luc doesn't bother to unravel that last portion of my soul. It's something useful to him, a means of control. He simply rips me free, and I feel more than see Irina's body fall away from mine. She slumps unconscious, face down upon the runway in her lovely dress, her pretty tiara, her damaged wings.

I look down at my gleaming limbs, the glowing, sleeveless raiment that I always wear when I am myself. Stare down at my burning left hand, the flames fully visible in the poor light. Disoriented, disbelieving, betrayed twice over by the one I'd loved more than anything. Itself a heresy, surely.

I'm still small, still mortal-sized. So dazed to find myself inhabiting my own skin after all these long years, these interminable centuries, that I do not know how to shape-shift, to make myself Luc's equal again.

'Rally to Mercy!' I hear Michael roar, defying the dark angels that threaten to engulf him, parrying their blades more swiftly than the human eye could follow. 'She must not fall to Luc. Rally!'

The air is full of the sound of opposing energies colliding.

Luc holds out his hand to my small one. And, for a moment, I wonder what would happen if I simply took it.

'Come with me,' he says almost kindly, 'and you shall live and prosper and be free. Nothing, none of the darkness to come, shall touch you. You shall always be untouchable in my court.'

I look up at him. 'Though not your queen,' I say softly. 'Never your queen.'

He shakes his head. 'That part of the history of us is done. It is over. But stay with me willingly, and every heart's desire shall be yours. Even that boy.' He gestures into the darkness behind us. 'For you, I will let him live. Let him be your ... pet. Your plaything. And when you tire of him ...' he shrugs. 'Throw him away.'

I move forward towards Luc, almost hypnotised. His right hand is still outstretched, still open to receive mine. What he promises is so much more tempting than the fate the Eight have always had mapped out for me. Ryan. I would get to keep Ryan.

'*No!*' I hear someone roar, and K'el seems to fall out of the air to stand between Luc and me. My watcher, the one I spurned so many years ago, who loves me still, despite the torment I've caused him. My protector, to the last.

'Mercy, get back!' K'el cries. 'The earth will no longer be enough to contain him if you submit now. Don't you understand who he is? What he wants?'

'He's the Devil,' I say simply, understanding at last, but too late. 'He's the one responsible for all the evil in this world, all the tribulation; who fuels the worst excesses, the darkest desires and perversions of human nature.'

'He goes by many names,' K'el says fiercely as he pushes me back towards the now abandoned press gallery at the far end of the catwalk, his fiery weapon all that stands between us and Luc. 'Shaitan, Belial, the adversary — these are only some of the names he is known by. But we have ever known him as Luc, or Lucifer, the day star.'

'The Archangel of Light.' I laugh despairingly.

'No more,' Luc snarls, stalking us in long, easy strides. 'When my *brother* Michael cast me down, I ceased to be *elohim*. The Archangel of Light is dead. And the Devil has arisen in his place.'

The air shimmers with smoke and flame and ambient heat and I scan the area around us for any sign of Ryan, but all I see littered around us are fallen bodies, overturned furniture.

We do not sense Gudrun until she leaps out of the flames beside us. K'el does not see her — so intent is he on me, on Luc — until the short, burning blade she's holding in her hand enters his side. He looks down in surprise at the light bleeding from his pierced side in bright drifts, in errant curls of pure energy. Shock distorts his features — in some ways we are naïve, we *elohim*. Always imagining we are inviolate, so far above everyone and everything that nothing could ever touch us. We deal in death, yes. But rarely glimpse it ourselves, face to face.

'K'el!' I sob, pulling the demon's blade free and twisting my hands into the energy of which Gudrun is made. Though she towers over me still, I swing her up and over my head before sending her flying down the length of the runway with a blast of pure energy fuelled by all the hatred, envy and rage in my body.

Before she hits the blank wall at the northern end of the building, she scatters into a billion pieces and disperses.

K'el's still looking down at the wound in his side when Luc moves forward suddenly, grabbing him by the throat with his left hand, forcing his head up with the tip of the long, burning dagger he's now holding in his right. Before I can speak or even raise my hand, Luc hisses, 'And the Devil always gets what he wants,' and cuts K'el's throat in one smooth arc from ear to ear.

I scream as K'el's head falls back and the light leaves his beautiful eyes. His form seems to waver, grows unbearably bright for an instant. Then, without a sound, his energy simply vanishes, dispersing, never to return.

I begin to shake. There are no words to express my horror, my grief. K'el was singular, and perfect, and no one like him will ever be made again.

Luc subsumes his weapon into the palm of his hand. 'Time presses,' he says caustically. 'Take my hand willingly and live. Or die — it is all one. Your soul is mine; I'll claim it either way.'

He holds his hand out to me, palm upward, and I stare at him blankly. Unable to move, unable to believe that he expects me to take the hand that just destroyed K'el.

He makes a snarling sound in the back of his throat and moves forward. But before he can reach out and take hold of me, I catch a fleeting movement behind him.

'Merce, get back!' Ryan cries, and he throws something at Luc's back then vaults clear of the runway.

An arc of clear, strong-smelling accelerant hits Luc squarely and goes up with a roar. Flames rise at least twenty feet into the air. Luc just starts to *laugh*. He is truly horrifying to behold. He could douse the fire in an instant, but instead he lets it take hold of him, his whole form burning, and within that blazing outline I glimpse all those things he once showed me

— cruelty, perversity, death and destruction — on such a grand scale that I scream and look away.

I see Ryan gesturing at me from the ground, from beyond the burning catwalk, telling me with his hands, his eyes, to go to him. And I shake my head at him in wordless horror, wanting him to run, to get as far away from me as possible if he wants to live. He deserves so much more than I could ever offer him. If he stays with me, he will be hunted down ruthlessly, like a dog. I know it.

Luc suddenly rises high into the air, arms outspread, still burning, still laughing, and ignites his long sword, ready for the killing blow.

'No mercy for you,' he roars, pointing his weapon at Ryan, at me. 'No mercy.'

But then a light of such blinding beauty and magnitude that even Luc must cover his eyes fills the interior of the Galleria, sending a beacon through the glass-roofed dome into the troubled skies above.

'*Flee!*' I hear the Archangel Michael cry. '*Fly.*'

As he says the word, the arched roof of the Galleria seems to shimmer, then more *elohim* — twelve in all — drift down through the solid canopy of glass and iron in a cruciform configuration, soaring straight towards Luc.

The blinding light extinguishes and I don't hesitate, I leap through the flames towards Ryan, moving easily, with a fierce sense of joy and purpose as if Luc's acts of betrayal have finally freed me. And Ryan closes his arms around me tightly, resting his chin briefly atop my head so that I close my eyes at the familiar, longed for gesture. The pain in my left hand seems to burn out, though not the pain in my heart. K'el hadn't stood a chance.

'You feel so real,' Ryan murmurs, looking into my eyes.

'I *am* real,' I reply. 'And you can't know how good this feels.'

I search his face. 'But we have to move, Ryan. It's not safe for us here.'

My sight is unerring though the darkness is lit only by fire now, by lightning. The Galleria looks as if an inland tsunami has swept through it, the ground strewn with chairs and video equipment, the bodies of the mortal fallen. As I look up at the knots of *elohim* and *daemonium* struggling and grappling in the air, I see Luc swiftly put his blade through one of Michael's reinforcements. The *eloah*'s energy disperses soundlessly as she dies, and another of her brethren engages Luc immediately.

I hear K'el's voice in my head. *We maintain, they destroy. That's roughly how it works.*

I grasp Ryan's shirt in my hand and pull him around to face the south entrance. As we start to move, Luc's voice penetrates the vast space from above. 'I want them *all*.'

Suddenly, Gudrun blocks our way, a new, more deadly weapon in her hand. A long, twisted, flaming blade, guaranteed to cause maximum damage on entry and exit.

When Ryan and I pivot towards the western axis, another demon stands before us. Another to the east. Those that are not bent on subduing the archangels who still live, move forward to block our way. Some are male, some are female. All their scars burn brightly, no matter how they might shift to disguise them.

I embrace Ryan tightly, feeling all his unspoken terror in the hard muscles of his arms, his torso, through his familiar, beaten-up leather jacket.

Michael bellows again, his voice disembodied, desperate: 'Fly, Mercy, *fly*.'

Then he seems to address Ryan directly. 'Guard her, human.' Michael's voice sounds throughout the vast Galleria like a tolling bell. 'Keep her safe in your human world when we cannot.'

Ryan gives me a hard shake. 'Can you do that?' he says urgently. 'Fly?'

I can't bring myself to answer him, just continue to watch, transfixed, as the reinforcements Michael has called here struggle to turn the tide of battle. Though the *daemonium* are roughly the equal of the *elohim* in number, they are extraordinarily vicious. As if they have been denied the chance to stretch their wings, to test their might, until now. One by one the *elohim* begin to go down. Each one singular and perfect, never to be made again.

Ryan is still shaking me insistently. 'Mercy, can you? Can you fly? You've got no wings.'

'Don't need wings,' I whisper. 'But I don't know if I can. It's been too ... long.'

I *know* now where my fear of heights comes from. When I recall that moment when Luc cast me out, cast me down, I feel that same terror all over again, the sensation of falling, the blinding, terrible impact. To know your enemy is to have some measure of control over that enemy — that was something Luc taught me, a long time ago. But I have no control over this fear. It seems boundless.

Luc loved me. Yet he tried to kill me. And for what? *Power.*

'Take them!' Luc screams at Gudrun as he and Michael spin towards each other, meeting with a sound like breaking waves.

'You have to try,' Ryan shouts, as Gudrun leaps through the air towards us, her twisted, deadly blade raised, her perfect teeth bared, a personal score to settle.

'Try, Mercy,' Ryan yells. 'For *us*.'

Us.

Though I'm nauseous and dizzy with fear, I embrace Ryan tightly with one arm, shut my eyes and leap off the ground.

No thought, just sensation. Against gravity, against every inclination, I'm *flying*.

My left hand burns and burns in agony. I make the mistake of looking at it, looking down at the ground falling away from us, and have to close my eyes again and swallow.

'Mercy, open your eyes!' Ryan screams. 'We're going to hit!'

My eyes flash open to see that majestic roof inches away from our upturned faces. It's pure reflex what I do next.

I curve my arms around to protect Ryan's mortal form, curve his face into the side of mine, clasp him even more tightly to me. And I take the full brunt of the glass and iron ceiling of the Galleria upon my forearm, upon my shoulders, my down bent head. Glass and steel shriek and rend as we burst outward into the storm-tossed night.

CHAPTER 20

The air is icy. Ryan inhales sharply, begins to cough and shudder.

I look back at the jagged hole torn in the roof of the Galleria, the fiery glow emanating from the building, and know that we have only minutes before Luc's forces come after us.

I glance down at the roadways — like human arteries, like veins — the emergency vehicles that look like toy cars and trucks, and have to close my eyes again, dry retching. All I can think about is falling. And I do fall.

It's a death spin. Gravity's got hold of me again, the way it did all those years ago, and I can't fight it. The wind's shrieking past us.

'Pull up!' Ryan yells, white-hot terror in his voice.

'Just look at me, Mercy! Look at me and you won't fall.'

When I open my eyes, I see people on the ground, getting bigger all the time. People I'm going to take out.

Ryan forces me to look at him, turning my face with the fingers of one frozen hand as we fall and fall. All I allow myself to see is the rain beating down on him, plastering his dark hair to his head, his clothes to his body; his dark eyes holding mine. The whole world, the whole sky, reduced to his dear face. My trajectory grows flat, begins, unsteadily, to climb.

'Okay?' he gasps, the icy air burning his mortal lungs with every breath.

I nod, the worst of the dizziness receding. My peripheral vision starts to return again and I look further and further afield. I rise higher, unsteadily, trying to get my bearings.

The battering rain, the hurricane winds, are buffeting us from side to side. The smallest downdraught sends me spinning out of control. A particularly violent updraught causes Ryan to slide through my arms, and only the iron grip of our entwined fingers keeps us together.

'So cold,' Ryan murmurs as I pull him close to me again, terrified I'll drop him; terrified of lightning strike, of air pockets, of wind currents — things no mortal should ever be subjected to at this altitude. But we need to leave Milan, to get as far away from here as possible, and this is the only way I know how.

It's a night for ironies, I think, too sick, too petrified by what I'm doing, to properly scan the ground for landmarks. I have powers, abilities, no human being could possibly comprehend, but I can't use even half of them. Because of Ryan.

I can't expect him to pass through solid matter. I can't expect him to become invisible on cue; to transport himself from place to place simply by wishing it. He was not made to counter science. He's made of a far different stuff than I am.

I'm weak, out of shape, out of practice. We're barely any distance at all from the Galleria as the crow flies when I see one gleaming, winged shape, then another, launch itself out of that wound in the iron and glasswork ceiling. They come straight after us, scars burning brightly in the midnight air.

'Mercy!' Ryan gasps.

'I see them,' I say through gritted teeth.

There's nowhere to go but down, and that alone is terrifying. I falter as I remember waking on that lonely hillside, broken, terrified, not understanding where I was or what had happened to me. But there's no getting around it. We need to go down. We need to lose ourselves in the human world, because there's no hiding up here, not when Ryan's with me.

A crack of thunder pierces the air, swiftly followed by lightning. In its glare, I turn to see that our pursuers have diverged, and that beyond them, above the burning Galleria, the battle has taken to the skies. Archangels and their glowing nemeses wrestle, falling and rising in the air, the tide of warfare turning and turning again. The air is lit by holy fire meeting its polar opposite.

No matter how I twist and fall, soar and feint, our pursuers close in steadily, driving me back towards the Galleria and to Luc. One of them is a lethally muscular male with short, auburn curls; the other has pale yellow hair that streams out behind her, a wicked, twisted blade in one hand. I have no doubt in my mind that it is Gudrun.

Ryan's teeth are chattering with cold, his lips have a bluish cast, and he's like a block of stone in my arms, head bowed against me, the rain sluicing off his soaked clothing. His eyes are closed now, as if he lacks the energy to keep them open.

'Stay with me,' I cry, gripping him even more tightly to me so that he struggles briefly, making a small sound of protest. 'Don't you dare die on me, not now. Not now we're finally together.'

'Sanctuary,' he mumbles, and he's barely audible, even to me. 'We need sanctuary.'

As he says the words, a bolt of lightning hits so close to us that it sends me into freefall. All I see is the Piazza del Duomo rushing up to meet us, and it's covered in a patchwork of emergency-service vehicles, tents, crash barriers, people, that lit-up Christmas tree that seems like something from another world, another time.

'Sanctuary,' Ryan mumbles. 'Sanctuary.'

I peel off at speed, skimming low over the flashing lights of all the vehicles, circling the square in frustration, Gudrun and the others in pursuit from above and below, closing in.

'Demons,' Ryan mumbles. 'No sanctuary for demons.'

And then I understand what my poor, battered, half-drowned human is trying to tell me.

'*Nullum asylum daemonibus!*' I shriek into the night. No sanctuary for demons.

I scream straight up the neo-Gothic face of the cathedral — hundreds of feet in the air — making for the crazy rooftop crowned by spires and tracery, gargoyles and statuary, the demons in pursuit. Gudrun's so close I can feel her hot breath upon my heels, feel the sizzle of energy her blade gives out.

As I burst above the roofline, all I see are human figures, each the size of giants, standing in rows upon the carved and fretted spires, hundreds of feet above the ground, their faces turned upon the city of Milan below.

I draw a sharp breath as lightning cracks behind me. For a moment, the figures seem alive, seem to move. I imagine I see disapproval upon their faces as I search frantically for the stairs. Stairs that lead down from the open roof of the cathedral to a walkway on the lower north side. There's a door there. And then another set of stairs — encased in a stone tower — that people use to access the roof from the ground.

I know it with a certainty born of true memory. I've walked those stairs before, been inside that tower. Years ago. The stairs must still be there.

I just need to get down onto the roof and the demons won't be able to touch me. No sanctuary for demons. No respite for demons in this place.

I feel a piercing pain as the edge of Gudrun's

blade meets my heel and blindly throw myself down at the field of saints and spires, Ryan held tightly in my arms.

Landing is always going to be a problem for me, I realise; it's that sense of falling, of losing control. We collide with the edge of a spire on the way down. Or, at least, I appear to collide with it. The sensation of solid stone passing straight through my body shocks me so much that I lose my hold on Ryan for the last few feet and he hits the roof at an awkward angle with a dull impact I can almost hear. He rolls a short distance down the pitched roof of the nave, then lies sprawled, face down, unmoving.

Without knowing how I got from where I lost hold of him to where he ended up, I'm already kneeling beside his still form, fear crowding my throat. I roll him over gently, take his face in my hands, and silver tears fall down my cheeks in gratitude, in praise, as I see his pain-filled eyes open.

He looks at me in wonder as he rasps, 'Are those for me? What happened to the hard ass I fell in love with?'

'We made it,' I say shakily. 'Think you can stand?'

He coughs, grimacing in pain. 'If you help me, sure.'

But then his eyes close, and I can't shake him awake. And I realise that there's blood on his mouth. He's badly hurt, and it's all my fault.

Why do I destroy everything I touch? Even the things I ... love?

Above me, the two demons wheel as close as they dare, shrieking in their inhuman voices. I know that we need to get on the move by daybreak; we can't stay here. I make everything around me a target. They will raze Milan around us while they wait for me.

I sling one of Ryan's arms around my neck, grasp him about his waist and pull him upright easily. He's a dead weight in my arms, his head of dark hair hanging forward, and I know that I'm running out of time. He's dying, I can feel it happening beneath my hands. His soul is beginning to cleave away from his body.

'Azraeil!' I call out despairingly. 'You keep away from him, you keep away, do you hear?'

Lightning illuminates the empty rooftop, the sea of slick and treacherous tiles on which we are marooned.

'Stay with me, Ryan,' I plead. 'Stay with me, my love.'

ACKNOWLEDGMENTS

With loving thanks to my husband, Michael, and my children, Oscar, Leni and Yve — for your unstinting love and great patience when I enter *the zone.*

Thanks also to Lisa Berryman, Liz Kemp, Rachel Denwood, Lizzie Ryley, Natalie Costa Bir, Mel Maxwell and Nicola O'Shea for helping me beat this sucker into shape. Again.

To the wonderful editorial and marketing teams at Disney-Hyperion and Ravensburger Buchverlag — especially Catherine Onder, Stephanie Lurie, Ann Dye, Hallie Patterson, Iris Prael and Marie Kubens — thank you for your expertise, enthusiasm and great care of me and Mercy.

To Teresa Fels — thank you for years of friendship, your out-of-this-world home cooking, and for fixing the Spanish, and the Spanglish.

And to Norma Pilling — thank you for reading the initial drafts of *Mercy*, *Exile* and *Muse* and cheerfully suggesting better Latin and Italian alternatives over cups of coffee and Portuguese custard tarts. Get set for the last one …

This is a work of fiction. Most of the locations described in this book are entirely fictional, as are all of the characters, outfits, artworks and events. Certain authorial liberties may have been taken with those buildings and places that do actually exist in the real world, for which the author apologises and begs your leave.

Mercy 'wakes' on a school bus bound for Paradise, a small town where everyone knows everyone else's business — or thinks they do. But they will never guess the secret Mercy is hiding ...

As an angel exiled from heaven and doomed to return repeatedly to Earth, Mercy is never sure whose life and body she will share each time. And her mind is filled with the desperate pleas of her beloved, Luc, who can only approach her in her dreams.

In Paradise, Mercy meets Ryan, whose sister was kidnapped two years ago and is now presumed dead. When another girl disappears, Mercy and Ryan know they must act before time runs out. But a host of angels are out for Mercy's blood and they won't rest until they find her and punish her — for a crime she doesn't remember committing ...

An electric combination of angels, mystery and romance, *Mercy* is the first book in a major new series.

REBECCA LIM

EXILE

An angel searching for answers, for her destiny...

All Mercy knows is that she is an angel, exiled from heaven for a crime she can't remember committing.

So when she 'wakes' inside the body and life of eighteen-year-old Lela Neill, Mercy has only limited recall of her past life. Her strongest memories are of Ryan, the mortal boy who'd begun to fall for her — and she for him.

Lela's life is divided between caring for her terminally ill mother and her work as a waitress at the Green Lantern, a busy city cafe frequented by suits, cab drivers, strippers, backpackers and the homeless, and Mercy quickly falls into the rhythm of this new life.

But when Mercy's beloved, Luc, reappears in her dreams, she begins to awaken to glimpses of her true nature and her true feelings for Ryan. How can she know that her attempts to contact Ryan will have explosive consequences?

Meanwhile, 'the Eight' — responsible for her banishment — hover near, determined to keep Mercy and Luc apart, forever …

Mercy's search continues in the second book of this major new series.

Everything that has happened to Mercy over millennia has made her who she is.

Love. Vengeance. Truth.
Hell hath no fury like Mercy ...

Fury *is the culmination of the spellbinding Mercy series.*

April 2012